# THE MASTER BUILDERS

## RICHARD NEER

## A RILEY KING MYSTERY

~~~~~~~~

## Also By Richard Neer

Something of the Night (2014)

FM: The Rise and Fall of Rock Radio (Villard, 2001)

# One

"Why am I here?"

"Philosophy from you. That's unexpected. Man has been asking that question throughout history," I said, trying to lighten the mood.

"No Riley, I'm not being philosophical. I just want to know why two goons I'd never laid eyes on before would kick the crap out of me."

The medication had lessened the pain --- it was only throbbing now, but I had no doubt that Derek Davis knew that the crushing blows that had been administered to his ribs and face would make their presence felt again. Being ragged on by me was just a continuation of our ongoing battle of verbal one-upmanship. The gravity of the situation would barely lessen our rapid fire jibes. But crashing in a hospital bed on this rainy Monday afternoon had dulled Davis' sense of humor.

"It was the right move not to call the cops," I said. "Their 'investigation' would consist of taking a statement. Once you say no money or credit cards were stolen, this case would be low priority. I think this is best dealt with through other means."

Despite the haze, Davis knew exactly where I was headed. By fortunate coincidence, I just happen to be the man at the right time for situations like this. My background includes a ten year stint with the FBI before leaving to work as a private investigator. I also still have friends within the Bureau who aren't adverse to trading information with me when our interests coincide. I use them for their science; they use me when the guys in suits can't make headway with the sleazier elements.

When I was alerted by the passerby who had found Davis semi-conscious and ferried him to Cornelius Medical Center, I rushed to the hospital. As the docs patched my friend up, I used the time in the waiting room to call a couple of contacts in the netherworld to see if the attack was something bigger or just a random event.

I said, "This kind of beat down, where you get roughed up but not killed, is intended to send a message. That's in the world that I sometimes have to operate in. I'd say whoever ordered this might have full time muscle at his disposal. But you don't gamble and you don't have any addictions I'm aware of. I'd know if you were boinking somebody's wife but that's not your style, boy scout that you are. So besides me, you know anybody who doesn't like you?"

Derek smiled wanly at my weak attempt to bring a grin to his battered face. If there was ever a man with no personal enemies, Derek Davis would head the list.

As a builder of upscale homes, I knew that Derek was a stranger to physical altercations. Cerebral by nature, he prefers to avoid confrontation and dreads the few occasions where he has to fire a subcontractor. In an industry that invites wild speculative ventures from dilettantes who think they could outsmart the market, Davis has never borrowed from sources other than legitimate banks.

A disgruntled customer seemed even more unlikely now, since Davis hasn't finished a new house in almost two years. After years of double digit growth, even his measured approach has fallen prey to the repercussions of the burst housing bubble that took so many contractors down with it. Now Derek Davis is hanging onto nothing but hope...hope that the market would recover and that when it does, he'll have the resources to capitalize on its renaissance.

"Hey, Riles, I'm sorry, man, nothing comes to mind," Derek said, after scouring his befuddled brain for recent unpleasantness. "I'm a little hazy now, but I think I'd know if someone had a bone to pick with me enough to want to hurt me.

Purple haze run through my brain. 'Scuse while, while I kiss the sky."

I wasn't sure the tranquilized Davis would remember this conversation. Once he started spouting song lyrics, it was a sure sign that his mind was giving way to the pain meds. His pale blue eyes were flitting between the thousand mile stare of the heavily medicated to the loopy gaze he often displayed after three cabernets. The rest of his face was distorted, bruised the color of rotten peaches.

I tried to get what I could before he succumbed any further. "So, other than the fact it was two muscular black dudes, anything else you remember about the attack itself?"

"It happened so fast. All I remember is I heard one of them say something like, 'Don't kill him or Johnny will be pissed.'"

"That's like that old joke Pat Cooper used to tell about how Sinatra once saved his life. A couple of creeps were beating on him and Frank says, 'that's enough, fellas'."

"Funny, Riles. But I'm not finding much humor in this yet. Besides, it wasn't Cooper, it was Shecky Green."

I shrugged. My six foot two inch frame has never experienced the short side of a brawl, although I've participated in my share. "Okay, all kidding aside, that's important. *Johnny, eh?* In time, maybe some more things will come back to you that will help. So, how many Johnnies do you know?"

A wave of curious thoughts overwhelmed Davis before he could answer, he later related to me. What was it they had given him exactly? *Oxyclean? Why would they shoot him up with a household detergent? Those wacky doctors!*

"Johnny Cash, Johnny Carson. Johnny Appleseed. Frankie and Johnny. They were sweethearts, you know. First gay romance celebrated in song and celebration. We are stardust, we are golden."

I knew that Derek wasn't trying to be silly; he was drifting toward his happy place. "Okay, you're working on a small job now, aren't you? Anything there that might be related to this?"

Davis gave me a blank look but answered coherently. "I'm doing a master bath remodel for a lady in South Charlotte. So your theory is what? I got beat up because she didn't like the grout color I suggested?" He guffawed, much louder than his sarcastic aside warranted.

"So you're telling me you've never had an unhappy client, Derek? Someone who didn't feel he got his money's worth or thought the work wasn't up to snuff?"

He had built a small business which, at its peak, had as many as six homes under construction at once. That was the maximum volume that Derek could handle while personally attending to all the important details. Things rarely slipped through the cracks, and if they did, he rectified the situation without question.

"I've been building houses for twenty five years. Of course I've had disputes, what builder hasn't? Worst case, if someone doesn't like the plan, it's not all that hard to throw in a change order. Ch-ch- changes. Turn and face the day. Oh, look out you rock and rollers."

I tried to ignore the radio playing in Derek's head. "Well, could be that she thinks you're overcharging already and doesn't want to add to it."

"Come on, you know me. Way I figure, I always give people more than they pay for. 'Sides, she and I get along g-g-g-g-great." Tony the Tiger would have cringed.

"Who is this rich bitch anyway?"

*Wow. That Oxyclean is nice.* Davis was feeling mellow, mellow yellow. "Her name is Serpente. Mrs. John J Serpente. Sweet Charlene. She's as sweet as Tupelo Honey. She's an angel of the first degree. She's all right, she's all right by me."

The weak Van Morrison impression was a clear sign that there was little to be gained by continuing. But through all of my friend's rambling, he had just revealed an obvious starting point to the investigation. For all his questions as to why, the *who* suddenly became clearer.

"John J. Serpente, eh? Surprise. Here's Johnny!"

Davis was slow at the moment but not altogether oblivious. "Johnny? Okay, got it. But it's got to be coincidence. I mean, I've never even met the man. Hey hey, my my. This is the story of Johnny Rotten."

He almost nodded out for a second. "Look, I have their number. I can clear this up in a minute. I'll call the dude." He picked up a plastic water bottle from the nightstand and held it to his ear. Hearing nothing of import, he set it back on the bedside table.

"I wouldn't advise talking to Serpente, mate. What do you know about him? " I said.

"Nada, really. Before this job, I hadn't worked in a month. I wasn't asking questions about her old man." Davis was almost lucid again, the wave subsiding one final time before engulfing his consciousness.

"So the short answer is, no, you didn't check them out."

He bounced back to lucidity, if only for a moment. "The new economy. On a big project, I might do a routine credit check if the realtor hadn't already done it, but this is small change."

Even in his diminished state, Davis had to laugh. He was reduced to taking nickel and dime jobs, handling most of the labor himself to keep the vultures away.

"Charlene Serpente is a good looking lady. I'd assume her husband is a man of wealth and taste. But just as heads is tales call him Lucifer, he'll lay your soul to waste."

*Sympathy for the Devil*, indeed. If Davis only knew how close his off key vocalizing came to pay dirt. There would be nothing further to gain from questioning him as he rambled on with whatever lyrics ran through his mind.

"You know, Riley, you're like Sherlock Holmes and Batman rolled into one. Da da da da da dada dada dada, Batman........"

I nodded. "And sexier than the two of them combined," I said to my friend, who'd already left the room and entered the Twilight Zone.

But my mind was working. J.J. Serpente. Last name means *snake* in Italian. And in his case, it was very apt. The man had a reputation as someone you didn't want to cross, even inadvertently. Our paths have never intersected, but rumor has it that Serpente was backed by some big mob boys up North. It was said that he had a nasty temper. And even something so inconsequential as an inappropriate grout color might set it off.

# Two

After leaving the hospital, I headed to the scene of the incident. I wasn't optimistic about finding anything helpful there, but if the two assailants were after something, they might have broken into his place to find it, since it hadn't been on his person. Might there be something in the paperwork on the Serpente job that could somehow be incriminating?

I dialed one of my local police contacts as I sped up I-77 toward Davis' condo in Davidson.

"Shabielski," a gruff voice on the other end responded.

"Hey, Pete, it's King. How goes it?"

"It goes. Sounds like you're in the car. I hope this is hands-free."

"Let me check. No. And there's still no law in North Carolina against it. Since when did you go all nanny state on us?"

"Next time a kid runs into a tree because they were texting, I'll invite you over to check out the body. I imagine you saw worse when you were a fed, but maybe you've forgotten."

"Busting your chops, pal. I'm on Bluetooth. And I'm not hanging with any of my extensive harem of voluptuous babes so you can speak freely."

"You really have forgotten a lot, former big brother. Since when do you think someone couldn't be listening to us right now if they wanted to?"

"Jeez, I never thought of that. Guess I'd better not say anything about you being gay, huh?"

Shabielski snorted. A veteran who'd done a tour in Desert Storm, married to a school teacher, and father of two girls, the gay jibe rolled off him. "So why the call, other than to bust balls, Riles?"

"What do you know about Johnny Serpente?"

There was silence for a moment. "Why you asking?"

The rugged cop had been a whistleblower in the small town in New Jersey where we'd first met. He had opted to report some payoffs he'd been offered rather than accept the gratuities as standard practice. When his chief took him aside and intimated that he was playing with fire, Shabielski didn't take the hint. Only some skillful legal work got him a settlement granting early retirement and a pension buyout to be paid over ten years. The provisions featured a strict non-disclosure clause, indicating that if any of this scenario was made public, Shabielski would lose the pension. So he took the money, moved South, and kept his mouth shut. The pay in Mecklenburg County wasn't nearly as generous as it was in Jersey, but along with the pension, he was able to get by.

But Shabielski wasn't a naïf about bending rules if the system failed to exact justice on the guilty. He had helped me in Charlotte on occasion, disclosing information that technically was not to be revealed to civilians. And if I chose to act on it and mete out punishment appropriate to the crime, well, shit happens.

I was surprised that Shabielski was so hesitant to comment on Johnny Serpente. "A friend of mine might have a small problem with Johnny."

"Is your friend alive and well?"

"He's alive yes. Well? No."

"Then he should be thankful and you should tell him to forget about the small problem. Live and let live."

Now I was doubly surprised. Shabielski generally was eager to help me go after bad guys, especially if his own involvement was easy to obscure. "Pietro, you don't want to hear what the problem is?"

"Sport, you may think I'm just a dumb cop. But I am capable of learning. Sometimes the hard way, but I learn."

For the first time since I'd known him, I detected a tentative note in Shabielski's voice.

"I'm surprised that some two bit gangster has you running scared."

"Not scared. Wise. Look, I'll say this much. This guy Serpente is pretty hot shit down here. He's got people on his payroll in influential places. Is he a bad guy? Yeah. I mean, I don't know that he's killed anybody, but he might have. He's the city's biggest builder of low cost housing."

All I had known about Serpente before the assault was that he was some kind of Triple-A hood. I didn't know the particulars, but through the grapevine I'd heard that Johnny the Snake was not a laugh riot. But the question arose: if Serpente was a builder, why hire Davis to do a minor renovation at his personal residence?

"Okay, so what you're saying is he builds slums and the government pays the freight. And maybe he charges a little more than he should, or bribes the inspectors. Is that what we're talking here? So if you know all this, why not go after him? I would think a decent forensic accountant could build a case in no time."

Shabielski exhaled. "Are you listening? He has friends. People who protect him."

"And you know this how?"

"Okay, I'll say this much and I'm only telling you this because I trust you. This can't go any further. I was called in on a domestic dispute, couple years after I came here. Routine shit, guy gets liquored up on a Saturday night, wife gives him some sass, he whacks her across the mouth, she locks herself in the john and calls 911. We get there, she says there's been a misunderstanding, no harm no foul. 'Course I see the bruise, but back then I can't write it up if she doesn't press charges."

"You didn't call social services? You just let it go?"

"Let's just say the next day, the guy almost drowned in that pond at Freedom Park. Don't know what he was doing there but I think his brush with mortality made him treat his wife with more respect. Funny how those things happen."

"Instant Karma. So the creep didn't know how to swim?"

"Yeah, good for him that some cop happened to be around at the time. Lucky break."

Not something in the procedures handbook. "Colorful story but what has this got to do with Serpente?"

"Getting to that. Anyway, I saw a hole in the wall the guy punched with his fists before he used them on her. No insulation at all. Checked around a little and found it wasn't just that apartment but the whole complex. I'm sure our fellow public servants in the building department inspected the premises carefully prior to issuing a certificate of occupancy, so I investigated the circumstances that would explain such an oversight."

I could visualize the little smirk on Shabielski's thin lips. I'd seen it before when Peter was regaling me other tales of happy accidents that had caused misguided souls to amend their ways. And he always resorted to the style of overly formal language he'd write on a report while describing his forays into the dark side.

"I did a little research on when the inspections were performed and the budget for various items like insulation. To make a long story short --- and it seems that money was being, shall we say, misappropriated. So I mentioned it to the boss, who said he'd get back to me. Next day he says, ain't nothing there, drop it. I proceed to explain how the numbers didn't add up. Next thing I know, he closes the door to the office and says, very quietly now, that we should just forget about it and move on."

"So knowing you, you didn't stop there."

"I pushed back a little, and it became pretty clear that he was about to write me up for insubordination if I didn't shut my yap. After what happened in Jersey, well, lesson learned."

"So you're saying that Serpente is so well connected that his tentacles reach all the way down to your boss?"

"All I'm saying is that he has enough juice to get rid of a chump like me in thirty seconds. Pay some sleazebag to claim I roughed him up during a bust."

"And you'd never do that."

"Hell, no. So I'm just saying, if your friend's beef with Serpente ain't no big deal, best let it go. You could be buying a world of trouble."

# Three

I consider myself a pragmatist. After trying to play strictly by the book in my early years as a fed in DC, I realized I'm never going to be comfortable taking orders from political types who are more concerned with image than results. I finally reached the breaking point after spending a decade in Washington, becoming increasingly frustrated with turf battles and the clogged bureaucracy.

So I pulled up stakes and worked as a private investigator on the Jersey shore for a few years, but the severe winters were not to my liking. While deciding on where to alight, I scouted areas throughout Virginia and North Carolina before landing in Charlotte, a city large and diverse enough to provide opportunities for my specialized skills. I soon found that the smaller town dynamic suited me and within a few months, I was convinced I'd made the right choice. I bought a small house on a large lot bordering Lake Norman, just a few miles from the energy of Uptown Charlotte.

That's when I met Derek Davis.

Since Derek's business had been a design/build firm, he could take my vague ideas on what I needed to work from home and turn them into a practical but attractive workplace. We immediately agreed on the concept --- use natural materials, create an energy efficient space, and make it as cutting edge as current technology would allow. Anticipate future use and wire the space for every contingency. Keep the rooms sizes modest but use top quality finishes ---- hickory floors, tall baseboards, wide moldings crowning the walls and surrounding the windows.

The final touch was a masculine office lined in cherry. We were careful to orient everything toward the stunning lake views that had drawn me to the property in the first place.

Davis did most of the work himself and was on site every day. I'm fairly handy and contributed sweat equity to the project whenever I could. New in town with few friends, I grew to look forward to the arrival of the contractor each morning, usually bearing coffee and doughnuts.

The only issue we had during construction was a wall that I wanted between the kitchen and gathering room. Since I had grown up in a fifties ranch house with a knotty pine kitchen, I believed that culinary workspace should be segregated from the rest of the house, so as not to show an ugly utilitarian area to guests and clients. Davis had grudgingly agreed to separate the rooms after pointing out that modern kitchens were something to be shown off, not hidden.

Once the remodel took shape, it became clear that Davis was right. I meekly brought it up on an overcast Saturday afternoon, as the job neared completion. I was taken aback when Davis bolted from the room.

*Great, I've done it now*, I thought. *This guy must think I'm a real jerk after insisting on having my way and then changing my mind at the last minute.* My fears were alleviated with Davis reappeared, carrying two 16 pound sledges and a six pack of Coors.

"Well, are we taking this bad boy down or what?" he said. "Could use your help."

With that, he swung one of the hammers into the offending wall, sending gypsum board rocketing across the room. I joined him, and within minutes the partition was down to its studs.

I was pleased but a little surprised at what I saw. "Wait a minute, Derek, I thought that you specified that all walls were to be 2x6, 16 on center. These are 2x4 and I'd guess there's three feet between them. I don't know that much about building, but this isn't what's in the spec sheet."

"Good catch. You see, I knew that you'd change your mind when you saw the final results, and rather than spend time and money re-routing plumbing and electrical and ripping out studs, I made this a curtain wall so we could knock it out easier when you came to your senses."

With that, we both fell about laughing, and after cleaning up the debris left from the false wall, made short work of the six pack Davis had brought. Another that I had stashed in the garage followed shortly thereafter.

# Four

## Derek Davis

Davis was wide awake at 3 a.m.

Time for some reflection on the state of Derek Davis. He was fifty five and this piecemeal contracting was causing him numerous aches and pains that come from trying to do a young man's job. He wanted out, but at this point in his life, it was all he knew how to do.

But Davis did have a master plan. He'd plowed his profits over the years into a large tract of land twenty miles outside the city. Eventually it would be his legacy...New Hope.

It was his dream development: a mixed use village designed to capture a small town Americana feel, with apartments over shops and everything within easy walking distance. Automobile traffic wouldn't mar the beauty of his little district. He had taken out a max loan to finance the project...at exactly the wrong time. The housing bubble burst, and Davis was in trouble.

Adding to his fiscal woes were those of a personal nature. He'd believed that his *almost* fiancée, Elizabeth Deveraux would stand by him no matter what, but when he sold his spacious house, she accurately observed that his temporary quarters really didn't suit two people very well. He sensed she resented that he was willing to sacrifice their comfortable lifestyle in his large lake house in order to keep making payments on two hundred acres in what she perceived as wilderness.

The turning point came after dining at Applebee's, followed by a movie rental; not her idea of a big night out. They had gone back to Liz's uptown condo, where he planned to stay the night.

"You know, Derek, there's something we need to talk about," Liz had said. "You've got a lot on your mind now, with the bank breathing down your neck and all. You're so preoccupied with that, I feel like I'm just an afterthought."

"That's not true." It came out quicker and more forcefully than he had intended. "Look, I am sorry if I seem distracted. I don't like this new job any more than you do."

He'd taken an interim position with a management company, responsible for maintaining several garden apartment complexes scattered around the city. When a call came in for an afterhours repair, Davis was invariably the one to answer it.

"It just seems that you're always thinking of something else. Even when we're making love."

Davis started to protest, but her words struck a chord. Nights were not his own anymore. Some spinster with a stopped up toilet had more purchase on his time than Liz did. But a minor plumbing leak left unattended could result in costly damage if not dealt with promptly.

"Liz, I'm sorry. This has nothing to do with you. I'm going through a rough patch now. Hate my job, and I'm doing everything I can to bid on some others where I have more control. But this is the best I can do at the moment."

She got off the brocade sofa she was perched on and poured herself another glass of wine, not asking if he needed a refill. When she returned, she sat opposite him on a chair that cost more than he made in a month at present.

"I understand when duty calls," she said. "but Sunday, at my mom's party, you answered your cell when I'd specifically asked you not to. Just this one time for a very special occasion. No one there could understand why you had to rush off to change a light bulb."

"Now come on Liz, that's not fair. The old guy thought there was a short in the wall and his place was about to burn down. He didn't know that you need to wear gloves when you replace a halogen bulb and his skin oil made it smell like an electrical fire."

"Yes, but I asked you to turn the phone off. Just for a few hours so we could celebrate my mom's seventieth. You couldn't even do that."

Now it was his turn to refill. Liz Deveraux came from money. Her dad had made his fortune in textiles in Fort Mill before the industry had shipped out to China. As it was he was looking for places to grow his holdings even further and he'd hinted that he might be willing to invest in New Hope, if Davis were to see his way clear toward marrying his daughter.

Befitting her status as rich Daddy's only daughter, her tastes ran to the top of the line. Derek was happy to indulge them when he could, but he was afraid that he wouldn't always be able to. A builder is always subject to the whims of the market.

"So what are you suggesting, Liz? Are we breaking up?"

"No, I still care about you very much."

Derek looked around. The cost of furnishing her small space was more than he'd spent on his first house. Money again. He couldn't help it. He'd like to think that the expensive bric-a-brac was less important to her than her undying love for him, but she was used to all of this. This was her default position; anything less would chafe.

"You know, Liz, when we first met, I thought you were the most beautiful thing I'd ever laid eyes on. I couldn't sleep that night. I was thinking about how to go about wooing you. Lunch, dinner or something imaginative. Should I call the next morning or wait a couple of days so I don't seem desperate. Remember?"

She was gazing out the window of the high rise at the spectacular view of their compact cityscape. Most of Charlotte's skyscrapers are clustered in a ten square block area, but the architecture is eclectic and interesting. At night, it is quite captivating, especially from twenty eight stories up. She looked over to him with distant eyes.

"Not really," she said with a wistful smile. "You called pretty soon, I do remember that. I remember going to that event with a rich guy that my dad set me up with. He doesn't like to see me between husbands very long."

The easy way out of his troubles would be to marry Liz Deveraux. Her father would invest enough to get New Hope shovel ready. He could have kept his house, live large on the lake. But that wasn't for him. He'd earned his way up the ladder and wasn't going to accept a handout now, however well meaning.

"You know, Liz. You deserve to be pampered." He saw where this was headed, and he wanted to make it as painless as he could for her, working on a variation of, *it's not you, it's me.*

"I'm not asking to be pampered. I work. I don't make a lot but I can't imagine not doing something." Her interior design business was more a hobby than an occupation, and she chose to work at it only when it suited her.

"My point is, you should have the freedom to work or not work. And not worry about it."

"You seem to think I'm some spoiled princess who'd be content to sit around waiting to go out to lunch with her girlfriends. That I wouldn't be willing to make sacrifices for your career. That's why you never asked me to marry you, right?"

"No, that's not it. All I've ever done my whole life is build. I can't do that now. I may never be able to do that again. But I'm not ready to give it up yet. So the best I can do is ask you to wait. Stay with me. Let me do what I have to do. Then when things turn around, well, that'll be the time."

"And if they don't turn around? What if this recession lasts for ten years like some think it will. I'm forty six years old, Derek."

"You look like you're thirty."

"Well, I'm not. I'm not thirty. If you really want me, why put things on hold? My daddy would lend us whatever we need to get started."

"Liz, I can't live like that, don't you see? I hate the idea of borrowing money I can't be sure of paying back. I only start a project when I know I have the finances to see it through. The one exception was buying that land for New Hope. And you see what that's doing to me now. If I hadn't over-reached to buy that property and borrowed the money, we'd be fine now."

"So let it go."

"I can't. The down payment was everything I'd saved. If they foreclose, I'm out all of it. I'm trying to refinance but even then, it's stop-gap."

"Then let my dad help."

"And let you wonder whether we got married because I love you or I love your dad's money?"

"I wouldn't."

"Oh really," he said, raising his voice for the first time tonight. "I couldn't make this decision on my own, but factor in your dad's money and that's the clincher? I have to be bribed to marry you. You want me on those terms?"

"I'm willing to be with you on whatever terms. Obviously, you don't feel the same way."

She'd called him on it. He wasn't ready now. He wasn't sure when he would be. It was possible that he was just using New Hope to forestall a decision he didn't want to make.

For the first time in the year that he'd known her, he saw tears forming. She was a strong independent woman who he'd watched take stitches without flinching when she cut her leg on some broken glass while hiking. Even sentimental movies elicited no more than a sniffle, and a sarcastic comment. She had remained stoic through family funerals. He envied her outward fortitude and worried that his own might not equal it under similar circumstances.

But now, covering her face, she stood and walked unsteadily into the bedroom.

# Five

It's against my nature to let slights pass. It's one reason I'm no longer a federal agent. I've never sent away an innocent man, but my unconventional methods resulted in two solid cases being overturned on procedural grounds. Although my superiors didn't have enough evidence to pursue charges, they knew I colored outside the lines and kept a wary eye on me.

I'd found a like minded friend on the Mecklenburg County force in Shabielski, but my pal had almost lost his career once already and was therefore wary of taking on powerful opponents.

I have other acquaintances who might be of service. I'm chary of kicking the hornet's nest, but I know a radio talk show host who is extremely well-informed when it comes to local matters, major and minor.

His real name was Bill Blockmon, but he's legally taken the nom de radio of Patrick Henry. He uses an overdramatized recorded oration of the famous "Give me Liberty or Give me Death" line to begin his daily afternoon program. He was instrumental in forming a chapter of the Tea Party in Charlotte and instinctively supported the police, right or wrong. He hated liberals, Democrats, and immigrants, the order depending on how outraged he happened to be on a given day.

The man told wild, politically incorrect jokes, any one of which would get him banished from the airwaves if uttered in the wrong company. He was also a history buff, but his knowledge was always colored by his right-wing politics. With his shock of dark hair, hawk like features and deep set brown eyes, he projected authority, whether he knew what he was talking about or not.

It couldn't hurt to explore Henry's connections. The man had friends in high places and was tuned in to everything and everybody who made Charlotte go. I figured Henry might know of a side door approach to the Serpente problem.

"Yeah King, what do you want? I'm on the air in a half hour, dildo." Caller ID. At least he'd answered instead of allowing it to go to voice mail, a minor victory.

"And a pleasant good day to you too, Patrick. Glad to see you're in such a good mood."

"Just spent an hour in that lame-ass program director's office. The frigging wimp wants me to tone it down. Claims we're alienating a couple of sponsors."

"And that's not good, I assume. Money talks."

"Fuck 'em. The little weasel doesn't get it. He is pissed that I make five times what he does and that all I have to do is march into the general manager's office and tell him I can't work with this asshole and he'll be on the unemployment line with the rest of the lazy bums."

Rather than butt heads with Henry about the benefits of the social safety net, my goal was to compile information and arguing society's ills wasn't going to help me get it. So I passed on opening that can of worms with a bland "Yeah, well..."

"And those sponsors who are upset? They can go advertise on some pantywaist soft rock station. Or maybe on that idiot's show who's on after me. Fucking clueless bastard told me he voted for Obama. Wouldn't listen when I told him he was a commie who wasn't even born here. Dickhead regrets it now."

I was nearing the point of wondering if listening to this rant was worth whatever kernel of insight Henry might provide. I marvel at how the man can censor his vocabulary the minute the microphone is switched on.

"King, cut to the frigging chase, will you? Why is it when people want something from you --- the real reason they call --- they wait till the second or third item on the list to tell you. Why not just be upfront? You want a favor. Tell me what it is. Ever hear of texting? Now why did you really call?"

*I* was called out for being circumspect when all I had done was offer an innocuous greeting, which somehow had caused Henry to erupt. "Okay, I surrender. I have a client who had a run in with Johnny Serpente. What do you know about him?"

"I know I'd like to fuck his wife. You ever see her? What a piece of ass. Looks wholesome but sexy as hell....like Faith Hill or maybe Meg Ryan before she fucked up her face with all that plastic surgery. Makes Angie Jolie look like a skank. On second thought, she is a skank, tattooed liberal bitch. But Serpente's wife is hot. Whew."

"What about Serpente, the man?"

"You gone homo on me, King? You don't want to hear about this chick? Word is, she spreads it around, too. The old man probably can't get it up without enough Viagra to choke a horse, so she'll do anybody she comes in contact with. I almost did her myself at a Tea Party dinner a couple months ago, but I had to give a speech and didn't want to get stains on the tux."

"Does Serpente know?"

"Look, gotta go. My asshole producer wants to map out the first segment of my show. Got Michelle Bachmann coming on later. Now there's another bitch I'd like to climb aboard. Henry out."

# Six

## Derek Davis

"Mr. Davis? Do you think you're up to making a decision?"

Derek slowly opened his eyes against the slatted light pouring through the blinds. He was rewarded with the apparition of an angel. Blonde, Grace Kelly features, framed against the backlit window.

"I'll take the Pearly Gates nonstop, angel," he murmured.

The angel answered. "That's a bit above my powers. I'm only here to see if you're up to talking with another doctor. "

"Sure, why not? Is this going to hurt?"

"Just a consult. I'll be right back."

"I'll count the seconds."

Consult? That didn't sound good. He was eager to be released, especially since he'd heard horror stories about what a night's stay in the hospital would cost. This was his first encounter with the health care system since he'd dropped his coverage upon dissolving the business. He was prepared for sticker shock when the bill came. Although is it really sticker shock if you're prepared for it?

"Mr. Davis. How are we feeling today?" A doctor entered the room, head buried in charts.

Derek thought it amusing how docs always ask how *we* are feeling, as if addressing a roomful of patients, or if they hurt just like you did.

"Your numbers look good. So you were beaten up. Aren't you a little old to be picking fights?" said the doctor, no reproach in his voice. He had jet black hair and sharp features, very white teeth. Tethered reading glasses were perched on the tip of his nose. He shook them off as he smiled at Davis. "Dr. Shamaylan," he announced with a clipped accent.

There was something vaguely familiar about the man, but he couldn't place it. "I'm feeling better today," was all Davis could reply.

"Well, let's get down to why I'm here. As you may know, I'm not your primary physician. I'm actually a plastic surgeon."

"Running a special on botox today? Sorry, not in the market."

Davis tried to make light of the idea that he'd need such a specialist. Was this guy trolling for business? In Davis' line of work, many unscrupulous contractors used a similar approach. *Excuse me, but I was just in the area doing some work for your neighbors, the Joneses.....*

"I wish that botox would be a solution to the problem. Much simpler that way. No, I imagine you haven't seen yourself this morning."

In fact, he hadn't. His trips to the bathroom were painful shuffles and he hadn't bothered to look in the mirror. *Plastic surgery.* This really didn't sound good.

Shaymalan continued. "You show no major cosmetic damage other than to your nose. It's been pretty badly smashed."

Davis exhaled, wondering if that mere act would cause pain once the drugs wore off. "How badly?"

"It could affect your breathing. Not that you'd be unable to breathe, but it could be noisy. We could just set it and it wouldn't be too bad, I suppose. We're not talking Phantom of the Opera here, but you'd always look like you'd just gotten the short end of a fight. Which I guess you did."

"Look, I know this isn't an auto body shop but can I get an estimate? Like, a little touch up, a little paint as opposed to a new bumper?" Damn. A couple of years ago, insurance or no, he'd have told Shaymalan to do whatever he could to restore his appearance. But now, everything revolved around money. Ugly for life versus making the payment on New Hope.

"You don't remember me, do you?" the good doctor asked.

"Sorry, when they brought me in, it's all kind of hazy. No offense, but I wasn't concentrating on who was doing what to where. It hurt all over."

Shaymalan laughed. "I don't mean just then. We've met before. Five years ago. You don't recall?"

*I would remember going to a plastic surgeon.* Had he accompanied an old girlfriend to a doctor's office? Nah, any work they might have had done had occurred before they hooked up with him. Although over the years, some of his brief encounters had clearly had some artificial enhancement, and not necessarily on the nose.

"Apologies. I don't recall. Refresh me."

A warm smile this time. "Like I said, it was about five years ago. Your company was doing some building in our neighborhood. We had a minor emergency. A pipe had burst on the second floor of our house and water was gushing through the kitchen ceiling. My wife ran to where you were working. This was during the day, I was at the office. You rushed over, turned the water off, and fixed the leak. When I arrived home, the wall was open, as was the ceiling. You said when things dried out that you'd send your drywall man over to patch it up and treat for mold if any had begun. You were good as your word."

It came back. Shamaylan lived in a very nice area known as The Peninsula, a newer development surrounding a golf course just north of the city. Davis had done several custom homes there, and must have been finishing one when the incident occurred.

"Glad to have been able to help. I do remember now, yes."

"And do you remember why I might have reason to be annoyed with you?"

*Great. I didn't even build the damn house, I merely fixed someone else's mistake and this guy is mad at me*, Davis thought. *Did Shaymalan come to gloat now that the shoe was on the other foot? Was his first name Johnny?*

"No, I thought we got everything back to normal. Didn't I send our painter over to blend in the wall and ceiling? I mean, it's hard to get an exact match, but if it wasn't right, we'd have come back to tweak it."

"It looks perfect, like nothing ever happened. No, I was annoyed because when I called to inquire about the charges, you said to forget about it, that your crews were nearby anyway."

Davis didn't remember that part but it sounded plausible. He'd sweated the pipe himself, and his drywall guys just used some scrap from the other project. Paint and spackle --- it wasn't worth sending a bill.

"That's right. I think I told you to keep us in mind if you need any work done. A remodel, addition or something. Still in that house?"

"We are. Frankly, I wish you had built it for us. We've had all sorts of things go wrong with it and our builder skipped out and changed his number. But it's not fair that you didn't charge us. If you hadn't come along when you did, we could have lost the whole kitchen."

Davis extended his palm outward. "Goodwill gesture. No big deal."

"All right, so you'll understand that I've got you scheduled for surgery tomorrow morning. I think we can get that nose looking even better than it did before. Consider my fee waived as a *goodwill gesture*."

"Now wait, doc, a little solder and some drywall..." he said to Shamaylan's back as he whisked out of the room.

# Seven

I let myself in to Davis' condo, using the extra key Derek had given me months before. While not wanting to intrude on my friend's privacy, I thumbed through his mail in case something required immediate attention. Just junk, investment seminar solicitations and a few bills. I placed the bundle on the kitchen counter, and walked about, testing the exterior doors and windows. No sign of forced entry and nothing seemed wildly out of place, not that I could make rhyme or reason out of the haphazard arrangement.

The condo was located in a small complex in Davidson, just off I-77. The nicer units faced Lake Norman, but the expansive vistas came with a price tag that Davis couldn't afford now. His space would have rented for a lot more if the main view hadn't been of a brick wall. The carpet and trim were old and worn and badly needed to be updated. But for now, the laminate counters and aging builder grade appliances served his purpose.

There was nothing in the apartment that shed any light on the beating. It was depressing to wade through the detritus of my friend's life. I thought back to the parties Derek had thrown at his prior home with its generous entertaining area and panoramic views of the water. But Davis had decided that the only way to stay solvent was to sell the house. It lingered on the market for nine months, the price dropping with each successive spate of bad news. Finally, he accepted an offer that allowed him to merely break even, adding insult to injury.

I locked up and walked over to the common area where the mugging took place. It was on a concrete walkway shielded somewhat from the upper floors by a vine covered pergola. Some of the branches were twisted and bruised, probably a result of the struggle. If I had my former FBI crime scene colleagues available, they might have been able to find some evidence. Luminol might reveal blood from the perps if Davis had gotten in a defensive blow, but Mecklenburg cops under budget constraints wouldn't have trotted out high tech DNA stuff for what appeared to be a routine mugging.

My main purpose in going over the scene was to figure out if there might have been any witnesses. There were eighteen condos in the L shaped three story building. I knew from Derek's laments that most were occupied by retirees. With no job or hobby to occupy their time, many oldsters just stare out their windows in contemplation. Maybe one of them had seen something useful. Some would be hesitant to come forward, not wanting to expose themselves to imagined retaliation.

A thought occurred. The Good Samaritan who'd taken Davis to the hospital and called me was a young black man, judging by the sound of his voice. Yeah, you could call that profiling but so what? I needed the name. I scrolled down *calls received* until I came to the number of the man who had dialed me from the hospital.

I jotted it down and rang Shabielski. "Pete, can you run a cell phone number for me? I'd do it myself but I'm not near a computer."

"You need a smarter phone, Caveman," my cop pal replied. "Mind me asking what's this for? I hope you're not ignoring what I told you about Serpente."

"Nah, this is something else. Minor league, but something I thought I could clean I up and make a quick buck," I said, lying through my teeth.

I never fail to be impressed by the speed of modern computers. Shabielski had my answer within thirty seconds.

"Okay, got it. Belongs to a Corey Wade. Address --- Eddy Hall, Room 320, Davidson College. Hey, I know that name. Kid plays hoops for the Davidson basketball team. Sophomore. What you do want with him? Got some kind of NCAA violation going here?"

"I can't tell you that now. Big kid, I'd imagine."

"Small forward. 6-7 maybe. Needs to fill out. Like you were, he's not first round NBA material but a nice college player. Good program they run up there. Made the big dance couple of years back. That Steph Curry turned out to be a great player, an MVP at Golden State."

I glanced around. Not a soul in sight. "Thanks Pete."

Another quick call. It didn't take an elaborate ruse to connect with the small college's athletic department and claim that I had misplaced the media schedule concerning when the basketball team would be available for interviews. The team had an afternoon practice scheduled to begin in a half hour, after which the locker room would be open to the media.

That would give me time to knock on some doors. Probably a waste of time, but part of the necessary grunt work of this glamour profession.

# Eight

If the dingy rooms Davis rented were not depressing enough, the neighbors tipped it over the edge. Although the complex wasn't billed as a senior community and there were no minimum age restrictions, he told me he'd yet to meet anyone under seventy. The rules stating *no dogs over twenty pounds allowed* were a tip off. There were more yappy poodles and Chihuahuas in residence than people and the animals looked like they would outlive their masters and take over. And from what I have seen, they were welcome to it.

After knocking on at least a dozen doors and being greeted with suspicious glares, sharp nips at my cuffs and no useful information, I hit upon a prospect. The woman who answered the door at 6C was bereft of canine accompaniment and flashed a smile instead of a scowl. Instead of peering carefully through a slender crack, she eased the door open and spoke first.

"What can I do for you, handsome?" she asked. Her voice bore no trace of the South. The accent was faint, but I guessed somewhere in the Northeast.

"Thank you, ma'am. I don't know if you are aware of it but there was a mugging on the premises this morning."

She seemed unimpressed. "Yes, young man, I heard. Hard for anything to happen around here without the local yentas jabbering about it. I'm sorry, yenta means gossip. Sometimes I forget where I am."

"I know the word."

"Funny thing is, I'm not Jewish. But having lived in Manhattan most of my life, I tend to automatically use certain words that just aren't part of the vernacular here. Just like I never realized that 'bless your heart' isn't a complimentary phrase down South until one of my neighbors explained."

"I'm fairly new here myself. Jersey. I'm a little shocked they'd reveal that to a Yankee."

"I must say, it did take a couple of tall bourbons before I was trusted with that little tidbit."

She must have been something in her day. She was fit and compact. Her face was pale with fine wrinkles that only showed when she gave a smile. Her blue eyes were clear. She was wearing jeans and a oversized cotton smock, and she gripped a sash brush flecked with light enamel in her right hand. No yappy dog, just an incurious cat who peered out initially and then went back to sleep.

"Pardon the mess. I'm painting some trim. The couple who lived here before wasn't very handy and I'm trying to fix the place up. Got it for a song. An apartment like this in Manhattan would rent for two thousand a month. And the view of the lake is superb." She caught her breath. "I was looking for an excuse to take a break anyway. Would you like to come in?"

I didn't have a lot of time before heading for the campus to interview the basketball kid, but after having doors slammed on me all afternoon, I could scarcely refuse the invitation. "If it's not too much trouble, I have a few questions."

"Are you with the police? Do you have identification?"

"Very wise of you to ask. No, I'm a private investigator. And actually, I'm a friend of the victim," he said, producing my license.

"Yes, that nice man in 1B. Poor thing. How's he doing?"

"Better, thanks. He might scare the children the way he looks, but hopefully no permanent damage."

"Nothing to fear on that score. No children in this place. That's one thing I miss."

"Were you a teacher?

"My, you are observant, detective. Yes, over forty years in the New York City system. Fifth grade."

"Well, I'd love to come in for a couple of minutes, if that's all right."

She smiled. Most of the teeth I'd seen here were either canine or spent their nocturnal hours in a glass, but hers were original equipment, and in mint condition.

"Forgive the mess again. I've only been here a few months and I'm tackling one job at a time."

Her apartment was a revelation. Same basic floor plan as Derek's but it looked twice as spacious. The walls had been freshly painted a soft golden color, and the molding was in the process of turning antique white. The kitchen boasted gleaming stainless steel appliances and granite counters. The floors were polished to a brilliant luster and the deliberately unembellished windows opened to an expanse of endless water, twinkling whitecaps in the afternoon sun.

"At the risk of sounding clichéd, I love what you've done with the place," was all I could think to say.

"Thank you," she said, not bothering to disguise the pride she so obviously felt. "It was pretty ratty when I moved in, but then if it wasn't, I probably wouldn't have been able to afford it. I'm pretty handy for an old bat, wouldn't you say?"

"Handy, yes. An old bat, no."

"And I feel that the area rug really ties the room together." She waited a beat for me to acknowledge *The Big Lebowski* reference but I wasn't biting.

She said, "Can I offer you some iced tea? Not that sweet tea they favor down here. That stuff will rot your teeth faster than battery acid."

"That would be nice, thanks. Look, I don't want to keep you from your work, so pardon me if I get right to the point."

"Certainly. I'll fetch the tea. Lemon, sugar?" She looked disappointed, as if she welcomed someone she could finally talk to on her own level. Given her years as a teacher, she must be sixty five at least. I could only pray I'll reach that age in such pristine condition.

"Artificial sweetener if you have it. Gotta keep my girlish figure."

"Nothing girlish about your figure, Mister," she said. "Funny, I haven't even asked your name. I guess I saw it on the ID but the short term memory isn't what it used to be. I hope that doesn't mean Alzheimer's is lurking around the corner."

"Don't worry, happens to us all. Just part of getting older. It's King, Riley King. And you are?"

"Randee. Randee Blankenship."

"A pleasure. Now, let me ask, Monday morning, between seven thirty and nine. Did you hear or see anything unusual?"

She laughed. Her voice had a warm, lilting quality, like sleigh bells. I found it utterly disarming. "That's an overly broad question. My fifth graders could come up with something more specific. Although maybe not. They probably never heard of *Dragnet*. I met Jack Webb once. Very nice man."

She was lonely. I would have asked about a husband, or how she came to move to the South from New York but that could lead to a long rambling conversation or a short awkward one, and I couldn't deal with either at the moment. "I'll try again. Did you see anyone or anything out of place?"

"I usually go out for a power walk or a jog around seven every morning. I see a couple of neighbors walking their pet rats. I generally cross the overpass and run along the lake on the other side of the highway. Lots of commuters. I very often see your friend. Seems like a nice man, always says hello. Let's see. Yesterday morning. Didn't see him."

"I'm just thinking of people in the immediate area. This complex. Do you remember seeing anyone different. Faces you hadn't seen before? Anything?"

"Actually I did. Didn't think much of it. Black men. Muscular. They seemed to be outdoor workers. Dressed like they were anyway."

She put two large glasses of iced tea down on the granite counter, which was flanked by three ash colored barstools. She alighted on one and gestured to me to make use of one of the others.

"And how was that? The way they were dressed, I mean."

"Dungarees. Tee shirts. Ball caps. I suppose they could have been anybody, not necessarily maintenance men but they had that look about them. You know, strong men who work with their hands."

"Would you recognize them if you saw them again?"

She laughed again. "Oh my, I could fall into the trap of saying they all look alike, couldn't I? I must say I've heard that more than once since I moved here. Lovely people for the most part, but some of them still haven't gotten over the Civil War. Or as they would insist, 'The War of Northern Aggression.'"

"But back to the men you saw. Nothing particularly noteworthy about them? Any distinguishing features? Above average size, build, would you say?"

"That might be why I said they seemed to be outdoor workers. They were strong looking men. Robust. The two older ones weren't particularly tall. But the other, well, he seemed a lot younger than the others."

Davis had been attacked by two men, at least that's what told me. Who was this other?

"So there were three of them. You're sure? Not two? How old were these guys, do you think?"

"Absolutely, there were three. The older two, were forty maybe. The kid, I don't know anywhere from sixteen to twenty. But tall. Very tall. Like a basketball player."

# Nine

### Derek Davis

There weren't many people Derek disliked at first contact. He was very much a 'live and let live' guy. Who would hate him so much that they would hire men to beat him up? As he sat up in his hospital bed seeking answers as to who his enemies might be, one of them appeared.

Todd Weller.

He was being liberal in according Weller enemy status since Weller had no idea that Davis didn't like him.

"Hey, Bucco, heard you were here. How's it hanging, dude?" Weller said.

Todd flashed a brilliant smile, befitting his role as television sportscaster. The smile was completely false, the kind you can see through if you're not blinded by the perfect teeth and chiseled features. The eyes were dead, shades drawn on the supposed windows of the soul.

The forced bonhomie was Weller's attempt at bucking up his spirits, and Davis felt a twinge at begrudging the man his good deed.

"Hey, Todd, nice of you to visit," he forced himself to say.

"Oh don't give me too much credit, my friend. I was doing a Thanksgiving piece on how the Panthers' players are giving back to the community by visiting sick kids, and I heard you were here so I wanted to pop up and extend my regards."

Davis had to admit that it was a thoughtful gesture and that his dislike for Weller had no grounds in anything the man had done to him. He had to admit that some of it was rooted in jealousy. Todd was in his mid thirties, a former quarterback for UNC who'd gotten a brief shot at the NFL fifteen years ago before being cut in training camp by the Eagles. But the Charlotte native was a local hero and had quickly parlayed his charm and handsomeness into a gig on Channel 36.

The guy was still built as if carved in marble. Not a ripple showed in his crisp blue suit, looking like he still could march a team down the field. His brown hair was thick as a teenager's and hadn't been tarnished by a hint of gray. His face was remarkably smooth, at least as far as Davis could tell behind the veil of lightly applied television make-up. At six four, two ten, he made Davis feel small and insignificant.

"So what happened, compadre? Get into a brawl defending my records at UNC?"

There was *that*. Everything in Weller's world revolved around Todd Weller. Despite his graciousness in visiting a man he barely knew in the hospital, Davis suspected there was an ulterior motive. He just couldn't imagine what it was.

His company had rehabbed a house for the quarterback and his wife a few years back. Weller had since dumped his college sweetheart wife for a minor but stunning television actress, who he then traded in for the freedom a celebrated bachelor could enjoy in a small city. The Charlotte Observer wasn't much on gossip, but the glossy monthly magazine inserts always featured pictures of Weller at another chi-chi event with a different hottie adorning his muscular arm.

"You played ball at UNC, Todd? I didn't know that. I'm more of an NFL fan myself." Davis knew that was a low blow, but he couldn't help himself. After the Eagles had cut him, no other pro team had even sniffed at the college gridiron star.

Weller blew it off. "Set school records that still stand. You must have seen the trophies when you were working for me. Always enjoyed coming home and finding you laboring diligently to make sure my cabinetry was plumb and level. Always had a joke and a kind word for me and Kirsten."

"And how is Kirsten these days?" Another cheap shot.

"We talk once in a while. She's fine. We split a few years ago, didn't you know? I imagine in your blue collar world you don't have time for that upper crust gossip. Well, it was all very amiable. No kids, thank god. She got the house, I'm living the life at the Rosewood now. You know, that luxury building near Myers Park. Don't have time to mow lawns these days."

Davis decided to stop with the snarkiness. This guy was Lancelot, too perfect to be true, but so what? He wasn't King Arthur. He saw Weller in person maybe four times a year at golf outings and the like. Business-wise, he'd been paid on time; there were no call backs at the former Weller residence. And Davis actually did know that Kirsten Weller was doing fine, engaged now to a pediatric physician.

Davis said, "Yeah, I heard you have a syndicated show."

"I do. It's low tech by today's standards. They want my personality to carry it and the numbers bear out that it was a wise decision."

Davis held back from voicing his real thoughts, that Weller was a superficial pretty boy who didn't provide one insight into whatever sport he was covering. But women loved him and that must be why his ratings superseded what could be expected from a Sunday night wrap-up show.

"How nice for you," was all he said.

Weller broke character. He seemed awkward and disjointed as he drew closer to Derek's bedside.

"Look, Davis, huddle up, I need to tell you something. I didn't want you to hear it second hand and I know that the lady feels funny about telling you. So I felt I needed to step up to the plate and man up about it."

Whatever it was that Weller had to tell him, couching it in sports clichés was the best he could do. He doubted that anything the man could tell him would affect him one way or another. But he decided to be gracious and cut the guy a break.

"Hey, I'd expect no less. What's up?"

Weller stumbled forward a little more. "Well, I'm sort of glad you're hooked up to that IV  because if you weren't, I'd expect you'd want to pop me in the mouth. And when you're up and around, I'd be happy to give you that satisfaction. Just don't leave a mark, okay?"

He smiled at his weak attempt at self effacement. But Davis was beginning to sense something coming that he definitely wouldn't like. Had Weller ordered the beating?

His tolerance for this fool was growing short. "Well, out with it, Todd. What's the problem?"

"I, ah, I know that for a while you and Liz Deveraux were an item and that you two hit a bad patch. And I wanted to honor our friendship, you know I've always considered you to be a friend even though we don't know each other all that well. But I might as well spit it out. I ran into Liz at BLT Steak a few months ago, and well, I don't know how to say this any other way except that, we're dating. Can we still be friends, dude?"

# Ten

I love Davidson. It fulfills everything small town Americana is all about, at least to my romantic notions.

Main Street was College Town USA, directly out of Norman Rockwell's *Saturday Evening Post* illustrations. There was even a soda shop with swiveling chrome stools topped in red vinyl. Fountain drinks, milkshakes, burgers with fries, and banana splits. Healthy eating. You half expected to see Ricky and David Nelson strolling down the street, books in hand, helping an old lady cross. Or maybe squiring a pony tailed lass in a plaid skirt, smiling coyly at the boys' innocent quips. That was before young Ricky grew his hair out and died freebasing on a plane.

It's hard to maintain quaintness in this cynical age, but the town fathers had done their best to resist modernity. They insisted that no new building rise taller than two stories, constructed of the same clay redbrick that lined Main Street a century ago. Chain stores were required to comply with these zoning ordinances, despite their protests that it compromised their brand. After a while, they began appreciate the cachet their shops gained by appearing to be managed by ma and pa, despite being bankrolled somewhere in China.

Ersatz artsy-craftsy galleries of kitsch had failed to invade the center of town, so everything colonial there was authentic. There was a used book store that had managed to survive Kindle and the big chains. Business was thriving at the outdoor cafes, especially during the warm weather which lingered for nine months in the Piedmont of the Carolinas. Even the musty antique shop somehow made a go of it. Its wide pine plank floors were scarred by fifty years of wear, boasting a rich patina that no amount of faux aging technique could quite capture. And the octogenarian owner still had a sharp eye for undiscovered treasures.

The college had been founded in the mid eighteen hundreds as a religious institution and still maintained its affiliation, although the school was now open to all faiths. Sports had quite a bit to do with the diversity on display, as the school recruited its jocks internationally, demanding academic as well as athletic excellence.

The crown jewel of the athletic department was the basketball team. They weren't able to match the consistent success of Duke, Wake Forest, UNC or NC State, but every few years they surprised the experts by playing deep into March Madness. I've attended a few games in their impeccably maintained field house and always come away impressed by the team. They play hard for forty minutes, and never fail to exhibit sportsmanship of the highest order, even in defeat.

The afternoon practice was just wrapping up as I arrived. Players were scattered about the court, some working on their free throw shooting, others tossing jump shots from three point range. There were a couple who were running up and down the bleacher stairs, a conditioning drill I've never tried and doubt my knees would tolerate. I like to think I'm in excellent shape, but these kids make me feel downright slothful.

I knew the sports information director was named Julie Monahan, and since there was only one woman present, using my super-sleuth powers of deduction, I guessed she was the one holding a clipboard courtside. There was an expensive looking Canon EOS strapped around her neck, which she occasionally raised to catch a player in a candid moment. "Excuse me, Miss Monahan?"

"Yes, sir. What can I do for you?" Her manner was brisk and businesslike. She had short blond hair and the build of an athlete. A swimmer? As she turned to me, a faint whiff of chlorine confirmed it.

"My name is Riley King," I said. "I wonder if I might have a word with you."

She was wearing khakis and a polo shirt, with Davidson emblazoned over her left breast. I figured her for late thirties, younger than me but old enough to have seen the world as it is, not as how she'd like it to be.

"May I ask what this pertains to?"

"I'm a private investigator. I have some questions regarding one of your athletes."

She frowned. "I'm not sure I'm the one to talk with. You may want to see the head of our department. I'll walk you over if you like and we can see if he's free. Mind me asking who your questions are about? And of what nature?"

If I come on too officiously, the school mucky-mucks might go into a defensive posture and clam up. That's the last thing I need. So I softened the tone. "Not at all. And I really don't think this rises to that level. Corey Wade. And this is probably a good thing."

She looked perplexed. She had a mild southern drawl, barely detectable in the way she stretched out certain vowels. "Corey was excused from practice today. A family matter. Does this relate to that at all?"

She wore no rings on either hand. I had left a lover behind in New Jersey. Jaime Johansen was a literary agent who I'd become involved with while on a case. This Monahan woman reminded me of Jaime, and with no small degree of guilt, I fantasized that she might serve as a surrogate.

"If you let me buy you a cup of coffee, I'll explain everything. And I promise that if I seem too nosy you can shunt me off to whatever bureaucrat you like."

She smiled at my irreverence. "Davidson isn't big on bureaucracy. But my practice notes aren't due for a bit so why don't we head over to the student center and I'll let you treat me to an overpriced latte."

"I'm sure I'll get my money's worth," I said, hoping she would sense that my interest wasn't merely business.

It was November but still mild. She carried a light fleece jacket to ward off the chill that might arrive later in the day, but for our three minute walk across the campus in the twilight, it was unnecessary. We spoke about the weather and how the leaves had turned late that fall.

The student center was warm and smelled of Starbucks. I ordered a dark roast and despite her earlier expressed desire for a latte, she settled on green tea. After we were seated at a corner table, she sipped the hot brew and looked up at me with eyes the color of turquoise. I'd never seen eyes that color before and told her so.

"Thanks. I have heard that before. Is that the best you got?" I was rusty at this and she quickly reacted to my downcast look. "Only kidding. So Mr. Private Eye, what do you want to know?"

"Everything and anything you're willing to tell me."

"Are we talking about Corey Wade now?" She flirted back.

"For now yes. Later maybe, no."

"Practice notes, big boy, remember? Got to get them out before deadline. I'm all yours for the moment but my time is limited so do your best."

"Okay, let's get business out of the way. A friend of mine was attacked not too far from here. Corey Wade happened by and helped. Drove my friend to Cornelius Medical Center."

"Really? Is your friend all right?"

"I'm surprised you didn't know about it. After all, you *are* the sports information director. I'd imagine a Good Samaritan act by one of your players would get some ink."

"You're right, it would. Our record's only 1-2 at the moment so a little human interest stuff would be welcome. I wonder why he didn't tell me. Or Coach for that matter."

I've interviewed plenty of suspects who were hiding information and I like to think I'm adept at extracting whatever I need to know. I sensed no guile here; she seemed genuinely surprised.

"Strange that Coach never mentioned it to me," she said. "I mean, there are personal things with the players that he won't tell me. Keeps their confidences to gain trust, makes a more cohesive unit. But something like this, I'm sure he would have told me. It's my job to get this kind of good stuff out. But why are you looking for Corey? Some kind of reward? We have to be careful about that kind of thing, NCAA and all."

"I know. I played a little for Georgetown, ages ago."

"Really? Wait, Riley King. I remember the name. Didn't you have a huge game once against Syracuse? Then busted up your knee and I guess I lost track after that."

"C'est moi. I'm flattered anyone remembers. Yeah, my senior year. They called me the token white guy. I rode the bench for most of it, starters got in foul trouble so I played a lot that night. I was lucky I was in the zone at the right time. Actually hurt the knee on the last play, after the game was iced. Never played again."

"A shame. You were certainly en fuego that night."

"How is it that you know so much about my short career?"

"I played some ball myself. UVA Charlottesville. Softball mostly. Pitcher. I wasn't great but got honorable mention All American my senior year. I loved basketball too but barely made varsity. Followed it pretty close, though. Obviously helped me get the job here. Not too many female SIDs at major schools."

I almost forgot the reason I'd sought her out. "Wow, I grew up in Charlottesville. Small world. Funny, I had you pegged for a swimmer."

"Oh, that's what I do now to stay in shape. They have a great pool one level below the basketball court here and I'm in it a lot. "

Back to business. "Well, regarding Corey. I know he lives in a dorm here. Think he's there now?"

"I know for a fact he's not. Left to attend family business and before you ask, we don't know exactly what it is, although I really couldn't tell you if I knew. We have to protect our student athletes."

"You wouldn't be stepping out of bounds if you could hook me up with Corey. You'd save me some trouble."

She frowned. It was a pretty frown.

I said, "Look, I just want to ask him a couple of questions. My friend didn't even get his name. He was pretty busted up at the time. My interest in Corey is to find out if he saw anything that might help in finding who attacked my friend. Maybe something he thought was inconsequential. And if there *is* a reward, although knowing my friend's finances I doubt there would be, I'd certainly run it past you."

She quickly came to a decision. "Maybe I'm being naive, but I think I can trust you. If you say that's all you need, I'll try to help. I need to get these notes done, then I can run over to the administrative building."

"Can I call you later?"

"About Corey?"

"For now. But once I know that, there's a lot more information I'd like to know about another employee of the college. Someone in the SID office." Clunky, but she didn't wince.

"I think I can accommodate those queries, sir. My cell number is on the card. I should be done by six thirty. Dinnertime. And I have no plans. Fancy that."

I gave a rakish tilt of an eyebrow as I took the card. This had worked in the past, but she showed no reaction to my best seductive gaze. "I get hungry around then too. Coincidence. I'll call you," I said.

I walked away. At the moment, Wade and Serpente were the last things on my mind.

# Eleven

## Johnny Serpente

Johnny the Snake was not having a good day. All he wanted to do was relax with a glass of his favorite beer after a frustrating day on the golf course. But his round was interrupted by a panicked call from one of his foremen informing him that a building site had failed its rough plumbing inspection. Apparently there was a new county assistant plumbing inspector who didn't understand how these things worked. To top it off, his playing partners were annoyed that the call had distracted the Snake at a crucial point in the match. After all, he was only a builder, and they were doctors, lawyers, politicians --- people who actually did something important.

The truth was many of his partners were deeply indebted to him for his clandestine contributions to their campaigns or very public donations to their hospitals and practices. Lacking his kickbacks, their sybaritic lifestyles might be compromised. The attorneys benefited by his deliberate lack of scrutiny of the billable hours charged to his interests. It was all handled discretely, with maximum insulation between parties. In exchange, his partners made sure that Johnny had free reign to build according to his standards, which often did not coincide with the law.

He viewed these "associates" as utter hypocrites, masquerading as upright members of the community when in fact they were small time extortionists. He allowed them to maintain the illusion mainly when it suited his purposes. He put up with their snobbery. His assumed last name ended in a vowel and he suspected they viewed him as some immigrant laborer just off the boat from Sicily. A man whose hands were calloused from manual labor, as opposed to the silky manicures their delicate occupations called for. Occasionally, he bristled at their condescension and contemplated payback, but he generally eschewed the immediate gratification for a more substantial price to be extracted at a time of his choosing.

John Serpente provided housing for the poor. He made a profit. *This is America, isn't it? Isn't that what it's all about, making a buck?* But the elites wanted to keep the poor working man in his place. They wanted to house him in ghettos far from their luxurious playgrounds. *Not in my backyard*! So Johnny Goombah was a mere step above a common laborer in their eyes.

The taxpayers didn't want to foot the bill for the working poor, at least on the books. So faced with ever shrinking budgets for public housing, he had to make the numbers work while still taking his cut. Building codes? They were for some Ivy League professors who thought they knew what was best for the great unwashed. He knew better what worked and what didn't. So he cut some corners --- no harm, no foul. He learned to provide more units for less cost by skimping on some things that in his mind, really didn't matter.

Another part of the charade Johnny truly resented on a daily basis was trying to dance to his wealthy friends' cultural standards. Born in Brooklyn, he fancied himself a meat and potatoes guy. His speech reflected his birthplace. He learned hard lessons on grimy city streets but now in this more genteel Southern setting, he was forced to make adjustments. He adapted the rules as he went along as he played the country club game.

This was reflected symbolically as he competed in their sport of choice. He didn't see anything wrong with teasing the ball into a better lie in the rough, or nudging it over a yard or two so that a tree wouldn't block his route to the green. If his first attempt left him in a bunker, well, it didn't count if no one saw it --- that was just practice, right? And you were entitled to a couple of unreported mulligans, weren't you?

But Johnny's jiggering the scorecard hadn't helped him much today. Even at a buck a hole plus junk, he hated to lose to these pricks and the added indignity of buying the drinks as a result of dropping both nines was adding to his distemper.

"Well, Serpy, you really took it on the chin today," one of his foursome, an attorney, said as he sipped an eighteen dollar glass of single malt. "I don't think I've seen you drive so erratically. Normally, a wiry Dago like you keeps in the short grass."

Serpente stiffened at the casual way the slur was tossed but held his tongue. A third member of their group, a prominent city councilman, was just returning from the locker room, bourbon and branch water waiting. Their fourth had begged off their customary post game round of drinks to attend to his wife's social calendar. Serpente played with these men regularly. They were the closest thing he had to friends at the club.

"Couldn't get that slice under control. Frigging wanted to bust my wrist, it was flying open so much." Johnny had conceded that "frigging" was more acceptable in their company than the more graphic expression whose use was reserved for dealing with subordinates.

"Maybe you should try a lesson. Our pro here is rated in the top fifty in the country. Really knows her stuff," the councilman added. He was a slim, fastidious man, always perfectly put together. Fresh from the locker room, he wore impeccably creased flannel slacks and an auburn cashmere sweater. His skin glowed under shower slicked hair. He sipped the bourbon appreciatively, closing his eyes as he savored the smoky aftertaste. "Fix that slice in no time."

Johnny's swing was homemade, and while not a thing of beauty, it worked for him most of the time. He didn't want some fancy pants female club pro messing with it.

He just grunted in reply.

"Well, you certainly weren't yourself today, Serpy." Johnny didn't like the nickname the country club set had given him. No one else dared call him "Serpy". By refusing to use his full name, it somehow diminished him; that was how he took it, anyway. His so-called friends thought by assigning him a pet name they were being inclusive, admitting a lesser creature into their pride. "By the way, I take it you will handle that matter with the plumbing inspector. We wouldn't want that to blow up in our face now, would we?"

"Yeah, I'll take care of this *stonado*. Guy never should have been hired in the first place unless he knew the rules going in. But I'll clean it up."

"As long as it's covered. Just get it done. How's the lovely missus, by the way?" the lawyer said.

"Actually, you want to know, right now I'm a little pissed at the old lady." Although he was almost twenty years her senior, he referred to her in this fashion to age-match them more appropriately.

His partners jumped at the chance to hear more about Serpente's wife. Although they themselves had once married to trophies befitting their standing, Johnny's bride topped them all. Even at forty plus, the former runner-up Miss North Carolina outshone every woman in their circle. With no job and nothing to do but shop and keep herself fit, she excelled at both. Her infidelities since her union with Serpente were an open secret. The male club members relished sharing rumors of her lascivious behavior when he was not within earshot, another unspoken advantage they had over him.

"Do tell, Serpy, what has the beautiful missus done to warrant your displeasure?" the legal eagle inquired, barely disguising his boyish zeal for gossip in grown up verbiage.

"You know the way these broads are." Enough already. He didn't need to explain the arrangement he had with Charlene to these snobs.

"Come on, you're among friends. And what are friends for if not to lend a sympathetic ear?" His associate, although bursting with curiosity, feigned impartial counsel.

"Ah, nothing. She wasn't happy with our master bath. Had brass colored fixtures, not oil rubbed bronze like the fag designers in the women's magazines are into now."

"So, change them. You're a builder, what's it going to set you back? You keep letting it bother you, you'll lose more than that to us on the links. Not that we mind," the attorney said, winking.

As much as he didn't want to provide more detail, Johnny didn't want to appear cheap either. "I wish that was all it was. Reading that damn SouthPark magazine, she decides the whole master bath is outdated. Ceramic tile instead of travertine. Frosted shower door instead of frameless. Big ass mirror over the vanity instead of those little dainty ones."

"Okay, friend, but again as a builder, these are minor items, no?"

Johnny was exasperated enough to finally give up his story. "Look, you don't know the whole deal here. She throws that builder thing in my face, too. 'How hard is it to fix the bath and make your wife happy?' she says." His imitation was a nasally whine, quite the opposite of Charlene's husky purr.

His partners suppressed a snicker. "So make your wife happy. And she'll make you happy in turn".

"Right. Well, I tell her, you think it's so easy, why don't you do it? Make up a budget, draw up a plan and a work schedule. I figured that would shut her up." He took a deep draught of his Bud light.

"And?"

"That's where I fucked up, pardon my French. She took me up on it. She hires this *gavone*, used to be a big time builder but got screwed by the recession. She gets him to do the whole job for practically his cost. I mean, I guess the guy might have had some material left over from other jobs, whatever, but she got a great deal."

"So you should be happy --- it's win-win. You get a new master bath, appease the wife, and pay less than the going rate. What's to be upset about?" They both were disappointed that there were no lewd stories to be mined.

Serpente was uncomfortable talking about Charlene with them. He was a small, bony man, no more than five seven. With dishwater gray, thinning hair, he looked every bit of his sixty some years. He'd over-corrected his jagged teeth, but hadn't bulked up his scrawny frame with any sport other than golf. Even the fifteen hours a week he spent on the links didn't increase his fitness level, since they always took electric carts.

He was naturally pale. Never a flashy dresser, his current sartorial sufficiency was a direct result of his wife's taste and insistence. Early in their dating cycle, she'd taken him shopping and to this day picked most of his wardrobe. He cleaned up well enough so that their pairing wasn't exactly *beauty and the beast*, but everyone who knew them agreed that if Johnny wasn't wealthy, there was no way she'd be seen with him. In low moments, he admitted this to himself. But he saw no need to share his insecurities.

Serpente now turned to his area of expertise. "Yeah, but if you're smart, you know that when a deal seems too good to be true, it always is. Like, she shows me samples of the stuff the guy was putting in and again, the numbers don't add up. Now, mind you, I never even met this builder, fellow name of Davis."

The attorney did recall a builder named Davis that he'd done a closing with. He thought, *uh-oh, if it's the same Davis, the handsome contractor might be accepting payment from Charlene Serpente in something other than cash.* He could be willing to barter some of his services in exchange for some extracurricular activity. He kept these suspicions to himself, for now, although he was dying to tell his cohorts. He knew Johnny had a sore spot when it came to his wife and didn't wish to provoke it too much in the lavishly appointed taproom.

All he said was, "So what happened?"

"I was right. Guy was doing the work himself, it was going slow. Then he doesn't show up the last three days. I haven't had a working john in the master for two weeks now. Three times a night, I dance around a 2 by 4 when I have to go down the hall to take a piss."

Serpente's partners exchanged glances, greatly amused by this predicament but loath to ridicule the little man in his presence. "No wonder your game was off. You chunked an easy wedge on nine that you normally can hit in your sleep. So what now?"

Serpente shrugged as if he hadn't already decided. "I don't know. I got guys I pulled off another job to finish this one. Teach the old lady a lesson."

His partners nodded, disappointed in the low grade salacious yield. "Oh well, just make sure you clean up that plumbing inspector situation quickly. I think another round is in order. Gentlemen?"

They went back to recounting their exploits on a particularly vexing par five that they had conquered. Serpente mumbled his excuses for skipping another beer and headed to the locker room, eager to get away from others' critical analysis of his marital woes. He thought he heard Charlene's name mentioned prior to a cackle of laughter but wrote it off to paranoia caused by his bad mood. No point in alienating men he did business with, however prying they might be. And this new inspector was a pain in the ass he didn't need at the moment.

# Twelve

## Derek Davis

"Mr. Davis, our network can't find an insurer for you but that's not unusual. If you would be kind enough to provide us with a name or policy number, we can get the ball rolling on resolving the business side of your stay with us."

The patient services administrator was a small man with a shock of gray hair. Rimless glasses, gray eyes. A light gray suit, and pearlescent shirt. The only splash of color was the crimson striping on the neatly knotted rep tie around his neck. Even his voice seemed gray, despite his efforts to inject a bit of lightness.

"You couldn't find an insurer because I dropped my coverage when my company folded a few months back." Derek's premiums had been over a thousand a month, an expense he felt he could do without, since he'd never missed a day due to illness in twenty years. Even with the ACA, he figured he'd rather pay the small fine than apply for subsidized coverage. When he took that gamble, he didn't anticipate spending two nights at Cornelius Medical.

"Oh, I see. Then why don't we see if we can work out a method of payment that will be comfortable for both you and the hospital."

Davis wondered which one would be more comfortable when all was said and done, the hospital or him. Even at his age, his experience with the health care system was extremely limited. None of Derek's subs had been seriously hurt on the job and he was proud of that. When he first began building, he was amazed how cavalier most of them were about safety. Within the organized chaos of construction, there is always the risk of injury. Therefore, he'd always insisted on hard hats, gloves and safety glasses for anyone on the job site. He warned his subs that if he caught anyone not wearing protective gear specific to their tasks, like masks or ear plugs, they would be immediately suspended for a day, without pay. Initially, this hard line stance spawned curses uttered sub voce in Spanish, that's how he learned what *mericon* meant. But in the end, the reduction in days lost to injury more than compensated for the fines, not to mention the human cost.

"Give me an idea of how much we're talking about."

The gray man consulted his tablet. "Well, up to this minute, we have one figure. If you were to stay an additional night, of course, you would incur further charges. But at the moment, including doctors' visits and lab fees, plus the room and medications, your total is $8245.78."

Davis flashed some quick numbers. He'd gotten a twelve thousand dollar advance to start the Serpente gig. Materials already accounted for half that. There was some marble and some bath fixtures on order---- hopefully he could cancel those. He'd be over two grand in the hole on this job, assuming Serpente didn't have the balls to demand his deposit back. Could the beating be applied as payment?

"Any discount for cash?"

"Oh and now I see Dr. Shamaylan has reserved a suite to perform a procedure tomorrow morning. That would be another $1456."

"But he indicated to me that there would be no charge for that."

The gray man shook his head. "Whatever fee arrangement you have with him is between the two of you. I don't see his charges here yet, but that is standard practice until the procedure is complete. And I should also warn you that there would be an additional charge for the anesthesiologist. I'm guessing that could be in the twelve hundred range. But the O.R. charge for the procedure is a fixed cost. That's the fourteen fifty six."

There was no way he could justify an additional three grand to indulge his vanity, not at this point. He'd have to speak to Shamaylan and see if postponing the work would cause any lasting disfigurement. Walking around sounding like Darth Vader wasn't something he relished, but maybe Shamaylan could suggest a more affordable alternative.

"So you know, this is coming directly out of pocket. Is there some way we can do this for a little less?"

The gray man gave him a practiced look of concern. "We can work out a payment plan. Given the figures we're dealing with here, a three year monthly payment at three percent per annum seems doable. How does that sound to you?"

Davis hated owing money to anyone. The only mortgage he was carrying now was on New Hope and the payments were breaking him as it was. He was loath to take on an extra three hundred a month even at a reasonable three percent. He told the gray man that his suggestion was a non-starter.

"The other course is --- if you'd agree to allow us to examine your financials. If you prove to be indigent, we have a program that could cover *all* of the expenses."

Davis hated that idea even more. He paid his debts. He wasn't about to accept charity even if he qualified. "Well, I don't want to do that, either. Is there any discount for cash? I asked you that before and I don't recall your answer."

"We do offer consideration for prompt payment. We could reduce your charges by twenty seven per cent if you pay within fifteen days, twenty five if you pay in full within thirty."

"That sounds like the way to go. I'm going to need to leave as soon as you can get me out of here."

"That's up to your doctors. We don't want financial considerations to affect your well-being."

"No, that's up to *me*. I'll sign whatever waiver you need, so you won't be liable if anything happens. Just get me out of here, asap. You'll have your money in two weeks."

He knew that his injuries were not life-threatening and even if they were, would it really make a difference at this point? Davis drew himself up, grimacing in pain. "Now, where are my pants?"

# Thirteen

"Man, there's sacrifices and then there's sacrifices," I said.

Davis was scrunched deep into the passenger's bucket in my Audi A5. The heated seat eased his discomfort somewhat, but the shoulder restraint dug onto his ribs whenever I took a turn too swiftly. The aggressive driving was payback for missing my date.

"Hey, pal, if it wasn't for me getting beat up, you wouldn't have met this chick anyway," Davis said. "So slow down, you'll have your shot."

I swung the Audi through a twenty five mph curve at 45. "Yeah, well... I can't follow up on Wade's family tonight anyway, but I was looking forward to spending some quality time with the fair Ms. Monahan. Until you insisted I give you a ride home, that is."

"From what you said, she must be a marvelous swimmer," Derek answered, channeling his inner George Harrison with a poor attempt at a Liverpool accent.

"Don't rub it in."

"Look, Riles, I do appreciate all you're doing. Hey, when I feel better in a couple of days, I'll start work on building those bookcases for your office. I'll sketch something out and you let me know how you want them finished."

Normally not one to extend sympathy, I had to admit Davis did look pretty pathetic curled up in the seat next to me. I eased off the accelerator, acknowledging that I had allowed lust to overcome compassion.

"We'll see about that. So did you get Shamaylan to reschedule?"

"Yeah, he was great about it. Said it could be an office procedure day after tomorrow and not to worry about the anesthesia."

"Yeah, tough guy like you, a shot of whiskey and a bullet to bite is all the numbing you'll need. Might even be an improvement over that craggy mug you've been sporting for the last hundred years."

Davis laughed softly but I knew his appearance *had* been a concern lately, even before the beating. The circles under his eyes which he always figured could be cured by a decent night sleep now seemed permanent fixtures. His cheeks were succumbing to gravity, sagging into small wattles on his neck. He was becoming alarmed at the parchment quality the skin on his legs was taking on. Small blemishes that had previously caused him no concern now were potential melanomas. Soap sting at the tip of his manhood could be a sign of prostate issues. Minor muscles aches in his extremities might signal an impending heart attack. I was only a couple years younger than he, so I had all these little signs of decay to look forward to. Whoop-de-do.

Derek had grown comfortable having Liz around. Facing a life without her meant years of loneliness or worse, trying to attract someone else, a game he was not eager to enter. He no longer was a prosperous young builder; he was now a middle aged day worker, living in a hovel compared to his previous digs. The package of affluence and physical attractiveness had made him a decent catch. Now with the money gone and the looks fading, his prospects seemed bleak.

He'd told me earlier about his misgivings concerning Todd Weller. He knew that he was smarter than Weller, more sophisticated, deeper. But Weller would give George Clooney a run for his money in the looks department. Physically, Weller was superior to Derek by every metric. He was younger than Liz, but envisioning them together, even Davis had to admit that no one would guess that almost a decade separated them. Indeed, the smaller gap between his own age and Liz's seemed more pronounced as the years progressed.

Davis said, "So, about my accident. If you've got other business Riles, don't let me keep you from it. In the scheme of things, it's not that important I guess. From what you've already pieced together, I doubt the cops would go after Serpente anyway. So why waste your time?"

I fed the accelerator again. "Feeling sorry for yourself? Man, you're a country song. Your woman ran off, you lost your job, you live in a shithole. All you need is a dead dog. I got a friend who knows Darius Rucker, maybe we sell your story to him and he can make a hit record out of it."

"Very funny. If we waste our time finding out why someone beat me up, where does that get us? Why escalate this into a war when we know we're up against bigger battalions?"

"Excuse me, but did they remove your balls in that hospital? Damn it man, somebody kicked the dung out of you. You don't even want to know who did it and why? And you can just move on?"

"All I'm saying is, let's say we find out who and why. Then what?"

I stared out at the winding road ahead, trying to disguise my disappointment in his spineless stance. "Depends. My gut says that Serpente is behind this. You were working for him --- his name is Johnny."

"But let's look at the big picture. Where is this going?"

I resisted raising my voice. "Less than two days ago, a couple guys leave you for dead on a sidewalk and you're looking at the big picture? Aren't you pissed? Aren't you outraged that someone could hurt you, cost you money you don't have and just skate away? Don't you want to make someone pay for what they did?"

"Sure, the primitive side of me does. The macho, dumb-ass, competitive jock side of me says bring it on, I'll kick butt. But what does that really accomplish for me? It takes time and resources away from what I need to do and that's rebuild my business and keep my project alive."

"I never took you for some candy-ass metrosexual, Derek," I shook my head. "Some things just have to be done. You can't let people get away with shit. Then next guy knows that, pulls even more shit. Next thing you know, you're up to your eyeballs in it and you can't dig your way out."

"What about karma, though? What goes around comes around. Turn the other cheek?"

"Yeah, Jesus said that. And look where it got him, hung up on a cross. I mean, if your goal is storing up brownie points for the next life --- "

"My point is, it's already paid off. Shamaylan is giving me several thousand dollars worth of repair work gratis. Because I helped him out when he needed it. Now I never expected to be repaid like this. Never thought I'd need his services. I didn't even remember who he was at first. So good deeds may not get rewarded immediately but they do get rewarded.

"Maybe it's all bullshit, I don't know. Riles, let me try to explain what I mean. It's like when a guy is on trial for murder, say he killed someone's brother. The bad guy gets convicted, gets a lethal injection. The family wants to witness the execution. Why? Because they claim it gives them *closure*. What the hell is closure? Killing one bad man doesn't bring the other man back to life. Still must hurt like hell. So how does it benefit the family to see someone else fry? It's primitive, barbaric."

I said, "I've been at executions and the victim's people *do* feel better about justice being served. It's human nature. If we find out who did this to you and why, you'll appreciate it, trust me on this one. And I think when you stop feeling sorry for yourself, you'll agree.

"Understand, I'm saying this as your friend. Look at your life a few years ago. You had a nice house, fully paid for. You had a great woman --- smart, gorgeous and oh by the way, rich. I get it, your business went south. Join the club. But you had work, maybe not the big bucks stuff you were used to but enough to stay afloat. In actuality, stay nicely afloat. So what happens? You sell the house, lose the woman, and for what? *A god damned housing development.* How many hundreds of those have gone belly up in the last two years? I mean is it worth losing everything you had for a housing development?"

"Riles, I thought you got it. This wasn't just a housing development, this was going to start a change in the way we live. This was a response to the techno age, where we don't need offices to commute to. A community that isn't electronic but uses electronics. This is how I make a mark on the world. Maybe make a better life for millions. My contribution to the earth."

"You're talking like some sorry ass hippie now. Don't you see, it's screwing up your whole life? Let it go for now. Let the bank have it. Start over. Fight for something other than this cause that may not even be worth it. It's a dream. Maybe you can pick it up in a few years, when the economy recovers."

"I let the banks foreclose, my credit is shot. I'd be sixty five before I can restore my name in the industry."

"That's bullshit. America loves people who get off the mat and fight. But pick your battles wisely. Fight for Liz. She's real. Fight for what you can have now, don't give up your manhood. If you just let people like Serpente push you around with no consequence, how are you ever going to achieve anything great? I thought you were stronger than that."

"I guess we have a different definition of strength. Tell you what, Riles, I've taken up enough of your time. You've got paying clients to attend to."

"But..."

"No. I mean it. Take me home now and let it drop."

# Fourteen

"Sorry about dinner. Had to take my friend home from the hospital. Does tomorrow work?"

I was home, relaxing with a single malt while channel surfing sports. This was my second call to Julie Monahan, the first, an effusive apology left on her service an hour prior.

"Your loss," she said. "Road trip to the New York area for a tournament in the Meadowlands. I won't be back until next Monday."

"The whole team going?"

"Including Corey Wade if that's what you're asking. I'm getting the impression you're only interested in me to get to him. Am I wrong?"

"As wrong as can be. Like I told you, five minutes with him is all I need. With you, I plan on taking considerably longer."

"Do lines like that work in the hot pickup spots in Charlotte?"

"I wouldn't know. I'm sorry, I *would* like to get in touch with Corey. And I would like to take you to dinner." I awaited a response and receiving none, I plowed ahead. "I like you. I'd like to see what develops. Corey Wade or no Corey Wade."

Again there was no response. "Still there?"

"Yeah."

"No reaction to what I just said?"

"I'm not sure what you want me to say."

"I want you to say whatever is on your mind. If it's go screw yourself, say it." I recalled something I'd read in a self improvement book some years back. Don't make vague proposals if you want an honest answer. Be specific. "Let's have dinner when you get back from New York Monday night. Seven o'clock. Mickey and Mooch in Huntersville. We can meet there or I can pick you up ---- whatever you're comfortable with."

Again silence.

"All right," he said. "I don't know what I did or said, but you seem different than you did this afternoon. This *is* Julie Monahan, right? If you're mad because I stood you up tonight, I thought I explained that it was important. I wouldn't have called you back to apologize again if I didn't feel bad about it."

"It's not that. It's not like we signed a contract or anything."

"What is it then?" I was about ready to give up. I already felt guilty for pursuing this woman when Jaime was still in the picture. She occasionally teased me about how she understood that men have *needs* but I knew how I'd react if she were having this same conversation with some sharp dressed man in New York. I was disappointed in Julie Monahan, but by writing her off now, I might save myself grief later.

"Okay, look, I'll find Corey on my own. Sorry to have bothered you," I said, in resignation.

"Riley, wait."

My finger was a split second from disengaging.

"Corey doesn't want to talk to you."

"So you spoke to him?"

"Yes. He called in. Wanted to know when and where he needed to be for the trip to New York tomorrow."

"Did he say why he wouldn't talk? I mean, he did something positive. He could have just called 911 and let the EMS folks take over. But he went out of his way for a guy he didn't know. Who knows, if the injuries had been more serious, the time he saved may have saved a life. Why wouldn't he want to help me find out who attacked my friend?"

"He thinks you want something else. I agreed to help you before under what I now consider false pretenses."

I couldn't ask for a more definitive declaration of why she was no longer an ally. Her job was shielding the student-athlete from harm, while burnishing the achievements of Davidson's sports programs and all who participated in them. It took precedence over helping me root out the truth. But why should Corey Wade become inhibited now when he could only improve his image by coming forward? Unless he was in on it.

"How did I lie?"

"Corey says he wasn't there. He didn't take anybody to the hospital. He thinks you're either from the NCAA or some kind of reporter trying to dig up dirt on him."

"My NCAA days ended at Georgetown years ago. And I'm as wary of the press as the next guy so don't confuse me with a reporter. Julie, hate to impugn the kid, but he's not telling you the truth. Corey or someone using his cell phone called me from the hospital to let me know what happened. I have it on caller ID. I also have a eyewitness statement that he was at the scene. So if he's denying it, it makes me wonder why."

"Like you say, maybe someone was using his cell. And how closely did this witness see him?"

"Fine, Miss Defense Counsel. I'll make you a deal. Tell him what I just told you. I don't even have to talk to him. If he'll tell you what happened and can point us toward whoever did this, and if you're convinced he's being honest, I'll accept that."

"You mean it?"

I didn't but it sounded good. "Julie, if you could see what these thugs did to my friend, you'd understand. If Corey Wade can lead me to the bad guys, there's no reason anyone has to know he was involved. But think about it, he's hiding something. I'm not accusing him of anything, I just want the truth."

She took a deep breath and exhaled. "Okay, let me talk to him again. He trusts me. There might be other explanations. Maybe he's scared that whoever did this will come back at him if he snitches. You know how kids think."

Sadly, I did. *Doing the right thing* meant not snitching on your friends. In my day, it meant, standing up to malevolence and accepting the consequences. "Like I said, his name doesn't have to come up. This isn't a police matter now and I protect my sources."

"I think he's a good kid. He came from a rough background but he has excellent grades and his high school coach vouched for his character, otherwise Davidson wouldn't have recruited him. We have high standards."

"I know that." This was true. They had plenty of eager recruits without baggage. They don't accept questionable characters to win. Their coach wasn't on notice every time they lost to a traditional rival. They run a clean program.

She said, "So let me spend some time with him while we're on the road and see what I can find out. If it's helpful, I'll pass it on. At dinner Monday night at Mickey and Mooch. Seven o'clock. Deal?

"I'm there."

# Fifteen

## Derek Davis

Davis awoke in his own bed, the sun struggling to pass through the condensation fogging his window. He was disoriented and it took a minute for him to realize that he was back home, or at least at the rental that he'd called home for the past few months. Just as slowly he absorbed the fact that the diffused light wasn't coming directly from the sun but from its reflection off the windows of the building opposite his.

Derek Davis might as well have been living in a storage bin. Moving from a spacious home on the lake to a nine hundred fifty square foot apartment that cost him seven hundred a month in rent had eased his cash flow worries somewhat, but it came at a price. The condo provided him with a small kitchen that worked well enough to heat the microwave dinners that were his staple now, and the single bath was all he needed to clean up after a dirty day's labor. But instead of a sizable basement workshop, his tools were stored in the single garage bay that the landlord provided. The few pieces of furniture that he hadn't sold to a consignment store at ten cents on the dollar or donated to Goodwill, sparsely furnished the multi-purpose main room of the condo. He kept his king sized bed on the off chance that it might be shared occasionally, but it took up over half of the inappropriately titled master bedroom.

The closet sized second bedroom was chock full of items that held some value to him--- monetary or sentimental. He'd saved an old sofa that he'd picked out with his mother twenty five years ago, and a few odd pieces of art. The rest of the room was filled with boxes containing business records, his collection of classic rock CDs, which he intended to translate to MP3s when he had the time. Anything else that couldn't be converted into immediate cash or might be valuable to him in the future packed the room to the gills.

He kept a laptop on the breakfast bar and cribbed onto a neighbor's unsecured wireless connection to get internet access. An amplified antenna allowed him to receive television signals from over the air broadcasts. He read more now, and had learned to patiently wait to download books from the public library as opposed to the days when he'd order a dozen titles from Amazon and think nothing of it.

His was a monk-like existence. He was gaining a perverse pleasure in finding ways to deny himself comforts, even if they saved him only pennies. Instead of subscribing to the Charlotte Observer, he would grab the previous day's edition at the town coffee shop before they disposed of the unsold copies. He especially liked the Sunday paper because it was overflowing with coupons that saved him meaningful dollars at the supermarket. He devised a game: he kept careful records of food expenditures, and the challenge was to top the previous week's savings by a greater percent each time out. It rankled that on their nights out together, King insisted on picking up the tab. His friend chided that when things got better, he knew that Derek would reciprocate.

Davis had tried to think of a creative way out of this crisis. He approached the banks he'd dealt with in his salad days, thinking they might lend him enough to do some flips on his own. But they all had tightened their lending standards and his proposals never gained traction, given his diminished assets and debt on the land. It seemed that New Hope might never come to fruition, despite his sacrifices.

Overnight, the overall pain had subsided into an ache approximating the soreness one gets the day after a vigorous but overdue workout. Clad in a tee shirt and briefs, he tiptoed around the clutter toward the bathroom.

He noted that his stream was pale, untainted by blood. A welcome improvement. The cheap, wavy mirror over the vanity reflected a face gradually returning to its normal hue, distorted nose notwithstanding. He threw on some jeans and a Davidson College sweatshirt and began his day.

He actually felt pretty good. Maybe it was a night in his own bed, but he felt a sense of renewal rising within him. Shaking the fog away, he consulted his mental day planner. He wanted to call King. They'd left things in a bad place last night and Derek felt the need to apologize. He didn't want his friend taking time from more profitable endeavors, especially if no satisfactory finale was possible. In the short term, petty revenge was a diversion from his ultimate goals.

He noticed that the LED display on his cell indicated an unanswered message. It was from a blocked number. Even though he had dutifully placed his phone on the government "do not call" list, charities, political robo-calls and even a few local scammers still managed to get through. Rather than deal with it now, he speed-dialed his tile supplier.

"Hey Chet, Derek here. How's it going?"

"Everything's good. Busy now. What do you need?"

"Real quick, I need to cancel the travertine on the Serpente job."

"Sorry, no can do, pal. We delivered it yesterday. You weren't there so the lady of the house signed for it."

"Yeah, well I'm not doing that job any more. Can you pick it back up? I'd be willing to pay for the delivery truck's time."

"Come on Derek, you know that was a custom order. The manufacturer won't take it back."

"Even if I pay a restocking fee?" In most cases, Derek knew that such levies were superfluous --- designed to discourage frivolous change orders. The dealer simply returned the items, as yet unpaid for, and stuck the manufacturer with the unwanted material. But in this case, Chet might have to absorb the outlay. He might be able to re-sell it as overstock at a discounted price but the odds were long that he would break even.

"I'd like to Derek, but I can't sell this stuff. I don't have room in the showroom and buried in the warehouse nobody is going to see it. Maybe some picker type would bite but you're talking cents on the dollar. Can't do it."

"How about on consignment? It's really nice stuff."

"Hey, I'd like to help but it's a custom order and a specific amount. It's either going to be too much or not enough for another job. Best I can do is send you the invoice in sixty days rather than thirty if money's tight now, but can't let you skate. You understand."

"Yeah, I'd appreciate that Chet. Thanks, I know you'd try if you could."

"Sorry I couldn't do more. But we're all hurting here. Later."

His optimistic mood had been dampened to a degree and subsequent calls to suppliers weren't much better. Fortunately the toilet, bidet and showerheads were stock items and he was able to cancel their delivery, but the other fixtures were custom ordered and the best he could do was agree to pay a restocking fee. His losses were mounting.

For a second, he contemplated calling Charlene Serpente and asking if he could remove the tile on his own. But calling Charlene brought to mind something he had avoided coming to grips with. The more he'd thought about it, the more he supposed it might have something to do with the violence that had been inflicted upon him. He had to tell Riley about the incident. He should have done it sooner.

# Sixteen

## Johnny Serpente

After the belittling badinage with his colleagues, Serpente headed for the men's locker room, where he found that his golf shoes had been dutifully placed in front of his cubicle by the attendant. The day's grime had been scrubbed away and the spikes cleaned. The polished cowhide uppers gleamed to a mirrored finish, but noticeable fissures were developing on the worn leather soles.

*Maybe they could refurbish these*, he thought, calling over to the clubhouse man's booth.

"Hey, Moses, got a minute?"

"Yes sir, Mr. Serpente. What's your pleasure?"

Moses Ginn was in his late sixties. His posture was still strong and underneath his gray blazer and neatly pressed slacks, he was all lean muscle. He approached with a mischievous, almost conspiratorial gleam in his eye. He'd been with the club for over forty years, and knew all of its deepest secrets. Most of the major movers and shakers in Charlotte had passed through this locker room, and Moses had served them all and heard all their stories. But if he had opinions on anything other than the weather, he kept them to himself, at least as far as Johnny could see. When it came to serving the members, no detail was beneath his attention. Despite his station, his mirthful eyes were full of worldly wisdom and dignity, in the fashion of an old blues musician. The kind of guy who knew all the important stuff about life but had too much grace to point out that you didn't.

The only time he'd been away from the club was during the early seventies when, as the story went, he spent two tours in Viet Nam. Upon returning home, the old job at the club was all that was offered to him, but he had acquired certain skills while away. Where Moses Ginn lived or what he did in his spare time was a mystery to Johnny, one that he wouldn't spend any time trying to solve.

"Moses, I want you to take a look at these shoes. You think they can be re-soled? I paid a good buck for them and I'd hate to throw them out."

Ginn's eyes grew wide at the suggestion. "Well, actually Mr. Serpente, I been having a hard time finding soft spikes that fit them shoes. They don't make 'em anymore but I been keeping a supply as best I could. Fact is, these were the last ones I had."

"Call me Johnny, Moses. I wasn't asking if you could fix the spikes, I was asking if you could replace the soles. Maybe with newer ones that could handle the spikes they make today. Understand?"

"Yes sir. Truth be told, they don't really make new soles for golf shoes. Folks just usually get a season out of them and chuck them. Now, I suppose it's possible to fix up some regular soles to fit these, but to be honest with you sir, it'd probably be a cob job. They wouldn't be comfortable and might not look sharp. I be afraid that retirement is coming soon for these shoes, sir."

"And you don't have to call me sir, Moses. Oh well, it was a thought. That's the trouble with things today. Everything is made to be disposable. You know what I do for a living?"

Moses had a hard time bringing himself to address any member by his first name, much less drop the titles of respect that he'd been so vigilant to reference. An air of subservience had become second nature to him.

He kept his answer vague. "I heard you work for the government. Building apartments."

"That's the gist of it. I'm a builder. You know we're under orders to recycle everything now. Guess that's part of why I asked you about the shoes."

"Recycling be a good inclination, sir."

"Let me tell you Moses, a lot of this recycling craze is a bunch of bullshit. By the time you melt something down and clean it up and make it into something else, you could have made it from scratch cheaper and better. You said it yourself about these shoes. Damn EPA makes you refine all this stuff so that it's purer than the driven snow. Back where my ancestors are from, they never had laws like that and people lived into their hundreds. Understand what I'm saying?"

"Surely do."

Serpente wasn't sure that the man knew or cared but he needed to express his frustration. He'd had those shoes since he became a member and had grown to cherish them. They represented his ascendance to a higher level, acceptance to a country club that only the privileged few could enjoy. They gave him a sense of permanence and now he was being told they were obsolete.

"You know, they make it so damned expensive with all their rules that you can't build shelter for common folks anymore. And what do they know about construction, anyway? You think any of them ever picked up a hammer in their lives? And they tell you upfront that you need to obey their codes, but that after they inspect, they couldn't care less if you tear everything down. So I recycle stuff my way, maybe not the way they'd approve of but it saves me dough and no one's the wiser. Now today, I get this new guy.

Doesn't know how things work. Flags me on a two million dollar job. Bastards. Sometimes I feel like I'm fighting a one man battle against the machine."

He'd worked himself into a full rant now. All his resentments about life were being shared with a simple man he doubted could understand.

"You know Moses, you need something, you come to me. Can't promise to handle it on my own, but I got friends that'll help, too. Just ask."

"That's kindly of you, but I put no truck in asking for charity."

Serpente wondered how much of the service fee in lieu of tips he paid the club monthly trickled down to the workers. They probably skimmed a nice chunk off the top for themselves and marked it as administrative fees or some such balderdash. Even though he was a member and technically one of *them*, he felt he had more in common with Ginn. Snooty bastards felt they had all the answers because daddy bequeathed them a fortune. Somehow that made them better than someone who actually sweated and earned his way up.

He didn't share his misgivings with Ginn. He knew club politics enough to figure that if Moses Ginn got *uppity*, he would soon be let go. But there might be another way out, and Serpente could chalk it up to his good deed for the day.

"If you don't mind me asking Moses, what do they pay you here?"

"No sir, I imagine you could find out if you so desired. I make two thousand a month from May to November, then one thousand from December to April. Things slow down round here in winter."

Serpente quickly ran the total in his head. "Nineteen thousand a year. Hard to make ends meet on that, I imagine."

"Just me and my dog now. Never had children. Spend most of my time here. Social security and Medicare. Big television in this room I watch when I'm not busy. I get by."

"Tell you what, Moses. My organization might have a place for a man like you. I can see you take your work seriously and you do a good job. Always on time, rain or shine. I think we might be able to find you a position in my organization that would pay maybe thirty thousand a year. How does that sound? No promises, but I'll let you know within the week. Sound good?"

Moses Ginn looked Serpente square in the eye for the first time. "Begging your pardon sir, but I'm content where I am now. I don't know what you'd have me doing for that much money, but I make honest wages now. I'll be staying right here, thank you kindly though."

Serpente started to say something but held back. He'd worked hard since coming to Charlotte to foster a reputation as a tough guy with lethal backing up North. So he left the locker room carrying his worn shoes, feeling isolated and alone. The rich lawyers, doctors and politicians didn't really accept him; he was too "salt of the earth" for their refined tastes. And those stationed below him were too intimidated to treat him with anything but deference. Feigned or real, what did it matter?

He'd made a lot of money over the years. He was a member of the most prestigious club in the area. He had a fine house, several cars and a beautiful wife that other men envied. Their relationship was a sham, but she looked great on his arm when such decoration was called for.

He was essentially alone in life and at times it made him melancholy. He had no one he could talk to on his own level. He couldn't go back home to Brooklyn. His associates in North Carolina dismissed him as a low rent Dago who had acquired dirty millions.

He had lost his place in the world.

# Seventeen

## Derek Davis

As he cast about how to present his little secret to King without sounding like a total jerk, Davis' doorbell rang. *Paranoia. Was it the two goons coming to finish the job?* Normally he wouldn't have thought twice about cheerily telling Jehovah's Witnesses at the door that he was fornicating at the moment and had no time for their nonsense, but things were different now. The small window in the guest room afforded an obstructed view of the front entry and he eased over to it for a peek. A little old lady with a package of some sort. *A disguise?* Were there others, awaiting in the shadows? *I'm being silly, it's just a neighbor, checking in on me.*

He opened the front door cautiously, keeping his left foot in a position to jam it closed if the old lady made a false move. "Can I help you?"

"Hello, Mr. Davis. My name is Randee Blankenship. The lady with the tabby. I live in the building across the way. I came to see how you were feeling. Of course, everyone here was worried when they heard you were attacked."

"Thank you. Miss Blankenship. I'm fine now. I appreciate your concern." *The old biddy probably wants the gory details of what happened so she could share it with her crone friends.*

"You're a builder by trade, aren't you?" she asked. He had no idea how old she was, he guessed anywhere from fifty five to seventy. *Fifty five and I'm labeling her an old biddy. We might be the same age. Yikes.*

"Do you mind if I come in? I brought you some cookies. I hope you like chocolate chip, just the Toll House recipe I'm afraid, but they are fresh from the oven."

He was reluctant to let her in, but he knew that he had to overcome this reticence if he was going to move forward. If an old lady bearing cookies scared him, how was he going to face a mouthy subcontractor. *Get over it, Derek!!*

"Please come in. I have some coffee. Let me clear a spot."

She entered the apartment, her bright blue eyes flitting about the chaotic scene. "Oh my, I didn't realize that those men trashed your apartment. I was under the impression you were attacked outside."

The tension burst like an overfilled balloon and laughter erupted from him. She was puzzled by his overreaction to her observation, but smiled sweetly nonetheless.

He said, "I'm sorry, I guess I'm just used to the clutter. No one trashed the place. I just have too much junk and no place to put it."

"I understand. I'm not so old as to forget what a bachelor's apartment looks like. Let's have some cookies while they're still warm. And could I trouble you for tea, not coffee, if you can manage?"

"Of course," he said, showing a false confidence that he could easily locate anything in the hurricane damage that was his kitchen. After rummaging a bit, he found two crumpled tea bags that he had lifted from a Japanese restaurant. He found a mostly clean pot and heated water on the one stove burner that still functioned.

"How extensive were your injuries, Mr. Davis?" she asked.

"Luckily, it seems my ribs were only bruised not broken. Nothing they could do about that anyway, they need to heal on their own. The worst damage is to my nose as you can see but have been kind enough not to point out. I've got an appointment to have that taken care of tomorrow."

"That's good. I'd be happy to take you over to wherever your appointment is tomorrow if you're not up to driving. No need to waste cab fare when you have neighbors."

"That's very kind of you but I think I'll be okay to drive." He poured the steaming water into the nicest clean mug he could find. Maybe she had come to dish to the whole neighborhood about his woes but she had the good taste to hold off the interrogation until they were settled. "I'm fresh out of milk. Sugar or artificial sweetener?"

"A Sweet N' Lo if you have it. Just one please." He brought the tea and two small plates to the table, which she had cleared sufficiently for them to sit.

His fear surfaced again. *I'll wait until she takes the first bite in case they're poisoned.* She didn't notice his reluctance and took a bite, again making him painfully aware of how far he had to go.

"Good," he said as he sampled the cookie. "This is very sweet of you, Ms. Blankenship."

"Call me Randee. But I have to admit, I have an agenda."

Here it comes. The *Crone Chronicle's* readers demand the truth. Chapter and verse of what happened Monday morning. Film at Eleven.

"An agenda? My, my. Well, these cookies are so good, they're worth at least me asking what I can do for you."

"How long before you can lift a hammer?"

"Doctors told me to let pain be my guide. If it hurts too much, close it down. I don't know. I expect the rhinoplasty or whatever it's called will set me back some but I imagine by the beginning of next week, I'll be able to do some light lifting. What do you have in mind?"

"I've been in my place just a few weeks now. It's too bad that such a lovely location has such dated apartments but I think this complex is prime for gentrification. A couple of my neighbors' units have been spruced up and they look great. "

Davis hadn't seen any of the nicer units. For him, this was a cheap resting spot until he could afford better so he didn't begrudge the builder grade quality. But the early part of the twenty-first century had seen a huge influx of Northerners who were nearing retirement age and looking for a nicer climate. Then as banking regulations loosened, Charlotte-based Bank of America and Wachovia grew exponentially, bringing wealth and thousands of new jobs to the area. Added to that were retirees who had migrated to Florida but found the summers too harsh for them. These so called "half backs" wanted to be closer to family members still in the Northeast and enjoy the mild four seasons the Piedmont enjoyed without extreme heat or cold.

"Here's my first proposal--- a trade. You help me fix up my place. In return, I'll clean up your condo, organize things in the kitchen. I'll do the unskilled work in both places and I'll pay you the going rate for your time."

A year ago he would have laughed. What did she think the going rate was? And what kind of work did she envision for her place? But now, maybe he could come home to something a little nicer than the sour conditions he was in. Possibly make a few bucks close to home doing some light carpentry, trim, tiling. Who knows, the way word spread amongst the oldsters, more of the neighbors might opt for an upgrade. Maybe he could even recoup some of the losses on the bathroom renovation by actually using the materials he was stuck with.

"Randee, your idea might work. Let's talk more."

"There's something else that might be even of more interest to you. I've been looking into a low income housing development that is up for auction soon. They've already moved the tenants out to other locations. The government subsidy is about to expire and a new owner could renovate them and sell the units at market value. I did a little research and you have a sterling reputation as a builder."

"Thank you. I guess you can fool some of the people...."

"Don't be so modest. Now, I've managed to put aside some money over the years. I was thinking that I could finance the project and you could supervise the renovations. A stipend and a percentage of the profits."

"Where is this place exactly?"

"Just the other side of the highway. Some of the units have a water view and they have riparian rights for dock space. What do you think?"

"I'd need to run some numbers, do some research of my own to see if this can pay off. We'd have to dig into the bones of this complex, see if the structures are worth saving or worth more as raw land. Probably visit town hall for the original plans and specs. They might not even have them. We might have to find the original builder."

She beamed. "I'm way ahead of you. I have the plans. They were actually pretty common to a lot of the low income housing built in this area over the last twenty years. All by one builder. A man named Serpente. Do you know him?"

# Eighteen

I spent the morning cleaning up some old work, making a respectable amount of money in the process. It still amazes me how much investigating I can do from the house, only leaving the home office to shuffle to the kitchen for another cup of coffee. Although the media often featured panicky stories about how much privacy was being sacrificed in the electronic age, they didn't reveal the half of it.

I can access property records within thirty seconds on the Mecklenburg County site by entering an address, a street, or a last name. I can check tax bills, paid or unpaid. These are items the public can avail themselves of. Less than five years ago, I might spend hours at the same task, travelling to and from town halls and county seats, plowing through dusty bins of often outdated records. Other than meeting a couple of randy female public servants, there was little advantage to probing in person.

The more revealing sites are not available to the average citizen. A few of these are obtainable openly --- you merely had to know where to look. But there is a treasure trove of protected materials online that need security codes or passwords to inspect. Through friends in the Bureau or local law enforcement agencies, I'm able to log in to many of these areas unnoticed. I have to be careful to find out which agencies can track my inquiries and which haven't the budget, expertise or manpower to be concerned with this data mining.

The most fruitful searches come through the credit bureaus, who ostensibly are only available to banks or health care organizations to protect their interests. I can inspect credit card charges and balances, home equity loans, unpaid taxes and a host of other debits that might prove useful.

I've become a self appointed gatekeeper --- judge and jury as to how this information can be used. If a client comes to me with what I consider a legitimate request, for a fee, I'll provide all the relevant evidence. The problem is there are people in my profession whose judgment is, shall we say, less morally incorruptible. Of course, an ethics professor might question my qualifications to make such decisions, and they would have a valid point.

The business is becoming less dependent on actual legwork and more on electronic snooping. My size and presence are assets that serve me not a whit on the internet. But the efficiency it offers has contributed mightily to my bottom line. I'm not a computer whiz or accomplished hacker by any definition, but I know several who are. In a nod to Sherlock Holmes, I call them my BS Irregulars, none of whom I've actually met. I suspect they're maladjusted teens working out of their parents' garage. Their folks probably think they're selling drugs to make all the cash they flash to spend injudiciously.

I glanced up at the old Seth Thomas studio clock I keep in the office as an artifact of days gone by. 11:30, almost lunchtime. There were two unresolved personal issues on my plate.

I needed to talk to my old friend Rick Stone, a sports talk show host in New Jersey. An ex-Marine (although those in the corps will tell you there is no such thing as an ex-), Stone has pulled me out of the fire a number of times. He saved Jaime's life in snowy Vermont, on a convoluted case that had helped convince me that it was finally time to get out of Dodge.

"Stone dude, how you be?"

"Hey Riles. What have you been up to?"

I sketched out the Derek Davis situation.

"Sounds like you're spending more time on this pro bono thing for your friend than on paying jobs. Business slow?" he said.

"If someone beat you up, I'd do the same. Business isn't bad. Spending a lot more time on the computer than I like these days. At least I can burn some shoe leather on this one. You still ripping the Jets on the radio?"

"Nothing they don't deserve, pal. You headed back north anytime soon?"

"No plans but you never know. I do miss my dog."

"Yeah, well Jaime takes Bosco to the office every day. He's kind of become a mascot for the agency. They have a picture of him on their Facebook page."

I had left my golden retriever with Jaime when I left Jersey. In a lot of ways, it was the hardest thing I had to do in leaving. Running a one man shop, I wasn't sure at first that I'd have enough time to care for an aging dog. The ulterior motive was that Bosco would be a constant reminder to Jaime of our relationship. I hoped that if she is tempted to succumb to the same *needs* that I have, Bosco's presence will guilt-trip her out of any infidelity. He might have that effect on me, too.

Given my current level of activity, I know that I should reclaim the dog, and that my large wooded property on the lake would afford the animal a better life than a semi-urban office in Fort Lee. Ms. Johansen had been hinting about that quite a bit of late.

"Have you seen Jaime recently, Rick?" I asked.

"Last week I was up in the city on a promotion for the station and we had dinner afterwards. She looks great. Misses you but I'll tell you, a woman that hot isn't going to wait around forever for you."

"I know. I'm hoping I can convince her that she can run her agency from here. Publishers are based mostly in New York, but with everything electronic these days, I'd bet she doesn't need to be physically present there for more than a few days a month. I know a big literary agent who lives in Dallas but doesn't miss a beat in New York."

"Well, good luck with that. Anything I can do up here to help you on this Davis case?"

"Can't think of anything now. But the guy who we like for it is from Brooklyn, so I may ask you to do some digging in your spare time. But not yet."

"Okay. Keep in touch. I miss taking your money on the golf course, man. You know with the technology today, like you were saying, I can do my show from anywhere. So a long visit isn't out of the question."

"Maybe we can work something out soon. I'll talk to Jaime and see what her schedule is. Holidays are coming. Talk soon."

I turned toward Derek's problem.

If Serpente was the one who made Davis suffer, he would need to be punished somehow. Generally, you want to send a message to the enemy that their pain is payback for a specific deed. The question was what would be more appropriate and what would hurt more --- a physical attack or damage to the man's business. But doing either posed risks ---- Shabielski had made it clear that 'the Snake' undoubtedly had larger forces to draw from, and probably fewer scruples about how to employ them.

The alternative was an anonymous attack, inflicting damage that could not be connected to Davis. I could live with that if there were no other choices but Davis would never endorse any such payback.

I grew up honoring the old school sense of justice where bad guys didn't get away unpunished. Maybe it was my father's love of old Western television ---- dad and I had bonded over countless hours of *Gunsmoke, Cheyenne, Maverick* and *Have Gun Will Travel*. There was a code of justice in those shows, a code now embedded deep within my psyche.

I wasn't looking to explore the psychological roots of my pathology, if that's what it is. The easy way out was the course Davis had resigned himself to --- let the whole matter drop, write off the losses and move on. But I couldn't let that stand even though there was more potential loss than gain by taking action.

I decided to call Derek now and invite him to lunch. I need a friend who was more than just a voice on the phone or a series of 1's and 0's.

# Nineteen

We sat in the early afternoon sun, looking out over the lake. For early November, the North Harbor Club was doing unusually brisk business on its waterside terrace. There would be few opportunities to enjoy al fresco dining again until spring; the place bustled with businessmen taking advantage of the unseasonably mild weather. The food was fine, the prices moderate and the setting was enticing ---- a small cove with a marina opening up to an expanse of water stretching nearly to the horizon.

"Glad there are no hard feelings, Riles," Davis said. "I know you're only trying to help. But you didn't have to buy lunch. Besides, I've got a two for one coupon anyway."

"Forget about it. My pleasure." I sipped unsweetened iced tea. The cool rustle of a gentle breeze reminded me that winter was approaching.

We'd engaged in small talk since arriving at the restaurant, avoiding the elephant in the room. I was enthused by the idea of Davis working with Randee Blankenship to flip the condos. There was a brightness in my friend's eyes that I haven't witnessed in months, a zest for a challenge that would utilize his more advanced skills, as opposed to the manual labor he'd recently taken on.

He said, "I've got something to tell you, Riley. I don't know why I didn't mention it sooner. I'm still not sure it's relevant to what happened, but then again, it might explain everything."

I speared another shrimp. "Do tell," I said, between bites.

"I told you that the missus hired me. I don't remember, with the medication and all if I told you much about her."

"You didn't say much about her. You know that radio guy, Patrick Henry? Apparently he knows her. Told me she was quite a looker."

"Well, I've finally found one thing I agree with Patrick Henry about. Charlene *is* very attractive. But why you give that asshole the time of day is beyond me. He and his listeners are total Neanderthals. Looking for a government conspiracy around every corner."

Although I agreed, I didn't want to debate talk radio. But I was happy to see some fire in Derek's belly again. The thing that had saddened me most about the previous night is that Davis had given up and accepted defeat without putting up a fight.

"What about Mrs. Serpente? What were you starting to tell me?"

This time it was Davis who tended to his meal. He'd ordered an open faced turkey Reuben, which was tasty but messy given his condition. He dribbled gravy from the corners of his mouth, constantly dabbing it off with a napkin.

"Her name is Charlene. Former Miss North Carolina runner-up. She's closer to fifty than forty but the years have been kind, with a little help, I'm sure."

"Those rich trophy wives usually do stay cutting edge when it comes to their looks. Otherwise, they can be replaced with a newer model. When my mom turned forty, my dad used to joke that he was thinking of trading her in for two twenties"

"Well, Charlene is far from her expiration date, I can tell you that," Derek said.

"So I've heard. So what does this have to do with you getting beat up, exactly?"

"Like I said, maybe nothing. But you know me, I don't kiss and tell. I feel a little weird telling you this."

Davis' love life was off limits for jest. His nocturnal activities with Elizabeth never were shared beyond the bedroom door.

I said, "Did Charlene Serpente come on to you? Is that what you're afraid to tell me?"

Even with this opening, Davis was reticent. "Understand, until recently I've been with Liz and we were exclusive. But when we were going over the details on the renovation, Charlene was touching me a lot, getting a little closer into my space than she needed to."

I waited for more but Derek was back gnawing at the Reuben. "Are you telling me that you succumbed to her charms, Lochinvar? Wouldn't blame you from what I've heard, but if the old man got wind of it, that explains quite a bit."

"No, but I may have pissed her off by not going there."

"Come on Derek, drop the shy maiden routine. So she touched your hand. Big deal. Is that it? Is that all you had to tell me? Unless Johnny saw more than that, even a scumbag like him wouldn't order a beating."

"There's more."

"Thought so. What?"

Davis began to rub his feet together under the table. He looked like he needed a drink, a real drink, but his doctors had warned him against mixing alcohol with his pills.

"All right, here it is. I just completed demo. Got the room all gutted out. I had sketched out plans for her, pulled the permits, and she approved them. Said she even had showed her husband and he thought they were cool. But I've found that very often that clients can't visualize things on paper. They need to actually be in the space physically to see what it's going to look like when it's done."

Derek's discomfort and intentional digressions were starting to bug me a little. He was taking his time getting to where he needed to go. But, it was a nice afternoon, the food was good and dessert beckoned so I saw no need to rush him along.

"So anyway, once I had the space cleared out, I thought it would be a good idea to go over where we were relocating the plumbing before I actually moved anything, just in case she wanted to reconsider when she saw the room in the flesh."

Even the term "in the flesh" seemed to unnerve Davis. For all his reluctance to swap tales of swordsmanship, I had never figured him for such a prude. "Makes sense, Derek. Then what?"

"Well, the bathroom overlooks the back yard. We were talking about enlarging the window over the Jacuzzi. You know, might be nice in the winter, candlelight bath while the snow is falling." He looked around as if some spy might be listening, then lowered his voice.

"Anyway, Charlene was in the backyard, sunbathing. Topless. I called down to her to come up and take a look at the room and give me her thoughts. I tried not to look, but it was hard not to. She is rather healthy."

He took another pull on his diet soft drink, again wishing it was something stronger. "So she came in to where I was working. She hadn't covered up. She came upstairs, uhh, without a shirt on."

The waitress came by to refresh our drinks, and Davis waited until she was out of earshot to continue. "To make a long story short, she started to come on to me."

"So what did you do?"

"I didn't know what to do. I was shocked. I mean, she's a beautiful woman and all but she's married. She kept touching me when we spoke. Finally she out and out said that her husband had not been very attentive to her and that she was lonely."

"Did you say anything?"

"I've never been with a married woman. Against my code. Not bragging, but as a contractor there have been opportunities. But it's bad business and can create problems especially if it gets around. Men would be pretty reluctant to hire you, as you can well imagine."

"And how did she react to that?"

"She seemed pissed. Like I was rejecting her."

I had to laugh. "Well, you were."

"What would you have done? Anyway, she turned on her heel and stomped off to the hall bath and slammed the door. It was late afternoon so I just figured I'd call it a day. Next morning I came back --- she wasn't home. The maid let me in. We were scheduled for sheetrock so I made sure all the plumbing and electric was in order."

"Spare me the construction details. So this was when?"

"Thursday. Friday, she wasn't there again but she left a note saying that the plans were fine and that if I needed anything at all from her, anything, she underlined, all I had to do was ask."

"So you hang drywall, didn't work the weekend and Monday, they got you."

"Yeah."

"And you had no further contact with her after the little tease?"

"No, and in answer to your next question, no one saw what happened. I don't know where the help was, but I didn't see anyone on the way out and no one could have seen her march from the master to the hall bath. The maid might have gone home already, but I'm sure no one was around to see or hear anything."

I gave Derek my best blank look, perfected by years of watching Johnny Carson. Right now, I couldn't picture anyone short of the Bride of Frankenstein going for him.

I said, "Hmmn. A woman scorned? Look, I've never met this babe, but I've heard this isn't the first time she's offered up the goodies. No offense. Maybe it wasn't your contracting expertise she was after all along, handsome. But it sounds like she's not used to being rejected and if she was pissed.... she tells a little fib to Johnny the Snake that it was you who came on to her, and he sets the dogs loose."

The seduction may have had nothing to do with the attack but the timing made sense. Somewhere over the weekend, Charlene might have spun her tale to Johnny, who in turn made sure that Davis wouldn't darken their door again. This complicated the revenge factor. Whereas Davis was still a wronged party, if Serpente truly believed the builder had made unwelcome advances toward his wife, I could understand how he would strike back. I might do the same thing if Jaime was the victim of unwanted attention, although I wouldn't delegate the mission. Now wasn't the time to share these misgivings with Derek, but discovering the truth would affect my reaction.

I said. "We've got a pretty circumstantial case going. We've connected some dots but I can't be a hundred per cent sure we're headed in the right direction. You know, the best way for me to get a bead on this is to meet Mrs. Serpente myself. See if she's the type to order a beat down based on a failed seduction. Although if she pulls the same act on me, it might not fail."

# Twenty

I was speeding down I-77, heading toward the southeast suburb of Charlotte known as Ballantyne, built in the mid-nineties by the real estate division of a local power company. I had little interest in urban planning prior to meeting Davis, and it still occupied a spot about fiftieth on the list of matters I thought about on a given day.

Charlotte is a sprawling city that had the sad example of Atlanta as a primer on how not to manage growth. While both were fast growing new metropolises, Atlanta had exploded a decade before Charlotte and had made all the missteps that a hot young town could make. The city fathers in North Carolina were wise enough to learn from this negative role model, and as a result had a more livable city.

Ballantyne was quite a beautiful place. The houses were large with no two alike; they had avoided the cookie cutter sameness of lower end tracts. The golf course was well maintained and nicely integrated into the landscaping. I could see why any young professional with a growing family would aspire to this exclusive subdivision. It couldn't be considered an enclave of the fabulously wealthy but it was near the top of the upper middle class.

Armed with our latest theory that Charlene Serpente might be the root cause of Derek's troubles, I wanted to observe her first hand. Davis provided me with the address, land line number and a description of her car, so I decided to stake out the lady in question. I called the house, disconnecting quickly when a honeyed woman's voice I assumed was Charlene's picked up.

Stakeouts have come a long way. In my early days with the feds, we had hewed to the classic two man approach, the tedious routine of sitting in a cramped vehicle all day with coffee and doughnuts, broken up by trips to the lavatory of a convenience store before returning to fill the just emptied bladders with more java.

Nowadays, a private investigator didn't even need to be physically present to conduct surveillance. Had I desired, I could watch Serpente's house from a nearby bistro. A miniature camera and transmitter, affixed to a telephone pole or street sign would provide a wide angle view of the property.

In this case, I went low tech --- parking a couple houses down from Serpente's, sitting in the car with the windows down. I'd traded vehicles with Davis, preferring the nondescript Escape to my A5. The curbsides were populated by landscapers' trailers or the cargo vans of plumbers, electricians or home theater specialists. The old Escape fit right in.

I had my Kindle, which allowed me entrée to more literature than the Library of Congress, not to mention any other publication that might pique my interest. My laptop with a 4G card gave me internet access in case I noticed something I wanted to research.

Chez Serpente was no more or less imposing than its neighbors. Situated on a wedge shaped piece of land at the end of a cul-de-sac, its architecture defied categorization. There were Italianate elements, which I expected given the surname, but it didn't stop there. There was a stone turret reminiscent of a medieval castle, which housed a circular staircase visible from the street. There was a nod to English Tudor with rough stucco, hand-planed half timbers and cross hatched brick accents. The steeply pitched roof was of a contemporary material that mimicked slate quite well. The double entry doors were massive, clad in rust colored metal, rising ten feet to their arched tops. Breaching them would be difficult given the full length mortised dead bolt system.

Davis had mentioned a pool and garden, but they were not visible from this vantage point. Although the street frontage was no more than eighty feet, given the shape of the lot, the rear property line stretched to over a hundred yards along the waters' edge.

Not a bad lifestyle. I could imagine retreating to the green after dinner to practice putting, followed by a dip in the pool and then a dip into Charlene if she was as hot as advertised.

I passed an hour perusing the sports columns of several papers in different cities, then did a little background on my target. In addition to her beauty contest exploits, Charlene had recorded a CD a while back. The sample tracks offered weren't bad --- a hybrid of folk, country and rock that many Nashville artists today favor. Given the release date of the CD, I could see where it must have been too avant-garde to do well commercially. The only online pictures displayed a tarted-up southern belle with big hair, too grotesquely overdone to be appealing. But the shots were a couple decades old, and there was nothing more recent for comparison.

I caught sight of movement in Serpente's driveway. A sleek late model BMW Z4, dark blue, cautiously backed out from the garage past a large pallet of what appeared to be thick slices of stone. This must be the delivery of travertine for the bathroom floor. I didn't envy whoever was going to be tasked with moving the heavy limestone into the house.

The Beemer K-turned in the courtyard and pulled out of the long narrow drive. As it passed the Escape, I caught a quick glimpse of a neat profile crowned by thick mane of blonde hair. *Charlene Serpente.* No false advertising here, she had it going on, in a big way.

The chase was on.

~~~~~~~~~~~

## Derek Davis

At home in his ramshackle apartment, Derek Davis made a phone call. With everything else coursing through his mind, he hadn't dwelt much Todd Weller's visit. But it *had* bothered him. He knew that he had no claim on Elizabeth Deveraux --- he'd let her walk away with very little protest.

She'd been raised in a wealthy family and luxuries were taken for granted. When his business was thriving, he had no problem providing her with the comforts she had gotten used to. But from the beginning, he had told her that his business was cyclical and a life with him meant that they might not always be able to afford the very best.

In retrospect, he was forced to acknowledge that much of the fault was due to his own outdated concept of chivalry. Anytime she offered to treat them to a night out or even to split the check for a meal, he resented her. It was a reminder that he couldn't live up to her expectations.

He hadn't spoken to Liz in weeks. Their last contact came when she called about a scarf she may have left in his car or at the condo. Obviously it was a pretense to open channels with him, but he stubbornly resisted her overture. He told her he hadn't seen it and after a few awkward moments, made an excuse that there was another matter he needed to tend to.

Damn. Weller had no right to be with her. She deserved better than some pretty boy ex-jock who probably hadn't cracked a book since high school. But he had no right to blame her for taking refuge wherever she could find it. The thought of her with Weller convinced him that he could no longer afford to play games. She needed to know how important she was to him.

He was reluctant to call her parents' home. He'd never really gotten close to her folks ---even after two years he never sensed he was part of their family, but he did have warm feelings toward her mother, who seemed to accept him more than her father had. He dialed their home in Rock Hill.

"Hello." The sweet southern accent belonged to Veronica Deveraux.

"Mrs. Deveraux. It's Derek Davis. How are you?"

"Fine, Derek." Matter of fact.

"I'm sorry to bother you. I've been trying to get in touch with Liz. Her cell doesn't pick up and when I called her apartment, it says her message box is full. Is everything all right?"

"Derek, I'm not able to talk to you now."

"I'm sure you're busy. I understand. But I'm just trying to see if Liz is all right."

"It's a little late for that."

"What do you mean? Has something happened to her? Where is she?"

"I'm hanging up now, sir. I don't know who you are or why you called. Please don't call here again. Take us off your list."

Dial tone.

Unfortunately, the last time he had seen her, at her seventieth birthday party, Davis had noticed her slipping. She had asked him the same question several times mere minutes apart, which he took as a sign that early stage Alzheimer's might be setting in. Liz did not want to consider the possibility when he told her about it.

Liz hadn't been all that close to her mother. She was clearly a Daddy's girl. She had told him that her mother was distant and moody, affectionate one moment and screaming at her the next.

But daddy was always there for Liz and always the final word. He was stern, but had a huge soft spot for his only daughter. He disapproved of Liz's two divorces, but allowed her to live back in his home between marriages. And during those times, he always came around to the view that his girl had been faultless and that these undeserving men had taken advantage of her.

Derek was intimidated by Jack Deveraux. His Southern patrician manner. His contempt for those who failed to live up to his standards. There was nothing overt in what he said that gave Derek this impression. Davis just felt that he never measured up to the level that Jack Deveraux set for his daughter's suitors. Liz had gradually convinced her father he was worthy of her hand, even though he had never asked. She emphasized how smart, how hard working Derek was, how his lineage traced back to the American Revolution. The old man had slowly come around, she said. It had reached the point where Mr. Deveraux had intimated that he'd invest in New Hope if it was built by his *son-in-law*. Despite his attempts to show enthusiasm for the concept, Derek knew that the offer wasn't extended because Deveraux shared his vision for a renewed American dream. He just wanted to make Liz happy. He supposed he couldn't blame him for that.

But now, Davis needed to know where Liz was. That she was all right. And he didn't know where to turn.

# Twenty One

Nice afternoon, nothing better to do than to follow a pretty woman through a fashionable mall. SouthPark had absolutely nothing to do with the irreverent cartoon that shared its name. Almost as opposing forces, the shopping there smelled of old money and the new South. Current chi-chi boutiques and revered old line department stores stood side by side in its directory. Since its inception in 1970, it had been gracefully updated several times. There was even a glossy monthly magazine named after it, consisting mostly of advertising extolling the elegant polish of its shops and the refinement of its high end clientele. It was where someone like Charlene Serpente shopped.

I followed the BMW from Ballantyne to SouthPark, casually breaking most of the rules I'd learned about surveillance. She had no reason to suspect that anyone would be stalking her, so I could afford to be a little careless. Derek's beat up old Escape would look out of place amongst the Cadillacs and Mercedes perched in the three story parking facility, but most of the patrons would ignore it as they would a homeless man seeking a handout.

And what would Madame's pleasure be this afternoon? A new pair of Manolos? Perhaps a little black dress from Ann Taylor? Or something that would stimulate the old man enough to skip his Cialis that night --- something from one of the ubiquitous Victoria's Secrets?

As I followed her through the Nordstrom entrance, I decided that any artificial stimulus Serpente might need was strictly on him, not her. Because as prepared as I was to dislike

Charlene, to find something off putting and artificial about this lady, just the sight of her from a distance excited me. Normally I'm very good at shutting off the old libido when it comes to unavailable women, whether they be married, the girlfriend of a buddy, or just out of my league. And then there is Jaime, who though six hundred miles away, is always a consideration when I encounter a potential playmate.

I had intended merely to observe, maybe pick up a snatch of conversation with a sales person, anything that might provide a hint as to whether she was the type of lady who would rain hell on a man for rejecting her. But after watching her walk, I envied Davis for catching even a stolen glance at her semi-naked form.

I began to feel like a modern day Ulysses, girding myself against the Sirens' song. *Dare I come closer? Dare I speak to her? Will it mean my ruin?*

Yet there was no overt effort on Charlene's part to attract me or anyone else she passed. The girl couldn't help it! She was dressed simply, in designer jeans that probably cost more than my entire wardrobe. A plain white cotton shirt, open at the neck, revealing a simple gold cross and the slightest wisp of cleavage. Medium heels, nothing kinky. All in all, her attire was tasteful and if anything understated.

The body it contained was not. The tight jeans accented her long legs and perfectly toned butt. It tapered to a tiny waist, then to a bosom that while abundant, did not distract the eye from her face.

And what a face it was. Strong straight nose, generously proportioned lips, cobalt blue eyes. Framed in long soft blonde curls. She seemed to be wearing little makeup; had I not known she was over forty, I would have guessed her age to be no more than twenty nine. She was lightly tanned, suggesting that she never surrendered her complexion to any exposure that wasn't attenuated by heavy sunscreen.

I stayed a safe distance behind her, the faintest whiff of her perfume trailing in the air. A mental picture of her attempted seduction of Davis formed in my mind. Was this truly low hanging fruit or did she reserve her charms only for the right man in the right place?

*Research, that's what this is.* If I can somehow get next to her, I can get closer to establishing who bore culpability for my friend's current condition. If there's a side benefit to be derived, well it's like giving an old lady your seat on the bus and later finding a twenty stuffed in your jacket pocket.

It might have been my head, heart or somewhere lower on my person that convinced me to take a more proactive approach. She entered a chain music store, one of the few that the internet had yet to shutter.

I tried to appear nonchalant as I drifted toward the area she was perusing. The store was large, and the rack of rock CDs stretched at least forty feet, returning the same distance in the opposite direction. Neatly alphabetized, I recognized many covers from my own collection, although quite a few of mine were vinyl.

Charlene stopped at the letter J and softly fingered through the pile. Her nails were clear coated and not long, a little gardening dirt soiled them on occasion, I suppose. She didn't notice me behind her --- she seemed entranced by something. Gazing over her shoulder at the item she held, I knew why.

The bit of plastic casing in her hand displayed a dazzling cover photo of Charlene Serpente, bedecked in full country babe regalia. Despite the twenty year disparity, she looked only slightly younger in the picture, big hair being the only divergence apparent. The bold yellow font proclaimed **Charlene Jones   Her Debut Album**.

I seized the opening. "Underrated. The fact she isn't more famous now is a crime. Best debut of that year, without a doubt."

She turned and looked up at me. She was tall, I was only a few inches taller. I noticed the slightest mist in her eye.

Playing the fan boy, I said "Oh my God, it's you. Imagine that, meeting Charlene Jones in a record store. It's an honor." Extending my hand, "Riley King."

I wasn't sure how large her ego was and how much stroking it required, but the fact she'd been a Miss North Carolina runner-up and a recording artist indicated that there had to be a bit of narcissism going on.

She took my hand and held it for a moment longer than was necessary. "Thanks. I didn't think anyone remembered that CD. The only reason they keep it in stock here is that I know the owner and he has a thing for me."

"I imagine that's a common occurrence. I'm sorry, but did you record a follow up to this one? I'm afraid I lost track."

"No, this was it. Can't say it went over very well. People wanted hip hop or grunge when it came out and this is rock and roll with a country twang."

"Damn, lady, you were ahead of your time. All the country music they play on the radio now is really rock and roll. Rocks harder than the Eagles did, until Joe Walsh joined them at least."

Her voice was smooth, seductive without trying. "I got lumped in as a lower case Stevie Nicks. One critic called me a 'bolder, less talented, Emmylou Harris'."

"Apples and Oranges. What unfair comparisons. You know, I think my copy of this is worn out. If I buy this one, would you sign it for me? I bet nobody I know will believe I just ran into you at a record store."

She grimaced. "CDs don't wear out, sir."

Would this have come out on vinyl, or was everything digital by the time it was released? "Got me. I just wanted your autograph. Funny, I've never asked for one before. I must seem like some sort of groupie to you but I can assure you, I'm not."

"What's wrong with groupies?" she said. "They serve a purpose."

"Rita Coolidge, *Superstar*. Great version on *Mad Dogs and Englishmen*."

She smiled. "Nice to find somebody who doesn't think Karen Carpenter did it originally."

I said, "Written by the great Leon Russell. Although you couldn't possibly know that. You weren't even born when it was released."

Rick Stone's devotion to classic rock had given me an education and an appreciation of the genre. It stopped short at constantly quoting lyrics, which he did incessantly, much to my annoyance.

"I was around but I admit, I was a little young to know much about Leon when it first came out. I learned later though, I love his stuff. Your name again was...."

"Riley King"

"Interesting. Of course, you must know that Riley King is B.B. King's real name."

"My dad was a big fan."

"And I'm Charlene Serpente now."

I managed to look crestfallen at the notion that she was married and it worked.

She said, "Hey. I skipped lunch and my tummy's rumbling. If I sign your CD, would you buy me a muffin and a coffee?"

"Least I could do for a fellow Leon fan. I'll pay for this and meet you at the coffee shop around the corner."

"It's a date," she said. "But I'm going to rummage around for a minute while you check out. Come back and meet me here."

"Wild horses couldn't tear me away."

"Rolling Stones. The song's about Maryanne Faithfull's overdose. Circa 1971."

I had to admit, she was nothing like the Jezebel I was expecting. I was totally captivated, but cognizant of the danger she posed. And I was willing to walk right into it.

# Twenty Two

## Derek Davis

Davis had called every mutual friend that he and Liz had during their relationship. They all gave him variations on the same answer. *No, we haven't heard from Liz in weeks. Gotta go.*

He sensed no overt hostility from any of them. They were mostly her friends, people she had socialized with before hooking up with him. They tolerated Davis solely because he was her man and now that he wasn't, they had no particular use for him. Everyone in her circle had money. Now that he was no longer in that group, he was even more irrelevant to them, unless they needed emergency plumbing work.

He hadn't much in common with them anyway. Whenever they'd meet another couple for dinner, the conversation consisted of comparing real estate values to what they had been three years ago or how the current administration was spending them into oblivion. Davis had learned early on to keep his political and religious non-leanings to himself, for fear of alienating not only her friends but potential clients.

But the discussion waned when it turned to things other than money.

WWKD. What would King do?

Davis already was too indebted to his friend to ask his help on this one. And whereas the beating he had suffered caused Riley to spring into action without asking permission, the little matter of misplacing his ex would be asking too much of his friend's time. Especially when Derek knew of a good source for information about Liz all along but was too embarrassed to follow through.

Todd Weller.

He was the last person Derek wanted to call, but the most likely to know exactly where Liz was. He couldn't let his pride overwhelm his need for her. He dialed the main number of Weller's television station and patiently waded through menus for five minutes until a real human voice answered.

He hoped that Weller would answer his secretary's page. Todd might want to talk to him about Liz even less than he wanted to talk about her to Weller.

"Hey, Derek, how the hell are you, babe? Still in the hospital or have they let you out yet?"

Weller's voice on the phone was impressive, a booming baritone full of resonant vowels. Davis dropped down an octave and replied, "I'm home now, Todd. Thanks for asking."

"I knew they couldn't keep a good man down. Hey, I'm not in my office now. I need to voice a piece I did with the Panthers coach. Can I get back with you?"

"Actually, I just need quick question. Won't take a second."

"Shoot."

"It's a little awkward. Liz had called me a while back about a scarf she thought she may have left with me. Pashmere or something."

"Pashmina, dude. Yeah?"

"Well, I had told her I didn't have it and well, cleaning out the car yesterday, it turned up --- wedged between the seats. I'd like to get it to her, it was her favorite and the weather will be turning soon. But I called and her message box is full and her cell isn't responding. Do you know how I could reach her?"

Anyone with a brain in their head would suspect that he was prying into his ex's personal life. They'd see through scarf pretext as if it were made of Irish lace.

"Liz is travelling in Europe. Left several weeks ago. Paris, then French wine country, maybe Germany for Christmas, skiing the Swiss Alps New Year's. I couldn't get away during football season or I'd have offered to tag along. Fact is, if the Panthers don't make the playoffs, I might try to catch up with her in January."

"I see. I'm glad to hear she's having a good time. She's really a terrific skier. If you do meet up with her, keep that in mind. She'll leave you eating her powder."

Weller gave a condescending chuckle. "I doubt that. Look, no offense, without me prying as to why.... well, I'm just not comfortable giving out information on her without her consent. She brought her computer so you could probably email her. If she really is attached to that scarf, I'm sure she would tell you where to send it."

As if email wasn't the first thing he had tried. "That's an idea. Or do you know what hotel she's staying in now? I could just FedEx it there and surprise her with it. Might come in handy on the slopes."

"Uh, I don't think she's at a hotel. Staying with friends, I think. I wanted to give her space so I didn't really pin her down on the itinerary too closely. Haven't spoken for a while, since she left actually. Hey, they're buzzing me. Got to go, pal. Good to hear you're feeling better."

Knowing she was somewhere in Europe didn't help very much in contacting her. Todd didn't even know where she was staying. Their romance must be cool indeed if she was willing to leave him for such an extended period early on. That coupled with the fact that if she hadn't reached out to Todd from Europe yet indicated she wasn't missing him all that much.

He didn't need King to tell him that this trip sounded like something rich girls do to overcome their broken hearts. After the final divorce decree came through on both her marriages, Liz had taken long journeys to distant lands to cleanse her mind and heart. Was she missing him as much as he missed her?

# Twenty Three

"So Mr. Riley King, what do you do? Other than collect albums from failed singers?"

I was paying the price now for my impulsive decision to approach Charlene Serpente. I hadn't set up a cover story that couldn't be broken with a quick Google search. We sat at a small cafe table in the sandwich shop, the only patrons in the establishment other than an occasional leisurely shopper picking up coffee at the 'to go' counter.

"A little of this, a little of that. I'm much more interested in your story. And don't ever refer to yourself as a *failed* singer. I'll never understand why you didn't do a follow up to your first record."

"Funny to hear a body call them records again. Or albums for that matter. Wasn't my choice. When I cut those sides, I was a twenty three year old virgin in more ways than one. Did you know I was a Miss North Carolina runner-up?

"If you came in second, I can't imagine how great the winner must have looked. You look like you could still give those girls a run for their money." I wanted to keep her talking about herself and not about me. Usually, feeding into someone's vanity does the trick.

"That's very nice of you to say. You look like you might have been an athlete. Football, maybe?"

"Played some hoops in college. Nothing serious. So how did you go from a beauty contestant to a record contract?"

Charlene had ordered a smoothie instead of a muffin and she was sipping it through a wide straw. Lascivious images floated through my head. Seductive poses came so naturally to her that she probably wasn't even aware of them.

"I was hit up by a small time hustler from Nashville. Handled a couple of country artists and he thought that I might have some chops after he heard me singing in the talent competition. Remember, we didn't have American Idol back then."

"Thank God for that. So this guy signed you?"

"I was young, grew up without a lot of money, I didn't know better."

The Charlene Serpente I was talking to was at odds with the image that Patrick Henry had painted. She was hot, no disputing that. But I had a hard time picturing her sidling up to an overweight right wing talk show host.

"Anyway, we wound up constantly tussling over the direction the music was taking. I wanted to use my own songs, he wanted to bring in some hack country guys he was fronting for. I wanted more electric stuff, he wanted pedal steel guitar. I had been taking voice lessons, trying to lose the twang, he wanted more of it. That's why the final record sounds so schizophrenic. I gave him his head on some songs, he let me have my way with others."

"So let me guess, the critics thought it was a mish-mash."

"Most of them, yes. A couple liked it, said it showed extraordinary range. *The courage to cross boundaries*. But by and large, they hated it and it didn't sell."

I had to remind myself that this was a fact finding mission. This uncommonly beautiful woman so far had been quite the opposite of what I expected. She seemed genuinely self-effacing; if it was an act, she was damn good at it.

If I was to help Derek, I needed to ease her into talking about her life as it stood today but I didn't have to rush it. "So I take it that with all the disagreements and the fact your record didn't sell, you and this manager parted ways. Did you give up after that?"

"No. In some ways I wish I had. Because even though the CD tanked, it opened doors. But little did I know that they were the wrong doors. There were some A&R guys who were interested, but they weren't interested in me for my music."

"Uh oh."

"You can guess the rest. They made it seem like sleeping with them was part of the deal, that all the new artists did that. It was just the way things worked. After I said no a couple of times and got shown the door, I finally made the sacrifice. I got deflowered in New York City on a stained sofa in a smelly office in the Flatiron Building. I'll never forget the hissing of the radiator. One of those big old silver cast iron thingies. It seemed that with every thrust, it burped out a burst of steam."

I fought the image. I'd met her ten minutes ago, and she was describing in detail how she lost her virginity. *I feel like frigging Oprah.* Even though her life story seemed off topic, it could give me insights as to how she might respond to rejection, in this case, Derek resisting her abundant charms. "So no help to your career, obviously?"

She exhaled dismissively. "No. I bounced around from one label's scout to the next. I guess word spreads when you're willing to give it up. I found out later on I was the exception, not the rule. Most female singers that the labels take seriously don't go the casting couch route. Some may wind up sleeping with producers or managers or A&R guys but that's after they make it, not before."

"You hear stories, but I never truly understood how sleazy it can be. So what did you do for money during all of this?"

"I got by for a couple of years as a Miss North Carolina stand in. You know, trade shows and stuff, they like to have a semi-famous pretty face around. You give inspirational speeches to civic groups. I did a few paying music gigs, opening act in small clubs. Actually played the Bottom Line in New York once when the act they had scheduled got stuck in the snow in another town. I suppose that was the highlight of my career."

"That's a shame. Like I told you at the music store, your timing was bad. If your CD came out today, you'd be another Miranda Lambert."

"Maybe I should hire you to do PR for me."

"I can think of worse gigs. Do you still have aspirations to be a singer? I actually do know some people in the business. Got a pal who is tight with Darius Rucker."

I caught her full bore smile for the first time. The corners of her eyes crinkling. Her perfect white teeth. Even dimples. The cascading hair. It was probably impossible for a woman in her mid forties to look this good without a little help, but whoever had done the work had a subtle touch.

"No, I'm 'fraid I'm just an old married lady now."

Finally, a way to get her to talk about Johnny Serpente. "How did you meet your husband?"

She took another sip of the smoothie and delicately dabbed a trace of the thick pale liquid from her lips. Down, Boy. "After I gave up on the music business, I got a job at the Capital Grille here in Charlotte. Not waitressing, but a greeter at the front desk. Johnny came in a lot, entertaining clients. My husband's a builder. He's quite a bit older than I am, but I was duly impressed by the company he kept, not to mention the tips he left."

"So how long have you been happily married?"

This time the smile was fleeting, embarrassed. "We tied the knot a long time ago. Seems like forever."

It wasn't necessary to push harder. It would come on its own.

She said, "My husband is a small man in every way. You know, the old Napoleon complex. The only thing big about him is his bank account. Which I guess is why I married him."

I let that sit for a moment.

I said, "Obvious question and I hope I'm not being too nosy. It sounds like you're pretty unhappy. Have you thought about splitting?"

"Thought about it, sure. But you remember what Michael Corleone did to Kay when she tried to leave him? "

A woman making a *Godfather* reference. This lady was a keeper. But back to my original purpose in meeting her. "Are you saying that your husband would try to harm you if you left? Has he hurt you before?"

A hard look before she decided to trust me any further. "No. He has a temper but he's never taken it out on me. I guess you could say we have an arrangement."

She obviously wanted to say more but hesitated. "We've never really written nothing down, but it's there, Riley. I have a nice home, a credit card. Anything I want. I guess I sound like a gold digger to you. Tryin' to sleep my way to a record contract. I couldn't make it on talent --- got me nowhere. So I used what I had, that's how I was told the game was played and even that didn't work. So I married a man who gives me refuge from the cruel world. I give him something glam to show off in public. More a business arrangement than a marriage."

"I'm really sorry to hear that. You deserve so much more."

"Well, don't feel too sorry for me. John does what he can. I wanted forty thousand dollars to redo our master bath. I mentioned it to John and next day, the money magically appears in my checking account."

Enter Derek Davis.

"Wow. Forty thousand for a bath. Lucky he's a builder, eh?"

"Not so lucky. I'm afraid my husband don't have much use for aesthetics. At least I got him dressing decently now. What a struggle that was. But no, he does low income housing. I wasn't going to let him bring in one of his schlock crews to remodel our master bath. The place would a looked like one of Donald Trump's lobbies. All glitz, no taste."

I smiled at the image.

"I hired a very sweet local builder to do the work. John fought the idea at first but gave in when I showed him the plans and the budget. He admitted I did a good job."

"That's a win for your column."

"Not for long. Things were going well, the project was taking shape nicely when the builder and I had what I guess you would call a little misunderstanding and he stopped showing up."

Finally!

I said, "What kind of misunderstanding? I know a couple of builders, nice guys, but I hear they can be brutal when it comes to inflating their bill. Load up with extras you thought were standard."

"No, nothing like that. I really liked the guy and he was honest as the day is long. But my husband got impatient. Fired him. He hadn't shown up for a couple of days and Johnny said that it happens all the time in building when you work with folks you don't know. You've got to check them out thoroughly. Get references. They take your money and disappear."

"So your husband was mad."

"Not mad so much. More like self satisfied, as in *See, I told you so*. He got his guys finishing the job now. They're flying through it --- should be done next week."

"So are you stuck with an ugly bathroom like you feared?"

"No, not really. The builder left the plans, so they couldn't mess it up too much. The only compromise I had to make is that they're using a cheap floor tile that sort of looks like travertine instead of the real thing. John's tile guys are Central American. He says that they're good for basic jobs but travertine is only for experts and he doesn't have anyone who can handle that at the moment."

"That's a shame."

"Yes, it is. But John won't tolerate the inconvenience any longer so I had to give in. Meanwhile, I've got this beautiful stone sitting in the driveway and it's going to waste. He said unless I get it out of the driveway on my own, he'll fix it so it's picked up and disposed of. It's an ego thing now. He thinks I screwed up with that builder. I guess in the end, it's a small price to pay to let him win. It'll be a big improvement over what we had, just not that perfect spa retreat I was craving."

At lunch, Davis had told me about how expensive the travertine was and how he couldn't return it. I had an idea that could at least salvage something for my pal.

"Tell you what, I'm not real busy this week. I could take the stuff out of your driveway and at least it won't go to waste. And who knows, I might find a buyer with one of my builder friends. Make chicken salad out of chicken shit, pardon the language. Worst case, at least it's out of your way."

"That would be really sweet of you. And look, if you manage to sell it, keep the money. I really don't need it."

"No, I couldn't take advantage of you that way," I lied. "But I'm sure we could devise something that will bring the whole affair to a climax that will leave us both satisfied."

*James Bond couldn't have delivered the double entendre better*. I was proud of myself for that one. Maybe recriminations would come later when I thought about Jaime, but hey, I'm human.

In case my earlier attempts at 007 wit didn't register, I said, "Just give me your address and I'll be at your service at the crack of dawn, ready to take care of your every need."

"Actually Riley King, I'd like it if you could come a little later. It would give me the chance to thank you properly. My husband is playing golf mid morning tomorrow. As I said, we have an arrangement."

# Twenty Four

"No. No. No. No. No."

"Tell me what you really think, Derek." I said, with a smirk.

We were having dinner at the Brickhouse Tavern, a Davidson landmark that once upon a time had been a cotton mill, a 120 year old relic of times gone by. Its walls were adorned by the classic red brick that characterized the town. It was a frequent hangout for the college crowd, undergrads and faculty alike. On weekends, they added live music to their standard mix of reasonably priced bar food and an eclectic selection of microbrews. Businessmen from the nearby Ingersoll-Rand facility inhabited the lunch hour, equally appreciative of its convenience and nubile young servers.

As funky and quaint as the interior was, upon entering the first time, Davis had commented that such a structure wouldn't pass code today. Over the years, he'd had many a friendly discussion with acquaintances who insisted that they "just don't build them like they used to." To which he replied, "and that's a good thing."

He'd then point out the advances in technology that made for better building at lower cost. National standards had been adopted for electrical wiring, plumbing fixtures, insulation and dozens of other products that were superior to anything the past could offer. The comeback would be something along the lines of how plaster walls trumped sheetrock or that back in the day, a two by four measured exactly that, not like today's three and a halves by one and a half. Pipes were cast iron or copper, not PVC.

All valid points if the building was attacked with artillery shells. Those old materials would offer slightly more resistance before crumbling. But today's buildings were highly energy efficient and engineered to be more structurally sound, unless you were talking granite cathedrals.

Architecture was the last thing on his mind now as he sat across from me in a scarred wooden booth. He said, "Look, I appreciate you retrieving the travertine for me. Even if I can't turn it into money right away, I'm sure I can find a use for it down the road."

I cut him off before he could add *but*. "You're welcome. I'm just surprised that a builder like Serpente wouldn't use it. According to his wife, the stuff they're installing is an inferior substitute. Why go that route when you can have the real thing? If someone can lay tile, they can lay tile. What's the difference?"

"Well, if it was me, I'd certainly wait to find someone to install the real stuff, especially since it's sitting right there and already paid for by someone else. A year from now, you won't even remember the extra time it took and the beauty of the travertine will be permanent. But saying that one tile installer is as good as another is like saying all detectives are equally skilled. Serpente builds low cost housing --- the key is to get in and out quickly and not sweat the small stuff. Look at this place, for example. The mortar joints are sloppy, the result of using cheap semi-skilled labor back in the day. The floors creak and sag, no doubt due to a substandard foundation. Even the bricks themselves were hastily manufactured from the least expensive local clay."

I said, "Okay but this place dates to the eighteen nineties."

I was sipping a local IPA; Davis was nursing a ginger ale with his Advil.

"My point is that good work takes time and attention to detail. The place I'm staying in now was done fast and sloppy. Almost anyone can put down builder grade ceramic tile on a plywood subfloor, but quality jobs now use cement board and a layer of corrugated plastic material that's totally waterproof. A good tile job will look the same a hundred years from now. It will never leak and rot the joists. Also, the travertine was 13x18, and the plan called for it to be used in a herringbone pattern. Tiles that large are a bitch to level. You work each piece with a rubber mallet so that the edges match with no uneven spots. If Serpente's in a hurry to use his commode, his guys could probably install and grout porcelain in a day or two. It's a perfectly fine product, but it's not travertine."

"Thanks for the lecture."

"Hey, maybe they'll do a decent job and the average person wouldn't notice the difference, but I'm glad my name won't be on it."

He grimaced at how easily he'd been distracted off his original charge. "But you got me sidetracked, Riles, with this talk about tile. What I don't like is you sleeping with a married woman."

"Wouldn't be the first time."

"That doesn't mean it's right. What about Jaime up in Jersey? Are you going to buy a little red Porsche convertible next?"

The food came. Davis had ordered a chef's salad and it practically overflowed its gigantic bowl. Any intent he might have had about saving calories would entail leaving the majority of it untouched. I opted for a half pound burger, topped with bleu cheese and bacon. I'd work it off at Charlene's, during and after the stonework.

I said, "In the first place, my relationship with Jaime is complicated. It's kind of up in the air now. It's not like she expects me to be a monk while I'm living six hundred miles away."

"If that's what you want to believe, okay. But that's not my only concern. Charlene is married."

"To a snake. Who I'm pretty sure busted up that mug of yours. And this wouldn't be the first time for her, either."

"When you left me earlier, you were working on the theory that she told Serpente that I attacked her and he retaliated. Is that still operational or are we off onto something else?"

"Working on it. I've got to play this out with her. Consider it my sacrifice in the line of duty. "

He sounded like he was giving a sermon now. "You're really working hard to rationalize something you know is wrong, aren't you?"

"Look, kudos to you for not giving in to her. And I'm not saying she wouldn't be temporarily pissed if she came on to you and you resisted her charms. But I don't think she'd retaliate by having hubby sic his goons on you. It's not like she'd have to wait very long to find someone else. And she clearly has found an upgrade in yours truly."

Davis ignored the insult and picked at his salad, removing a couple of strips of mysterious marbled meat that looked like spam.

He said, "I'm not following. You told me you're pretty sure Serpente put out the hit. Yet now you're saying that it wasn't because of anything to do with Charlene."

"Ah, but it has *everything* to do with her. Let me play armchair shrink. Serpente grew up as a runt in Brooklyn. The real paisanos wanted nothing to do with him. The only way he could be a big cheese was a change of venue. So he moved down here. He probably came down with some money to spread around, so the combination of cash and implied muscle gives him status that he could never achieve back where he's from."

"I know you studied profiling with the FBI, but how solid is this?"

"Follow me, Derek, it's all of a piece. He marries this beautiful woman, way out of his league. She dresses him up to fit in with the rich southern dudes he hangs with. Deep down, he knows he's a fraud. Same with his bride. She doesn't respect him or what he's doing. She's a hustler who latched on to a rich guy for security. He knows that. The one thing he has over her is his money. Money that he got by being smarter than all these rich assholes who look down on him. So when she belittles what he does for a living by suggesting that he couldn't even remodel a bathroom up to her standards... well, that is hitting him where it really hurts. So he goes along with it to a point, let's you draw up a plan and specs, then pow. You don't show up for three days and you don't call. So he's the hero now, says he'll fire you, which he sort of did by beating you up. *See honey, I told you my job isn't easy. I'll rescue you this time with my guys, but don't ever think you're smarter at what I do than I am.*"

"So I get beat up so this guy can show his wife who's boss. Is that it? And you got all this from spending ten minutes with Charlene?"

"It started me thinking. So tomorrow, I probe a little deeper, no pun intended, and I test the theory a little more. "

"I feel like a pimp putting you two together. You'd be sleeping with another man's wife."

I brushed a crumb off my jeans. "Ok, mister pacifist. This is payback, then. You get your expensive tile back. This creep's wife gets used by a stranger. I get remunerated in a way that beats whatever petty cash you could give me. It's a winner all around. Now you're right in that I need more evidence to be sure my little profile of this guy is accurate, but as I told you from the get-go, this isn't going to be dealt with by a court of law."

"I'm also a little worried what could happen to you if Serpente finds out you did his wife. What if she gets mad at you and tells him?'

"I'm not worried. No offense, but I'd welcome it if he sends the same guys who roughed you up to deal with me. Then I could punish them for their role in this, too."

Davis tried to eat more but he'd lost his appetite." All right. I appreciate you getting my material back. Use my Escape, don't mess up your Audi; that stuff is heavy. But anything you do with Charlene Serpente is on you. I take no responsibility for it. It's your call. Don't pretend you're doing it for me. I can't endorse it. I'm willing to just let the whole thing go."

"And if it proves my theory?"

"I'm done with it. I'll write a letter of apology to Charlene in a week or so. Sounds like she was caught up in something she had no knowledge of. I'll tell her I was mugged and in the hospital and I'm sorry I couldn't complete the job. I've got referrals to worry about."

"That's up to you. Damn, you're sounding so wimpy you should be eating a hamburger, not me." The *Popeye* reference went over his head, or he chose not to acknowledge my attempt to make him laugh and spit out his food.

I said, "It would be more poetic if you were the one to enjoy the favors of the lovely Charlene but I'm honored to be your surrogate. I'll consider it revenge with a blunt instrument."

"Don't put it like that. It's not funny and you're not acting on my behalf."

"Hey man, don't be mad at me. I'm about to boink the best looking female I've ever had. It will be a blow against a bad man. Sorry that doesn't make it right in your book, but it does in mine."

Davis smiled wanly in absolution. "Wouldn't be the first time we disagree. Won't be the last."

"Then we can put our long local nightmare behind us. Hey, what's with you and that Miss Blankenship? Maybe a seventy year old is more your speed. I bet she was hot in her day. She's probably been celibate almost as long as you have. Another win-win."

"We may be doing some business together, that's all. Rehabbing condos. We'll see."

"Maybe a little monkey business, eh. Nudge, nudge, wink wink. Hey, it works for Demi Moore and Ashton Ritchie. It can work for you."

"You big slob. If you're going to make jokes with pop culture references, at least get them right. It's Ashton Kutcher. Ashton Ritchie is the guy that does fertilizer commercials for Scotts."

"I knew that."

# Twenty Five

## Derek Davis

Derek was up early, in fact he'd been up every hour on the hour all night. He was weaning himself off painkillers, bypassing the prescription meds that his doctors had given him. He was even phasing out the over the counter stuff. The discomfort hadn't reached the unbearable level for a couple of days now, and he would rather put up with some minor aches than become dependent on some chemical.

He'd called Randee Blankenship after dinner and she insisted on driving him to Shamaylan's office. He thanked her by agreeing to inspect one of the buildings she was interested in investing in. Perhaps by keeping occupied right up until the moment he went under the knife, he could stop worrying about it.

The whole idea upset him. He'd known of people who had never awakened --- an unknown allergic reaction to an anesthetic or a careless mistake by an overworked surgeon, even for minor surgery. Look what happened to poor Joan Rivers. If he joined that group, he tried to convince himself that it was the best way to go. Falling asleep and not getting up. Beats rotting away from the inside over a period of years.

Was there something awaiting him on the other side? That would be nice but he wasn't counting on it. *To sleep, perchance to dream, there's the rub*? Well, his dreams hadn't been so great lately and they wouldn't be missed.

The sun was extending russet colored tendrils on the eastern skyline and he gave up trying to go back to sleep. He made coffee and by rote almost made some breakfast before he remembered that Shamaylan's nurse had called yesterday instructing him not to eat within eight hours of the operation. He need a distraction, work that he could immerse himself in to take his mind off the surgery. Researching the condos might be the answer.

He started by checking the online tax records for the prices of recently sold properties in the area. He knew that just looking at raw numbers could lead to some major errors when appraising a property's true value. There was the matter of condition. Location. Views. Many factors that tax assessments couldn't tell him. When investing time and effort into a real estate project these unknowns can be the critical difference between a venture that will pay dividends and an expensive albatross.

As if by wizardry, his computer barked out a Skype notification --- a friend of his had just signed on. Maggie Holmes had been the real estate agent he had most often used to represent him in his golden days. They hadn't spoken much recently --- after she had found buyers for his personal home they'd had little contact. He still got her monthly emails, all her optimistic predictions on why *now is a great time to invest because interest rates are at record lows and prices are below replacement value. And prices are sure to rise soon, so don't miss out!*

Davis clicked on her name and she picked up after two rings.

"Hi Derek, how are you? Your video isn't working. Check your camera, hon."

Davis had deliberately called on the **audio only** setting. He didn't want to scare her with his appearance and didn't want to waste time explaining how he got that way if she hadn't already heard.

"Yeah Mags, my camera's on the fritz. Plus, you told me a long time ago that your husband wouldn't approve if my face was the first thing you saw in the morning."

"You are an incorrigible flirt, Derek." He felt at ease teasing Maggie. Although they were the same age, she seemed far older. She had been happily married to an attorney for thirty years, and to put it gently, they both enjoyed eating. Not a petite woman to begin with, she had entered the realm of plus sizes two decades earlier and was making her way upward through double digits. Her husband was on a similar journey but they were so smitten that they didn't seem to mind the other's avoirdupois.

"Well I can see by your video that you're as lovely as ever," Derek replied. Despite her size, she cut an impressive figure. He had never seen her in anything less than stylish business attire. Always made up, her straightened black hair was perfectly coiffed, in a stiffly sprayed style. Flowery perfume telegraphed her grand entrance from several meters away.

Her ambition was prodigious. She worked constantly, tethered to a cell phone and looking to advance her next deal. As a result of her hard work, she had double the listings of any agent in her office. She did three times the marketing --- full page color ads in Saturday's paper, her weekly newsletter, emails and virtual tours. There wasn't a promotional opportunity she turned down. A fixture at charity events and civic meetings, Maggie was constantly on the lookout for new contacts who might tip her off to potential clients. In her business, information is precious and getting an hour's jump on a new project could be decisive. If anyone could flesh out the information he sought on the condo market, it was Magnolia C. Holmes. She had copyrighted *Holmes on Homes* long before the Canadian television builder, but she agreed to share the title with him ---- for a fee of course.

I said, "So Mags, I'm looking for a little info and you're just the person I need. Good to see you're up and at 'em with the sunrise."

"Early bird catches the worm. Everything all right? I'm afraid I haven't been a very good friend to you but I've really been busy. I know you know the market and not much is selling, but now I have to work twice as hard for half the business. "

"I understand. You'll always be a good friend. What do you know about those low income condos in Davidson, Mags?"

"A shorter conversation might be about what I don't know. Lots of older folks were living there on public assistance. Great location but they haven't aged well, not well maintained."

"How much do you think they'll go for?"

"Depends on who has money to bid. I toured a couple there this year, and the condition between them was night and day. One was an end unit --- it hadn't been touched since the day it was built. Lady had a small dog. Carpets were ruined, baseboard chewed up. The place smelled. The other was neat as a pin but very dated."

"Are they prime for gentrification? Make money flipping them?"

"Honestly, no, unless you can get them for a song. Condos these days move too slowly. I think they have rental potential but as a flip, uh uh."

"So upgrading them wouldn't pay off?"

"In this market, I doubt you'd get your money back."

"Well, as always Maggie, you have all the answers. Let's have dinner soon."

"Wonderful. I look forward to seeing you and Liz again. Miss you guys. Bye."

Magnolia C. Holmes didn't know everything after all.

# Twenty Six

My mid morning drive to Ballantyne to seduce or be seduced by the lovely Charlene now was troubling me. I tried to remember a similar situation from my past and couldn't come up with one. Essentially, I had an appointment to have sex with a woman I don't know.

One night stands are no mystery me. This was different. My earlier dalliances were spontaneous, generally after copious consumption of adult beverages by both parties. There was no planning involved.

It brought to mind the Woody Allen line, from *Annie Hall* I think, when he said, "I really feel strongly both ways about this."

I'd lied to Davis about a couple of things. I had never had an assignation with a married woman. Never even been tempted. Like he, I regard poaching another man's wife the same way I look at shoplifting, strictly off limits. The other lie involves Jaime, who wouldn't be happy if she knew that I was sowing wild oats in Charlotte while she remained steadfast in New Jersey.

In this case, I told myself I was like a latter day Robin Hood. Stealing from a rich man, something he didn't deserve and had attained strictly because he *was* rich. I wasn't exactly giving to the poor, but I could rationalize it as achieving a form of justice for my friend. What other way made sense to repay Serpente for ordering the beat-down? This might hurt him more than direct eye for an eye.

But Davis had said that he wanted no part of this crude form of revenge. So while I drove, mindlessly listening to music Dan-o was spinning on Sirius/XM, I gave up trying to justify what I was about to do. It was driven by lust, pure and simple. A bewitching, beautiful woman seemed willing to sleep with me, no questions asked. The rest were side benefits.

But still, I was starting to feel dirty. Would it happen in the marital bed? Somehow the thought of fornicating in the same place that Serpente had been was anathema. It hadn't occurred to me until now that I'd be enjoying the same body parts the Snake had visited. Not a pleasant image. Although the curse of ED had never visited me, carrying that picture into the kip might provoke a first-time embarrassment.

I pulled Davis' Escape onto the cobblestone driveway at the pre-arranged time. As instructed, I pushed the intercom button at the garage and was greeted by Charlene's husky morning voice.

"Riley. I'll be right down." She was off before I had a chance to reply.

Thirty seconds later the massive wooden door silently drew open, revealing a Jag and two other cars, her BMW Z4 convertible and a Lexus SUV in a third bay off to the side. What did Serpente drive? I guessed it was the Lexus and if so, why was it still here?

"Is your husband gone? Is that his car?" I said.

"Nervous Nellie. He left for golfing a half hour ago. He took the Mercedes."

"You make him park it outside?"

"No, Sugar. See the way the driveway curls around the house? We have room for more cars underneath. That's where he keeps his Mercedes and his Harley. Of course he never uses the Harley. Strictly for image."

The sight of her made me forget the earlier recriminations. Her blonde hair was tousled, as if she'd just arisen and hadn't bothered to run a brush through it. She was wearing running shorts and a powder blue UNC tee shirt. Barefoot, no bra. Her legs were everything I'd imagined them to be, and the loose fitting tee shirt barely traced the outline of her breasts. Even without makeup, it was hard to believe that she was on the long side of forty.

"So what's on the agenda today?" I asked. The awkwardness I felt at the question was at odds with my witty riposte of the previous day.

"It's clouding up. Why don't you load up that limestone so you don't have to do it in the rain later."

"I could do that. Might get a little gamy though. That stuff isn't exactly made of Styrofoam."

She smiled at my attempt at being gentlemanly in a decidedly ungentlemanly situation. "The cabana has a shower. You could meet me there when you're through. See that truck on the street? My husband's drywall guys. They're doing the final sanding today but they should be out soon."

"Uh, aren't you worried that they might say something about me being here?"

"Not really. As far as they know, you're just some guy I hired to take the tile away. *No habla Ingles* very well anyway." She started toward the back yard. "The pool is heated. I'm going to take a morning swim. You could join me if you're finished with the tile fast enough. Otherwise, I'll be in the cabana."

"You sure know how to incentivize your workers. Unfortunately, I didn't bring a suit."

"Neither did I." With that, she opened the aluminum fence gate leading to the back yard. After she stepped through it, she turned to me and winked. "I'll be a-waiting." She pulled the tee shirt over her head as she started toward the pool.

Evidently, she wasn't concerned about the drywall workers enjoying the show. I wouldn't be the only laborer treated to a casual striptease act. Part of her standard routine? Things had sure changed since yesterday. The mild flirtation had become blatant and to my mind, a bit forced. Knowing that she had pulled the same act on Davis didn't do much for my ego.

This was too easy and things that were this easy usually come at a higher hidden cost later. I opened the lift gate of the Escape and began loading the Travertine. Davis had ordered 300 square feet, roughly two hundred pieces. Even a strong man used to such labor could barely manage more than five at a time. Let's see, forty trips at 30 seconds each....

I gave up my calculations and just hoped she'd still be in the water when I finished. The sky was getting dark, ominous thunderheads approaching. Tempting though she was, I didn't fancy being naked in a pool during one of Charlotte's notorious cloudbursts.

The lifting and loading was mindless grunt work, so I channeled my thoughts toward a gauzy fantasy of what awaited me. The cabana looked pretty spacious --- I imagined it would be equipped with every amenity the house boasted --- heat, power, satellite TV, Wi-Fi and a well turned out kitchen. Sofa bed? Probably. I had visions of Charlene lying beneath me with rain pounding the metal roof to hasten me along and help erase my doubts. I finished in twenty five minutes.

The workers' truck was still on the street and despite her casual attitude, the fewer people who knew about this, the better. There was a gate to the pool area adjacent to the back of the cabana, well shielded from the house. From there I could see that no one was in the pool, so I slipped into the back entrance of the cabana.

The room was much as I'd expected. A compact space with stamped concrete floors, a kitchen bar, and wood paneling. Glass doors overlooked the pool. There was another door which I assumed led to a bath and shower area. Charlene was blow drying as I entered, her head down. She was wearing a long white terrycloth robe, falling open in the front.

"Oh, Riley. You surprised me. I heard thunder so I got out of the pool."

"My loss. Well, the tile's all loaded. I'm at your service."

"You worked like a Russian peasant. Like my husband told me he was in his early days."

"You said your married name is Serpente. Your husband is Italian, no?"

"No. Serpente isn't his real name."

This was news and quite counterintuitive. Why would anyone select a name that meant *the snake* by choice?

She saw the question in my widened eyes and answered it. "John is Russian. His real name is Zubov. Dmitry Zubov. "

"Okay, you've tickled my curiosity. Why would a Russian named Zubov change his name to something equally ethnic? I mean, don't most assimilated Americans go for Anglicized names? I don't get it."

"Blame Francis Ford Coppola. My husband grew up in Brooklyn. There's a big section of Russian émigrés there. "

I had dealt with the *Russkaya Mafiya* while with the Bureau and soon developed a distaste for my occasional forays into Brighton Beach, where most of them were based. I found them to be more brutal than the Sicilians --- they didn't even abide by the perverted code of honor that binds most organized criminals. I imagined elaborate Mafiya tattoos covering Serpente's back.

"Coppola? Your husband's a Mafioso?" I said this with a smile, as if this couldn't possibly be true.

She sucked her tongue against her front teeth. "My husband's a wannabe."

"Oh. So you're telling me he's a successful builder who wants to be Don Corleone?"

"Among other things. But I'm afraid I been putting off telling you some bad news. John called. Seems his golfing was cancelled 'cause of the storm coming. He'll be home in a half hour. I was going to come out and tell you if you were still working."

"Oh."

"I'm just as disappointed as you are. At least you got the tile," she said, as she shrugged her glorious shoulders, causing the robe to drop even lower.

Was Serpente really due home soon? Or had she just wanted me to dispose of the tile with a promissory note that would never be cashed in? It was a relief actually, since I was starting to feel guilty again. I'd retrieved the travertine. I learned that Serpente was Russian, not Sicilian. His real name might be useful.

I was actually relieved that my libido had been squelched --- there were too many unintended consequences. This was the best outcome in the long run, but still, I didn't have to feign disappointment. "Well, you got what you wanted. I guess I'll be on my way."

"Is that what you think? That all I wanted from you was muscle?"

"Not the ones I had in mind. Yeah. But that's cool. Fool me once."

"Well, you couldn't be more wrong. I thought even if it rained that John would hang out at the club for drinks and lunch but he said he needed to take care of some business and wanted to come home and work from here. Rain check?"

"Yeah, sure."

"Riley, I just had me a wild idea. What are you doing this weekend? John's got this silly member-guest tournament at the club. A lot of drinking and cigar smoking and man talk. He'll be tied up with that all weekend."

"Look, I know you think you have some kind of enlightened marriage but honestly I'm uncomfortable here. It's too exposed and besides, it could rain."

She showed absolutely no concern that the robe was wide open and her considerable assets were on display. "Well, listen up to what I was going to suggest. We have a condo on Hilton Head Island. I've already told John I was going to go down there to check on it. We haven't used it in a while and they had a tropical storm pass close last weekend. I was going to go with a girlfriend but I could get out of that no sweat. Are you in?"

"I'm not sure." I'd been granted a temporary reprieve from doing something that made me uncomfortable. But looking at the exquisite naked body in front of me and imagining what it would be like to make love to her, if only once --- well, it was hard to resist the invitation.

"I promise you, it will be worth it", she said, pecking me on the cheek. She scribbled an address on a sticky note. "I'll be there by noon Saturday. Scram now, big fellow."

Game postponed because of rain, but the home team had offered better tickets to a doubleheader in exchange. I had time to come up with an excuse. Either to her or to myself.

# Twenty Seven

## Derek Davis

Even though he informed Randee that his realtor thought the building was a poor investment, the retired teacher wanted to see for herself, so he agreed to stop there on the way to the plastic surgeon's office. Davis brought along his emergency toolbox, outfitted with the bare essentials. Included were a hammer, two screwdrivers, a compact handsaw, stud finder, an adjustable wrench, pliers, and assorted packets of screws and nails.

Upon arriving at the complex, he said, "We've got about forty five minutes before we need to leave for the doctor. That should be enough time to go through this place thoroughly enough. Why don't you follow me and take notes?"

"Okay. I was worried about lead paint. Is there any way you can tell about that with the equipment you have or would you have to send it out to a lab?"

It was a rather inexpert question but Davis chalked it up to her Upper West Side mentality. "Not really an issue. Lead paint hasn't been used since the seventies and these buildings are less than twenty years old. That was quite a problem in some of the post-war buildings in New York. Don't have much of a rat problem here either. Let's check out the mechanical room."

It was more like a closet than a room and both of them couldn't fit. It housed an older furnace and a thirty gallon hot water heater. It was typical of any small apartment, and since these were low income units, he expected to find the least expensive appliances offered at the time.

"This ductwork looks like it's coated in asbestos; this stuff has been banned since 1979. How'd they get away with this?"

He scanned the furnace for the boilerplate, which contained the year it had been manufactured.

"1973? How can that be? You mentioned these buildings were built in the nineties."

"That's what the auction website says. Isn't asbestos dangerous?"

"Only if it flakes off. Breathing it in is carcinogenic. In this enclosed space, it's probably not too risky, but it should be encapsulated or removed. Nasty stuff, best handled by pros. As for the furnace, only thing it can think of is that some slick plumber sold the old folks who lived here a used replacement furnace. But that wouldn't explain the asbestos."

He moved around the apartment with Blankenship trailing, taking notes in her small precise handwriting. He found numerous hazardous violations --- incandescent bulbs in closets too close to shelves, no carbon monoxide detector, no gas shut offs. Most were easy fixes that should have been done right initially. The trim work was sloppy --- wide gaps at the miter joints were plastered over with caulk. Not against code, but if the finish work was done this carelessly, the labor that was hidden most likely was worse. The electrical box was a maze of unlabeled wires, several of which weren't properly stapled and therefore attached to the breakers too loosely. A violation indicative of buried junction boxes or exposed splices beneath the walls. The bath surround was sided with the cheapest thin four inch square plastic tile available, and making matters worse, they had been applied indifferently. The joints didn't line up in the corners, and they had used grout rather than caulk at stress points, resulting in numerous cracks and splits. No doubt there was mold and rot underneath. This confirmed why Serpente's tile contractors weren't to be trusted with expensive travertine.

He ran his stud detector over an outside wall. "Twenty four on center. I need to see if they're 2x6s, in which case, it's probably okay. I can tell for sure if I open up a wall and then I can check the insulation too. Your call."

"We'd be repainting anyway, if we buy. Go for it, Mr. Davis."

"I think we've reached the point where you should call me Derek."

Davis poked his drywall saw into the wall, and the sheetrock yielded instantly. He probed further, removing a foot square chunk of wallboard and peered inside the cavity.

He said, "Holy shit! Pardon my language but this is three eighths drywall. Half inch is standard and they mandate five eighths on the ceilings. My Lord! There's no insulation here. None at all. They'd need a minimum of R-13."

There was a look of shock on Blankenship's face. "Aren't these buildings inspected?"

"They are. I'm amazed that the county gave them a certificate of occupancy. The inspectors are supposed to look at each unit, but sometimes there isn't enough time to do that, so they go with random spot checks. But no insulation? Inadequate framing?"

He pulled out a wire. "Look at this. No staples. And this is aluminum, extremely light gauge. Reacts badly with copper fittings and it corrodes them. One big cause of electrical fires. Unbelievable!"

Randee Blankenship appeared stricken. "Did these people have any recourse? Sue the builder? Or the subcontractors?"

"Technically, we're trespassing here so I don't know what the legal status would be. The residents weren't owners though, just people in subsidized public housing. No, the taxpayers were the ones who were ripped off here. That and the safety issues. Thank God the place didn't burn to the ground with this wiring. Coupled with what my real estate lady told me this morning, I'd stay away from this place. You'd be throwing good money after bad. Lucky we found these problems before you plunked down any cash."

"You may have just saved me my life savings. I'd be happy to pay you and clean up your place too. But we have a few minutes before we have to go. Can we check out another unit, just to be sure?"

He nodded. Even though he had come to terms with moving on from the beating, he now had another reason to go after Serpente. Somehow, the man had managed to circumvent the law and provide substandard housing to low income families and old people. And how many others were still in use, others that contained dangerous conditions that could result in tragedy?

Contractors were already respected less than disc jockeys and used car salesmen. This made it worse.

# Twenty Eight

After the surgery, I met Derek and Randee at his place and I couldn't get over the transformation. Not of Davis, since the bandages and swelling obscured the plastic surgeon's work. It was the condo: clean, uncluttered and appearing almost livable.

"Doctor Shamaylan said you'll need to come in next week, but that within a month, you'll be even more handsome than you were before. Hollywood awaits," Randee said.

"That's not the only thing that's improved," I added. "When did you have time to clean up this place? It looks great."

Blankenship said, "The doctor said it would be a good six hours or so before Derek would be ready to go home, so he suggested that I leave and come back to pick him up later. I started organizing this place. Still have a ways to go. Funny, the doctor called me Mrs. Davis."

Had Randee not been present, Davis would have fired back that Mrs. Davis meant she was his mother, not his wife. His gratitude and good sense prevailed.

"You should be so lucky Derek," I said. "She's got your hovel looking almost presentable.   Props to you, Ms. Blankenship. "

Derek asked, "So how long am I going to be out of commission?"

"Over the weekend, for sure. He prescribed rest. By Monday you should be around and about. The Midazolam has already worn off, " Randee said.

"I don't remember anything of that."

She knew the answer to that. "That's the effect of the Midazolam. I looked it up. Short term memory loss. I'm going to leave you with Mr. King now. I took the liberty of entering my cell number into your speed dial. Just hold down 7 and I'll be here. Lucky 7. Can you remember that?"

"If I can't, I'm sure King will drill it into me. Hey, thanks for all you've done."

She said, "Now that I'm retired I look for ways to contribute something. Glad I could be of service. Now if you'll excuse me, I have an appointment. I'll be over in the morning to make you breakfast. Bruising will be gone in a couple of weeks. Then we'll have Rock Hudson in our midst. Good night, gentlemen."

I suppressed a giggle. The moment Blankenship was out of earshot, I had a homophobic line about the late matinee idol I couldn't wait to use on Davis.

~~~~~~~~~~~~

## Randee Blankenship

It was a short drive to the Flatiron building in downtown Davidson where Blankenship was meeting a man. She was certain that Davis and King wouldn't approve, but she was used to getting things done. She had plowed ahead in school politics, despite warnings that she was ill suited for the task. She'd taken many unpopular stands within the city teachers union but it wasn't until she had retired that headway had been made in the causes she had prematurely championed.

She had met with City Council members and Congressmen to gain allies in her fight, but even though most of them agreed with her in theory, no one had the nerve to take on her causes. She continued the battle until her retirement.

She wanted to try out her new hobby of rehabbing undervalued properties on a small scale and see if it really was something that could both hold her interest and be profitable. Davis could prove to be a valuable asset, perhaps even a partner. But now, the man she was about to meet had altered her mission. She had overstated her case on the phone setting up this meeting, but it had worked to open the door.

The Flatiron building in Davidson is a small replica of its namesake in Manhattan. It is triangular in shape, necessitated by a fork in the main thoroughfare in town. One branch led south toward Charlotte, the other southeast toward Concord and Davidson's more expansive suburbs. The building was mainly comprised of vacant office space but the ground floor had been converted into a trendy restaurant with an active bar scene.

It was there that she met Johnny Serpente.

He was waiting at the bar when she arrived, greeting her with a tight smile that conveyed more menace than welcome. He was attired in a well tailored Italian suit, a crisp white shirt and red regimental necktie. He wasn't much taller than she, and if he outweighed her, it wasn't by much. She had insisted the meeting be in a public place and she clutched the Taser in her purse, its cold presence a comfort if things got testy.

"Mr. Serpente? Randee Blankenship. Thank you for agreeing to see me so quickly. You must be a busy man, and I appreciate it."

"I don't respond well to threats. Normally, I'd refer you to one of my attorneys but since we both come from New York, I thought we might find some common ground without getting too messy."

Randee was prepared for his reaction. "Dear, dear. I hope you didn't view my queries as threatening, sir. I merely want to make you aware of a situation that I'm sure you had no part of or had merely overlooked."

This was a tactic she had used before with some success. By bringing a problem to the attention of the person responsible for it without a specific accusation, innocent parties were accorded the opportunity to correct their errors without penalty. Even some guilty ones made restitution, fearing that otherwise, matters might escalate. In this case, it was hard to imagine that Serpente wasn't fully cognizant of the violations, but she wanted to offer him honorable terms of surrender before declaring all out war.

He pointed to a corner table, isolated from the bar area. It was still too early for the place to swarm with the drinks and dinner crowd, and quiet conversation could still be had. "Let's head for a more private spot. Can I order you something?"

She said, "Not at the moment. Shall we?"

He carried his beer to the table and they sat. "You said that you represented the homeowners' interests at Lakeside. Those tenants were relocated sixty days ago. So right away, I've caught you in a lie."

She shifted in her chair. "I'm unofficially speaking on their behalf. And on behalf of many others, I fear. "

"Look, miss, as someone who grew up in New York, don't play with words with me. You were right, I'm a busy man. Can we cut to the chase? What do you want?"

She had dealt with union leaders and politicians who had tried to intimidate her, and she hadn't backed down. This man was slippery to be sure, but his attempts at intimidation were laughable. "All right, if that's the way you want to play it Mr. Serpente. Here's the deal. I had a reputable builder inspect those buildings and he found several code violations."

"Let me stop you right there. Building codes change. What they might require today, they didn't twenty years ago. Any one of the tenants could have made changes to the joint. I can promise you that those units were inspected and they all passed with flying colors. So I have no responsibility if someone made changes after I left."

"If that's the case, why are you here? And besides, I checked several others. Same problems. You're telling me that welfare tenants at their own volition and expense would replace newer furnaces with older ones? Re-wire the place and remove the insulation? Really?"

"*Marrone*! I've had AC units stolen from properties after they were hooked up, copper pipe stripped and sold for scrap by the leeches that live there. I wouldn't put it past some of those moolies to take a brand new furnace and sell it and replace it with an older one. The city pays for the gas anyway so they don't give a shit how high the utility bills are. Either way, folks down here don't cotton to no New Yorker coming down and upsetting their apple cart. You start making noise about class action, people get annoyed. I wouldn't want to see you get into trouble."

"I can handle myself, don't worry about me. But let's be real here. There's no insulation in the walls. No previous owner would have removed insulation to sell it, where's the market for that? No tenant would have rewired the place or removed shut off valves. No one would have *added* asbestos. I have a lovely but dumb tabby cat, and I'd have a hard time selling her on that argument. Need I go on?"

Serpente exhaled impatiently. He didn't need to be an attorney to know she had no legal standing. His liability for any repairs had lapsed long ago. *But a nosy bitch like this could stir up trouble and cause his partners grief*, he thought. They were already agitated about the kid plumbing inspector who didn't know the ropes.

He needed to eliminate these distractions. His veiled warning hadn't backed her off --- he'd try another tack.

"Listen, I didn't get to where I am by ignoring my customers' complaints, valid or no. I'm sure we can take care of this without getting your panties twisted in a knot. If what you say is true, something may have slipped through the cracks."

"What about the other buildings? The tax records show that since you've been active in Charlotte, you've built over three thousand units for the county."

"You wanna scare me? Hey, I got lawyers with connections in this town. You make all the noise you want, nobody will listen."

He took a big sip of his beer and mopped his mouth with his hand. "But if you're so concerned about those buildings in Davidson, how 'bout I make it worth your while? Maybe I can speak to some associates. You said you got interested in this building for re-habbing and flipping. How about I arrange for you to buy them at a steep discount?"

"Out of the goodness of your heart. Where have I heard that before? Usually before getting screwed somehow."

"Ma'am I can't help what happened to you in the past. I'm just saying, I don't need the aggravation. Don't help my agita."

"Sounds like a bribe to me. Buy me off so I'll shut up?"

"You're trying my patience, lady. I'm a reputable business man trying to do the right thing here. Ask around about me. I think you'll find my offer the best option you got. Don't press your luck."

"Or?"

"You know, in spite of the fact we come from the same place, we don't communicate very well. What we have here is failure to communicate. Remember that movie? *Cool Hand Luke*. Remember what happened to Luke?"

"Now you *are* threatening me."

Serpente suddenly grabbed her hand across the table. "See what I mean. I'm trying to reach out here, do the right thing and you see it as a threat. Like I said, this ain't my problem. The building passed inspections, got its CO, and that's that. I'd get crucified by other builders if I started going back and bringing everything up to today's codes, woman. Be real. I'm willing to help you out in good faith."

His Brooklyn accent was started to show as he became agitated and his voice rose. This could get out of hand, forcing his partners to re-think their arrangement. Not worth the risk.

The bartender glanced in their direction and she nodded that everything was under control.

Randee sensed it was time for a strategic retreat before emotions got the better of the man. There was no amount of money he could offer her to back away, but if he believed there was, it could buy her the time she would need to build her case.

She said, "All right Mr. Serpente, maybe we do have a failure to communicate. I'll consider your offer. I was just trying to do some good here. I'll let you know in, say, a week. The auction isn't until next month anyway. And I'm sure you have knowledge of other properties to flip, as well."

"See that wasn't so hard. Now I hope you understand here that I made you no threats."

She grimaced. "So that line about *Cool Hand Luke* and what happened to him? What was that?" She remembered that right after Paul Newman repeated that phrase at the end of the film, he was shot in the neck by a sniper.

"Just a line from a movie." He winked at her as he got up to leave.

*That went well,* he thought. *Why pay a lawyer four hundred an hour when I can handle these things* myself. The old lady owns a lovely tabby cat, eh? Maybe if something happens to it, she'll think twice about messing with the big boys. Hopefully she'll get the message before I have to make her go away for good.

# Twenty Nine

*Went for a walk on the beach. Find me.*

"I'm paying for sins I have yet to commit," I said aloud to no one but me. I'd driven four and a half hours to Hilton Head Island along a stretch of uninteresting South Carolina highway, gotten a forty dollar speeding ticket in Bluffton, and now Charlene was not even here. The note taped to the condo's door may have well said, *I'm somewhere on the planet. Good Luck.*

I had to admit, I was impressed by the surroundings. This was my first time on the island and Harbour Town was truly the playground of the super rich, as evidenced by the size of the yachts in the boat basin below. I'd never seen so many huge watercraft clustered in one area. It had cost six dollars just to drive past the guard through the gated entrance into Sea Pines. From there it was a winding three mile journey on a narrow two lane path across shady mangrove lowlands with Spanish moss hanging from the sheltering oak trees. I caught sight of two large alligators sunning themselves near an estuary, and I wondered if the small Berretta I carry in the glove compartment should accompany me when I leave the Audi in case one of them is hungry.

I asked for guidance at one of the shops and was told the nearest beach access was at the Ocean Club, back down Lighthouse Drive, which I found easily. I parked the car and followed a long boardwalk over the dunes to the water. The pristine white sand stretched for miles in both directions and despite the time of year, the beach was far from deserted. Charlene's cryptic note hadn't indicated exactly which direction she would be walking, or even if this was the right beach. I had no idea what she was wearing. I envisioned shuttling up and down for hours while we moved in opposite directions.

As much as I cling to the masculine trait of refusing to seek help, I decided to approach a small grouping of older folks. It was just past one in the afternoon, but the sun hadn't warmed enough to allow me to shed my jacket.

"Hi folks," I said. "Beautiful, isn't it?"

"Aye-ah, lovely here year round," answered a slight white haired gentleman.

"Do I detect a bit of Maine in that accent?"

"You might, stranger."

"I was wondering if you had seen a lady walking alone through here a short while ago. Blonde, very pretty. Slender."

There were two couples, both on the plus side of eighty. They were all dressed in loose fitting white trousers, Labor Day rules notwithstanding. They sported deep tans on their creased faces. The women were wearing paisley scarves of bright red, the men yellow cotton jackets, crested with polo players on horseback over the left breast. All four smiled, revealing gleaming white teeth that looked as natural as Pamela Anderson's chest.

"Have you seen her?"

"Seen who?"

The next time my male instincts *not to engage* spoke to me, I'd heed their warning. "Thanks. Have a nice day," I said.

They dismissed me with a wave and went back to their conversation about the best early bird dining on the island. I was two hundred fifty miles from home. Bad cell reception. I had no idea where the woman who had invited me here was. I was hungry. It was chilly. Worst case --- I'd burned fifty bucks worth of gas and ten hours chasing an elusive skirt. To keep the day from being a total loss, I'd find a nice place for lunch, see if I could rent some clubs and talk my way onto the famous Harbour

Town Golf Links, where they play that cool tournament after the Masters every year with that red and white striped lighthouse looming over the eighteenth hole. Matter of fact, if I headed toward the lighthouse now, there had to be a decent restaurant at the marina. I could eat and still have time for nine holes before dark. Sounds like a plan. Chicken salad out of chicken shit again.

My thoughts were interrupted by a tap on the shoulder.

"You didn't find me, detective. I found you." It was Charlene, looking radiant.

"Next time you go for a walk at the time you're supposed to meet me, it might be a good idea to at least give me a hint where you'll be. It's a mighty big beach." I tried to fill my voice with reproach but the sight of her in white Capri pants and a snug navy polo shirt was disarming. She had some sort of jacket or sweater tied around her waist.

"You're the private eye, I figured you'd be able to use your deductive powers," she said.

It was the second time she had mentioned my profession. I'd never told her, so she had done some research. What else did she know?

"What's with the private eye bit? I don't call you rock star."

She turned and walked toward the water, beckoning me to follow. "I don't like being played, Riley."

"Who does? You invite me down here, tease me with glimpses of that tight little frame of yours and send me on a search mission. That's being played."

She gave me a trace smile, holding back candlepower. "Let's lay our cards out, shall we and not waste a perfectly lovely weekend. Our meeting at the record shop the other day wasn't by chance was it?"

"What do you think you know, Charlene?"

I glanced around. The group of oldsters had made their way up the beach and were barely in sight. In the other direction, a man was tossing a stick into the water, playing with his Golden Retriever. It reminded me for a second of Jaime, who was fostering my own golden, Bosco. The wave of remorse lessened my patience for the two step we were doing.

I said, "I'm going to sit down here in the sand. If you want to talk, sit next to me. If not, just walk away and I'll go home."

I could see her mind working, evaluating options. "Okay, but I prefer to stand. Sand fleas. You're a private detective."

"Yes, I am. Stipulated. If I didn't want you to know that, I wouldn't have given you my real name."

"So am I under investigation?"

"Not you."

"Does it have to do with Derek Davis?'

She had caught me off guard with that one. "Why do you think that?"

"When you came by to pick up the tile, you drove a white Ford Escape. It didn't register at the time. But the more I thought about it, it struck me as familiar. So I checked our security discs and the tag number was the same as Derek's."

What an idiot --- so enthralled by the prospect of boffing her that I ignored all precautions. She knew my real name, and probably had my face on a disc. I hadn't bothered to check for security cameras. I was so eager to get laid and get Davis' travertine back that I drove the same truck that my friend had parked in the driveway the week before. If she could inspect security discs, so could her husband. And seeing the same truck in the driveway might put Davis in peril again.

"Okay, Charlene, I'll lay it out for you. But you're not going to like it."

"I already don't."

"Derek Davis was attacked Monday and beaten silly. It wasn't a random act, nothing was stolen. Derek and I, we're good friends. I wanted to find out why he'd been beaten and who did it."

"And you think I had something to do with it? Heavens, why would I? I like Derek a lot. Why would I?"

"Not you. Your husband. At first, we thought it was jealousy. Since we're being honest here, Derek told me about your little tease. Same act you pulled on me."

If she was embarrassed it didn't show. She waited for me to continue.

"Your husband is a criminal. I don't know how aware you are of his activities. But given his background, he was the only person we could imagine who would come after Derek. We figured he was jealous. Maybe you let on that Derek was interested in doing more than your bathroom."

Despite the sand fleas, she sat down. She held her head between her hands and stared at the water.

"Let's get a few things straight," she said, her voice hoarse. "I would never do that. It's true, I'm not used to being dumped these days. I know what you must think, that I came on to your friend and now to you and that I'm some desperate housewife slut who sleeps with the help, but it's not that at all. I'm not some common whore."

I had just told her that her husband was a criminal and she was more concerned about allegations of serial infidelities.

I said, "After what you told me the other day, I came to the conclusion that your husband ordered the beat down to teach you a lesson."

She took it all in, while her eyes drifted to a flock of seagulls wailing in the distance. "How is Derek? That sweet man. Is he all right?"

"Nothing permanent. Bruised ribs. Rearranged that mug of his but he got a great plastic surgeon. In the end, he'll be even prettier than before. But he spent two days in the hospital in a lot of pain. And he has no insurance so it's all coming out of pocket. He can ill afford it."

"Send me the bill. I feel awful about that. I had no idea. But why didn't someone call and let me know? We just assumed he wasn't showing up because of another job or he just took off. My husband says it happens all the time in the business."

"Of course he'd say that. But Derek is the most dependable guy I know. His word is the gold standard. And the reason no one called you was that we got the message. Your husband didn't want him to finish the job."

She stood up, brushing sand from the bottom of her pants. "I can't believe that my Johnny would do that. Look, he's in the construction business. I have no doubt that over the years he may have busted a few rules, maybe even greased a few officials to get a project, but he wouldn't be beating a man up just to teach me a lesson."

"We think he did. Look at you. You're way out of his league. Why are you with him?"

"I thought you got that the day we met. I was honest with you, I don't know why, but I told you things about myself that even my girlfriends don't know. I was screwed around in the music business. I had no money, no talent, other than music. I was gonna be a greeter all my life, or at least until I got so old that nobody even wanted me to do that. Then I met Johnny and he showed me respect and offered me a life. You bet I went for it."

"I get that, Charlene, but come on. You'd be a prize catch for any man. And if you worked at the Capital Grille, there must have been dozens of handsome rich guys. Why Serpente?"

"Yeah, I met lots of men. Most of them married. The ones that weren't figured I was some brainless hostess. But Johnny was different. He seemed interested in me like a real person, not a sex object. He treats me like a queen most of the time. So we get along, better sometimes than others but overall, it works for me."

"If you're so grateful to him, why do you cheat on him?"

"Why do you think?"

"Charlene, I don't know what to believe at this point. I think you gave up on life too soon. I listened to your CD on the drive here and you were good, really good. I wasn't lying when I said I know Darius Rucker's people. I hate to see you trapped in a marriage that obviously doesn't make you happy, just so you can have an updated master bath."

"You know, Riley King, I've done seen this movie already. What, you going to take me away from all this and make me a star?"

"You're right. You don't know me. But I'm not some hustler, offering you a recording contract. We met under some unusual circumstances. I'm trying to get a little justice for a friend. That's my only stake in this. I admit, my initial interest in you was to find out about your husband. But it just pains me to see someone as beautiful and talented as you becoming a *Real Housewife of Charlotte* when you could be so much more. "

"Riley, forgive me for saying this, but don't you think I've heard that line before, like a hundred times? From men who want to get into my pants?"

"Sleep with me, don't sleep with me, at this point I don't really care. But the thought of you going to bed every night with a little snake sickens me."

"Johnny and I have never consummated our marriage. He won't have sex with me in what you might consider the normal way. Again, I don't know why I'm telling you this. I didn't know about his problems before we got married. I thought the fact we didn't sleep together was that he was like religious or something. I don't know what I thought, I just saw a way out. But we've come to an understanding. I satisfy my needs elsewhere, long as it doesn't come back at him. None of his friends, business acquaintances, you get it? There's no way he'd hurt your friend out of jealousy."

She had just made her case believable to me. Admitting to a loveless and sexless marriage was a degrading way to deflect blame, not something a proud woman would do lightly. I'd already been more careless with this woman than I ever had. She was smart, but was she Machiavellian enough to construct such an elaborate and humiliating ruse if it weren't the truth? I had the rest of the weekend to find out.

"Any place to eat lunch around here?"

"New Orleans Road has a couple of good places."

"You free for dinner tonight, too?"

"Let's go one step at a time. Lunch first. What do you think, I'm easy?"

# Thirty

## Derek Davis

Davis was wearing flannel pajamas with a teddy bear pattern that an old girlfriend had bought him twenty years ago. They were the only pajamas he owned --- normally he slept in a tee shirt and boxers but felt he needed something more modest in Randee Blankenship's presence.

"When I entered my number in your speed dial, I couldn't help but notice that you had two unchecked messages from a few days ago," Randee said.

"Well, I've been a little preoccupied. And they were from a blocked number and usually those are solicitations. I'm on the *do not call* list but somehow these shady operators get through. Like, 'you recently requested a quote for car insurance and we're returning your call'. I wonder how many fall for that scam?"

"Well, you should check it out. It could be someone offering you work. You can always delete it if it's not legit. It's not like you can get a virus like you could by opening a bad email."

"I've been a little paranoid lately, since the attack."

It struck him that maybe Liz had tried to reach him from Europe. Not being a world traveler, he wasn't sure what the prefixes were over there, wherever over there was. But he seemed to recall that there was a country code or some such notation if the call came from overseas, so it likely wasn't her.

"Would you retrieve them for me? You can put them on speaker. If it's private I'll tell you and you can plug your ears or hum or something."

"Don't worry. If it's a lady, I'll discreetly fade into the woodwork."

She picked up his phone from the counter and expertly plugged into the message center. She asked for his password and punched it in. The first message was from late Tuesday afternoon, when he was still in the hospital.

"Mr. Davis. It seems we have a little problem. Call me."

He gave her a quizzical look. "I have no idea who that was."

She played the second message. The voice was the same.

"Mr. Davis. John Serpente. I sent a message yesterday, by now you must have gotten it. I have very little patience for people who don't respond to my calls. You obviously aren't planning to finish our bathroom in a timely manner. So in the words of the great Donald Trump, you're fired."

Davis paled beneath the bruises. *What the hell*?

Randee looked perplexed as well. "What was that about?"

"Uh, that's a guy I was working for. His wife actually. Then I got beat up and didn't show."

"I recognized his voice, too."

"How do you know his voice?"

"I wasn't going to tell you this right now but I met with him."

"You what?"

"With you in recovery and Mr. King leaving town, I wanted to follow up on that condo situation. So I called Mr. Serpente and I told him about what we discovered. He agreed to meet with me in person."

"God, I wish you had told me first. You don't know who you're dealing with here. Did you mention my name?"

"No, your name didn't come up. But what's this about firing you? You never told me you worked for him. You didn't react one way or the other when I told you he built that place. What's going on?"

"I worked for his wife. But Jesus, Randee what were you trying to accomplish? King and I think that Serpente was the one who ordered my beating."

"I've dealt with tougher characters than he. He struck me as a phony tough guy. I wanted him to know we were onto him and that if he had any decency and wanted to save his reputation, he'd go back and correct the safety violations in his buildings."

"Randee, this guy is dangerous. He might have mob backing up North. You think you can intimidate a guy like that? All you've done is make yourself a target."

"I'm sure you're exaggerating. He seems a harmless little man. Maybe he's a bully with his wife or employees, but call him out and he backs down right away."

"Maybe. But you heard the implied threat in his message. And we're pretty sure he followed through on it."

"Why would he call to fire you if he'd already beaten you up?"

Davis pondered that for a moment. "The message he sent was when he kicked the living shit out of me. The firing was for emphasis."

"Well, I'm on speaking terms with him. He offered me a bribe. Essentially to rig the auction so that I could get that building across the highway at little or no cost. Maybe I can do a little undercover work and find out."

"We need to talk to King before you do anything more. All you may have done is given Serpente a reason to dispose of you. In fact, right now I want you to gather up some clothes and whatever else you need for the weekend and hunker down here. I'll call King and try to get us some protection. Now get your stuff quickly and be careful. Don't even cross the courtyard if you see anybody you don't recognize. Make that anybody at all. Got that?"

"I think you're being paranoid Derek. I'm telling you, this man is all bark and no bite."

"Are you willing to bet your life on that?"

# Thirty One

"Can't rightly say I've had a better meal anywhere, and I used to live in New York," Charlene said, wiping the last remnants of Chilean Sea Bass from her lips.

"I can't disagree." I was feeling mellow, the result of polishing off three quarters of the pinot noir that sat in the silver wine bucket next to the table. Despite my encouragement, Charlene had sampled but one glass, most of which still remained.

We were having an early dinner at a restaurant called Red Fish, in a strip mall on Hilton Head. The very term strip mall begs for amplification in this lush setting. Some forward thinking planners decades ago had decreed that commercial space on the island be set back from the main roadway and separated from passing motorists by a buffer of vegetation, generally tall loblolly pines, willow oaks and magnolias native to the area. Discrete signage was tastefully designed to fit the elegant style proscribed. The net effect was that drivers on any of the major thoroughfares may as well have been passing through an undisturbed forest rather than a densely populated resort community.

I finally gave voice to what I'd been thinking about throughout the meal. "I came here expecting a scene out of *Body Heat*."

"Me, too. When I first invited you, sex was on my agenda for sure. Then, this detective thing began to bother me. I didn't think I'd start to like you. And liking my extramural partners doesn't fit very well into my business model."

"Business model?"

She lifted her glass with long elegant fingers and raised it to her lips. Even the simple act of sipping wine was seductive, and again I wondered whether her actions were conscious or just a result of her native allure.

She said, "I know it sounds cold blooded. But like I told you, my marriage is a business arrangement. I'd never do anything to outright embarrass him, and I'll keep his little secrets. He keeps me safe and warm and dry and looks the other way when I act on my, shall I say, impulses. I suppose you'd say we're living a lie, but it's safe. I never worry about wanting for nothing, and I guess I fill a void in his life in some way."

"Okay. What's this got to do with liking me?"

She drank again, this time draining the glass as if seeking the fortitude to delve into areas of her psyche best left unexamined. "The lovers I've taken during my marriage, *perennials*, I call them. They don't need conversation. We satisfy our needs and then we move on."

"That seems to be a pretty cynical way to live." I knew I might be eliminating my chances of becoming one of her *perennials*, but the clinical way she explained it made me less eager to join their ranks.

"Why? Western society has got this myth going that one person can provide for everything we need. That's why the divorce rate is so high. They teach us that there's a soul mate out there who's the perfect partner. We spend our youth seeking that mythological being. Then, if we trick ourselves enough to think that we were lucky enough to stumble on that person, what's to say it's got to be forever? We change as we get older, only natural. You thought at one time that the FBI was going to be the be all and end all of your dreams. When you learned that it wasn't you moved on."

I had nothing to add, merely staring into her cobalt blue eyes, soaking her sad story in.

"So," Charlene continued, "why do we try to pigeonhole our lovers into a one size fits all bag? How can one person know our deep thoughts, give us with food and shelter, share our creative side and tend to our needs, like we was talking before? How can one person do all of that? When we're courting, we try to twist ourselves into all those roles to please the other. Then when that initial flame flickers, we morph into who we really are. And the combination of all these pieces never fit into the other's crevices to make it perfect. Just ain't in the cards, honeychile."

"At the risk of quoting some syrupy pop song, *that's what friends are for*. Charlene, I can't pretend to know you very well. But you've given up on romance because all anyone ever sees are your looks. There are men out there who can appreciate *everything* you bring to the table. I imagine the beauty pageant people, despite the talent competition and those inane questions about world peace, just really wanted to see what you look like in a swim suit. The music biz? I was part of a payola investigation when I was with the FBI and it was hard to imagine a more rotten bunch. So you latched onto Johnny, a non threatening eunuch who makes few demands and gives more than he takes. Too bad you didn't hold out for a real man who would give you so much more."

"Like you?"

"Yeah, like me --- once upon a time. I'm afraid you'd have to be deprogrammed of all the bullshit you've suffered. Might even be too late for that, given the damage it's done. "

"That's assuming I'd even want to try," she sniffed. "My life ain't so bad as it is, you know."

"Maybe now it isn't. But here's some breaking news --- you're not going to be beautiful forever. You've done a remarkable job so far. But in twenty years? You'd better hope that science takes great leaps by then, or you'll go from being an eleven to a five. And there are a lot of younger fives around."

"And I suppose you think that far ahead? You're pretty hot yourself. Big man, all muscle, clever, I'll give you that. But who's gonna be feeding you warm milk when you need a diaper?"

I stared at her hard, trying not to be seduced. "Look, can't someone give you eighty per cent of what you need and have friends and family fill in the rest? I'm talking emotionally. Then you throw work into the mix, something that's fulfilling and not just a way to stay alive. But here's the bottom line, Charlene, after all the new age bullshit we've both been spouting. You're married to a criminal. He not only scams the taxpayers but he endangers the tenants who live in his buildings. You can deny it all you want. And hey, maybe Johnny wasn't behind the beat down of my pal. But he is crooked and I think you know that. And you can punish him all you want by screwing around behind his back, but he's still always going to be who he is. A snake."

That harsh assessment crossed the line with her. I might have put things more diplomatically were it not for the wine but my better judgment had taken the rest of the night off. She got up abruptly and threw her napkin onto the table, almost knocking over the fake candle.

She was succinct. "Do me a favor. Eat shit and die."

She stormed out. I didn't follow. At this point, sleeping with her was out of the question, since it was likely I'd never see her again. I learned everything I needed to know about her relationship with Serpente. There was nothing to be gained by striking back at him through her now. He wouldn't care. I was beginning to agree with Derek that it wasn't worth it.

Depending on how drunk and tired I felt, I could either drive back tonight or sleep it off somewhere until morning. I finished my wine, ordered coffee and called for the check. The waiter explained that the lady had taken care of it when she had made the reservation. I pressed a twenty into the man's hand as I left.

I walked out of the restaurant, past the open wine storage in the front lobby and into the starless South Carolina night. The November chill sobered me further as I searched the lot for my car. Between the drink and my earlier eagerness to jump on Charlene, I had forgotten where I parked it. I was surprised at what I saw when I finally located the A5.

Charlene, her makeup streaked with dried tears, stood waiting. "Since you see me as such a hard-assed businesswoman, I'll cut you a deal," she said, leaning against the Audi. "Take me home, do want you want and then get out of my life. I don't need soul baring nights like this, it's depressing as hell. I've got a feeling that if I get involved with you, it would become a common occurrence."

*Not like love that you feel in your heart*, I thought, recalling the great Linda Ronstadt song that Karla Bonoff wrote. Maybe tonight we both need someone to lay down beside.

# Thirty Two

Randee Blankenship was angry. It was Sunday morning and she, Derek and I were in Davis' condo, the three of us pacing across his now neatly organized living room.

"Look, maybe one thing doesn't have anything to do with the other. Your tabby may have just gotten into something you were using to strip paint in the condo." said Davis.

"And your beat down was just a coincidence too? Who was it that said, 'One time is a happenstance, twice a coincidence but three times is an enemy action' ?" said Randee.

I was exhausted and not a little annoyed that my erotic plans for the weekend had been disrupted over a sick cat. The panicked call from these two came before I had a chance to take Charlene up on her offer. Parts of me still ached as a reminder.

I said, "Look guys, I drove most of the night to get here from Hilton Head after you called. I checked and found scratches on your door lock, Randee. Somebody did break in, but I can't say for sure when. It might have been a month ago. Or a year. It's just lucky for you the emergency vet was available right away."

Davis said, "That guy is aces. I used him for a dog I once had. If he says the cat will be back to normal in forty eight hours, you can count on it."

Randee's voice was stern, as if reprimanding one of her students. There was a steely resolve to her that had been tested over decades, fighting for her core principles against larger forces.

"I think Serpente was sending me a message, just like the one he sent you, Derek. Next time, it won't be the cat. Now you listen, boys. You think I've been scared off? Is that what you think? Well, you don't know me at all. I don't take shit from anybody."

Our jaws dropped in unison.

"I intend to fight. If low income folks and taxpayers are being screwed over by this builder, he's going to rue the day he ever tried to cross Randee Blankenship. I've been in contact with a young building official who is about to file a report claiming that Serpente tried to bribe him. He may have some pretty damning evidence."

It was clear that the focus had shifted from retaliating for the attack on Derek to the larger issue of Serpente's dangerous and corrupt building practices. They had told me about what they had uncovered at the condos and I had to agree that there were greater consequences at stake than Davis' bruised ribs and broken nose. But a sick tabby and an attack by unknown assailants wasn't actual proof of anything that could be tied to the Snake. We'd need to put together a much stronger case against him to gain any traction. My resolve to make it right had been strengthened but it paled by comparison to Randee's.

She wasn't finished releasing her fury. "I haven't decided exactly how I'll get him yet. Maybe the mainstream media. I'm sure someone at the Observer will be interested in how this man has bribed his way to the top. Or maybe there's an honest district attorney interested in making a name for himself. If not, there's the internet. But as sure as I'm looking at you, this will not stand. I guaren-fucking-tee it. How do you like them apples?"

# Thirty Three

I immediately sensed something was off with Julie Monahan. The woman sounded stiff and formal when I called to confirm our date. Charlene had demoted her in my pecking order of desirable females, but I was still looking forward to a nice dinner with an attractive and much less complicated lady.

I said, "Julie. How was New York?"

"I guess you saw the results. We got to the finals. Lost to Duke. No surprise there."

"But you kept it close. That's a plus."

"No medals for trying. Bill Parcells said it and I agree."

I had seen some highlights from the final game. Corey Wade had played poorly, turning the ball over three times and committing two dumb fouls early in the first half. He was subsequently benched and wound up playing just twelve minutes and scoring only three points, a far cry from his average of thirty minutes and eighteen points.

"Well, overall, you guys looked pretty good. Maybe you'll see them again in the Big Dance and beat them when it really counts."

"Yeah, well. Look, I'm afraid I'll have to cancel dinner tonight. I've got a lot of stuff to catch up on that I wasn't able to do over the weekend."

She said cancel, not postpone. Poor choice of words or reflective of what she really meant?

"Sorry to hear that. When can we reschedule?"

"Really can't say now. Lots going on."

I knew when he was being summarily blown off. Something had changed in New York and he wasn't sure what it could be. But fickle me, now that Charlene was occupying my lustful desires, Julie might merely serve as a conduit to reach Wade. That could lead to leverage against Serpente if the baller would identify the crew that attacked Davis.

"Okay, Julie. Let me know when it eases up. By the way, did you have a chance to talk to Corey Wade?"

"I did."

She was making me work for it. "And?"

"And he says he doesn't know what you're talking about."

"And last week, we both agreed that he does, didn't we?"

She cleared her throat. "I'll be honest with you. I talked to my AD about the situation. I didn't get into specifics because I didn't want to insinuate anything negative about Corey. Just gave him a theoretical situation Saturday afternoon. He led me to a conclusion that I think I knew all along."

Years ago, I would have ended the conversation right there. But I had learned to force people to say potentially unpleasant things out loud. Whereas certain concepts might pass muster within the mind's inner dialogue, actually giving voice to them might prove them irrational. So I waited a beat and opened myself up for the barrage that could follow.

"Treat me like I'm dumb. Julie. Spell it out. What exactly are you saying?"

"I work for the college. My job is to promote Davidson athletics. We raise a considerable amount of money for the school through the positive image that sports provide. At first, I thought that getting a story out about Corey helping save a life might be a good thing for him and for the school and him. But I don't trust that's your real agenda here."

"My only agenda is the truth, Julie. If Corey's involved in something bad, I'll find out. I was hoping that we could work together on this. But if I uncover something on my own, it's possible you'll be blindsided."

"So I help you or else? That sounds like a threat."

"Julie, come on. I wanted your help so we could handle this matter delicately. There may be nothing wrong with what Corey did. You think I'm out to hurt the kid?"

"I'm not sure what you're out to do, Riley."

"All right. Truce. You're right, we don't owe each other anything. All I can say is this: I will pursue this matter wherever it leads. I have no desire to hurt Corey or the program if he's innocent. Okay?"

"Do I have a choice?"

"What do you want me to say? We all have choices. Apparently you've made yours. My alternative would be to drop a solid lead because --- worst case --- it might reflect badly on a college athletic program. Again, I'm sympathetic. But I can't allow what happened to my friend to go unanswered for."

"This is a boy's life that we're talking about. Someone I'm entrusted with. I can't be a party to this in any way. I'm hanging up now."

There was now no reason ever to contact Julie Monahan again. She saw us as natural adversaries, and I had too many other priorities to continue to try to convince her otherwise. Any little spark that might have been there between us had been extinguished. Julie was the polar opposite of Charlene, and I wondered how such disparate females had managed to attract me.

Although Derek's beating and Randee's cat pointed toward Serpente, I needed more. Merely having my way with his wife wouldn't cause him any pain, at least that's the way she saw it. They had an *arrangement*. And if that weren't the case, it would serve as precious little revenge for all the folk who stood to die because lining his pockets was more important to Serpente than public safety.

Unfortunately, Randee's amateur bungling had escalated the urgency of the battle that now must be fought on multiple fronts. She'd tipped her hand, naively thinking that this gangster would observe the same rules of engagement that her scholastic adversaries would. Blankenship needed to back off, lest she become collateral damage. And in a way, convincing her of that might be the more difficult challenge.

# Thirty Four

## Derek Davis

Davis rubbed the back of his neck, then slammed the door to the utility closet. Randee Blankenship had shamed him into gathering more evidence to retaliate against Serpente. Whether the builder was responsible for the cat's poisoning or his own travails, the man was exposing his tenants to danger, either immediate or long term and it was a clarion call to Derek's conscience that he could not ignore.

Along with King, he had tried to dissuade Randee from charging ahead but other than physically restraining the woman, he couldn't prevent her. He *did* convince her to let him compile more evidence before she made her next move. After a couple of phone calls, he was able to locate a project nearby that Serpente had under construction. He dressed as a carpenter, hardly a stretch. Girding himself with a tool belt and a tiny video camera, he tried to blend in with the other laborers as they bustled about the site.

Davis was appalled at what he was seeing. One of the workers installing ductwork was wielding a box cutter and slicing into asbestos as if carving a Thanksgiving turkey.

"What are you guys doing?" he tried to ask casually, as a curious carpenter might to an HVAC man.

"Ducts," was the reply.

"Isn't that stuff dangerous? Cutting it like that?"

"I no understand."

"Muy peligroso. If that's asbestos, you're exposing yourself to cancer or mesothelioma. Long and painful death."

"Boss tell us is not dangerous."

"Let him do it then. You guys have respirators? Masks?"

"Si. We do."

"Good. You might try using them." At least, they would offer minimal protection, but small particles that stuck to their clothing could be just as deadly if eventually inhaled.

The worker shrugged. Got some good footage there, Davis thought. He then joined the men who were hanging drywall along an interior wall. He could tell immediately that it was too thin to conform to multiple dwelling code. He also didn't see any metal plates over the studs where the electrical wiring was woven. Davis identified the crew chief, who spoke English better than his subordinates.

"What's your plan here? Are you going to be working all day?

"Si, senor. Be finished this unit tonight, or boss dock us."

Davis was in another universe. Although he prided himself on keeping costs under control and working more efficiently than his competitors, this was a whole new level of irresponsible frugality. Asbestos was not something to be taken lightly. Davis couldn't imagine where you could even find the stuff unless you were mining a hazardous waste dump or removing it from old buildings about to be demolished.

And it was even crazier allowing untrained and unprotected workers to install it, years after it had been banned in all fifty states. He was playing Russian Roulette with their health. Tiny particles lodged in the lungs could show up years later and prove fatal. In Davis' view, any contractor who would allow unskilled workers to work with asbestos was guilty of negligent homicide.

This was clearly a serious offense. But poking through walls with drywall screws could be even more risky, with more immediate consequences. A screw driven into a twenty amp live circuit will ruin someone's day. Davis used the camera to take video of the obvious violations when the men weren't looking.

Randee Blankenship was building her case by chronicling and compiling the raw footage Davis was gathering into a cohesive presentation. She would move ahead, with or without their help. Davis was certain that he could blend in at a jobsite better than she could. But if any of the workers reported back to Serpente that an unfamiliar gringo carpenter was asking a lot of questions about safety, the Snake might escalate to another level. Davis feared that it wouldn't be a cat in harm's way this time.

# Thirty Five

## Johnny Serpente

Serpente had just come back from his golf outing and was surprised to find Charlene at home. He was dressed in a light cotton sweater; its pale yellow color was of her choosing. His face was reddish from the late autumn sun, doubtless because she hadn't been around to remind him to use sunscreen.

He'd played well today and was proud of how he had acquitted himself under pressure, but still a bit cranky because his playing partner had let him down. "I thought you weren't back until tonight. How was Myrtle Beach?'

She was used to his willful ignorance when it came to things she valued. "Hilton Head. I went to check on the condo. Remember?"

He shrugged. "Didn't you sign up for a timeshare at Myrtle? I must have misunderstood. You went with Doris right? How is the old bat?"

Doris Nevin was one of Charlene's closest friends, who, at a well preserved fifty, was hardly an old bat. "She had something come up and couldn't make it." She knew he didn't care enough to follow through and expose her lie. "I went by my lonesome. The condo is fine by the way. The storm missed the island. The worst of it hit the Outer Banks."

"Oh." He was now preoccupied with his nails. She had asked him to clip them in the bathroom over the sink and not in the bedroom, where the clippings fell to the floor. She decided not to bring it up, since it would raise the issue of the unfinished room.

They descended into an uneasy silence, a condition that happened a lot these days. Their interests had never really been compatible and finally, they'd given up the charade of trying to sound engrossed in each other's affairs, such as they were. They were civil for the most part --- they rarely had loud disagreements, but Charlene could feel one brewing.

"So how did the member-guest turn out?" she asked, more to break the silence than out of curiosity about his golf game, a sport she hadn't played lately.

"We finished second. Would have won the damn thing but Terry screwed up an easy chip on eighteen. I left him a couple feet off the green, an easy up and down. But he skulled it into the hazard. After the penalty, we double bogeyed and lost by a stroke. Asshole."

Too much information. But as always, he took no responsibility --- he blamed his partner. And that irritated her. That's all it took to get things started.

"So, did you cheat?"

He glared. "What kind of question is that?"

"A fair one. When we used to play together, you don't think I saw you fixing up your lie? Or dropping another ball down when you can't find yours and pretending like you did?"

He pulled the sweater off over his head. "Come on Char, everybody does that."

"Not when it counts, they don't."

"What's it to you? It's not like you play with me anymore."

She was starting to heat up. "Even in an open cart, I can't deal with those God-awful smelly cigars."

He sat on the edge of the bed and removed his shoes. They were Johnston and Murphy, three hundred a pair, and again, her choice. "I like them."

"More than me it seems."

He stopped changing and stared at her. "Okay, you're on the rag about something. What?"

"You're so sensitive. On the rag." She walked out of the room only to turn around after passing the threshold. "You know Johnny, there *is* something vexing me. They say that golf is a window into the soul."

"What the fuck is that supposed to mean?" he snorted.

"It means that the way you play golf is kinda like of your philosophy of life. If you cheat at golf, you cheat at other things. If you have a strict honor code in sport, you live your life that way. If you was to break the rules but don't get caught because nobody's looking, that doesn't mean that it's the right thing to do."

"What kind of bullshit feminist crap is that? Where did you see that, on Oprah? You think because I kick it back into the fairway once in a while, I don't have honor? What a load of shit."

"Not just once in a while. You're always doing something. You mark your ball on the green, then move it closer to the hole. I've watched you. All so as you can take a few bucks off your partners."

"Let me tell you something, lady. If you don't give yourself an edge in life, you lose. You think those sharks out there would give me the time of day if I didn't put myself in that position? You think this house, the condos, the cars were just handed to me because I'm so good looking? No. I worked for them. And yeah, maybe I cut a few corners here and there. Nobody gets hurt. Everybody makes out. "

"Nobody gets hurt, huh? Not a zero sum game."

"I don't know what that means but yeah, everybody wins."

She was still wearing the same outfit she'd travelled from the island in. She was dying for a shower but wasn't about to disrobe in front of him. She hadn't done that lately.

"Johnny, listen to yourself. Everybody doesn't win. You take something you don't deserve, it comes back on someone else's bill."

"What they don't know don't hurt them."

"What are you sayin'? You're a builder. What don't your clients know that won't hurt them?"

He pushed his shoes under the bed and removed his socks. "We don't need to have this discussion now. End of story."

"No, not end of story. There's been some talk around about your ethics. Some people have been saying what you're doing is criminal."

She now stood directly in front of him, looking down as he sat on the bed. "I need to know if the man I married is a criminal."

"Who says that? Where are you hearing this?' His face reddened further, not from the sun. She had pushed the magic button that had gotten his full attention.

"It don't matter where I heard it. I'm asking you, as your wife, is it true?"

"Yeah, wife. What a joke. Is what true? What do you know about what I do? What does anyone know? You think those building inspectors have a clue? If they did, they'd be making money building, not criticizing somebody else's work."

"They're supposed to enforce the law. That's their job. Laws are in place for public safety."

"Oh, please. You think some lawyer in Raleigh knows more about building than I do. I'll tell you what they know. They know how to make money. Every permit I pull costs me money, costs me time. Every bullshit regulation they pass costs me money, money that goes into the pockets of guys who grease the politicians. Doesn't make for a better house. And these inspectors. You wouldn't believe the grief I have to put up with from these nimrods. Just this week, this new guy fails the rough plumbing on an entire complex. Now I got to track this little *ciadrolo* down and find out what he really wants. And because of your little bathroom adventure, I haven't got the job done."

"Save the fake Italian slang for your weasel friends. So you just follow the rules you like?"

"Damn straight, *gnocca*" he smirked. "Hey, I build the greenest housing around."

This she had to hear. All she could remember him declaring about green building was that it was a hoax. *We have all the natural resources we need but those damn environmentalists are out to sell their products instead of the traditional ones, and at a premium.*

"I recycle. I take the old, and make it new again. Now the regulations don't go for it. But if I can save a few dollars by using material from another building that was torn down, everybody wins. Except the suppliers of new material. So maybe I slip the inspectors some coin to look away when they see re-used material. Still comes out ahead in the long run. Save the frigging planet." He laughed derisively.

"But it *is* cheating." She wanted him to acknowledge that much.

"Who am I cheating? So I put in a used boiler. By the time the forty-seven per centers get back what I've saved them on initial cost, they'll be old and gray. We got plenty of natural gas in this country. Hell, they're even trying to make cars run on it. Now, can I take a shower and have a drink?"

She wasn't conversant with the building codes. She'd never really thought about it, even though that's what he did for a living. Maybe he was right. But the easy way he rationalized bribing public officials didn't sit well. And she hadn't really thought much about golf being indicative of what kind of person you were. She had read it somewhere, maybe online.

"One more thing, Johnny. That builder who was doing our bathroom. Do you know what happened to him?"

"What happened is he didn't show up for three days. I called him once. He didn't answer. So the next day I fired him. Been doing without a frigging john for too long already. Did you see they finished the tile Saturday. Looks good, no?"

No sign of anything on his face. "So you didn't know that he was beat upside the head last Monday? Sent to the hospital? You didn't know anything about that?"

"Oh, really," he said casually. "Too bad. Wish I had known. I'd have sent flowers." He pulled his golf shirt over his head. His back was scarred and mottled from the tattoos that had been removed. "Price was right on that job. Too late now, though. My guys will have it finished, Tuesday latest."

No remorse. No reaction. Nothing. "That's all you have to say? Too bad?"

"Hey, I never met the guy. Now, I did check him out when you hired him. I know I told you it was your project but I just wanted to protect you in case this guy turned out to be a con man. Lots of them in this business. Turns out he was some hot shit builder who got over extended and like a lot of them, was doing hands-on stuff now. So I let you move ahead."

"And you told me that I was in charge. This was my project. But you were lording it over me all the way, weren't you?"

"What do you know about building? It was for your own good. And I didn't really step in until the guy didn't show for a few days. We were ahead of him on the draw. So I figured my guys could get it done quicker and just as good. I didn't know he got beat up, but I can't say it would have made any difference. You cruise, you lose."

"You really don't think I could have handled it, do you? You give me no credit for having a brain."

"Let's stop pretending, okay? I don't have time for this. I do what I do, you do what you do. That's the deal. I don't ask you about who you're fucking, and you keep your pretty little nose out of my business. You want to boff a contractor to get a better deal, I leave it be. But then the *gavone* doesn't show up for work, it becomes my business. You keep your little secrets, I'll keep mine. Capeesh?"

She didn't answer. She stared ahead without seeing for a moment as he continued to undress. He had never spelled out their agreement in such naked terms. To hear her husband express no jealousy about her occasional forays into adultery hammered home how hollow their marriage had become, if it ever was anything more to begin with.

And his blasé attitude about a good man who had worked for them and suffered a misfortune spoke volumes about his lack of normal human emotions. His inconvenience, having to walk a few more steps to use the hall bathroom outweighed his concern for an innocent man's suffering. And being able to save a few bucks in the process made it doubly worthwhile to him and doubly despicable to her.

It confirmed what King had told her about him. It was the dictionary definition of a sociopath. He may not have sent his goons to rough up Derek Davis, but as long as it didn't cost him money or time, it was no skin off his back. She would have hoped for a husband who would at least show some compassion, someone who might even offer to make it up to the poor guy in some way. Any way. A future job. A rebate for time spent. A few bucks to help pay for the hospital.

Instead she got, *You cruise, you lose*.

She had him pegged now. He had no concern for the consequences of his actions. He might never actually pull a trigger or sink a blade, or even order a goon to do so, but his willful neglect of public safety measures might result in more carnage than the most blood thirsty don. It would just take longer and cause more pain.

# Thirty Six

I was driving back home when my cell barked. I toyed with letting Charlene go to voicemail, but since I had left Hilton Head so suddenly after receiving Davis' call, I at least owed her an apology for not accepting the generous offer of her lush bod. Much of what she had told me about her life was a turn-off that convinced me further contacts with her weren't going to be productive on any level. Away from her, this was an easy conclusion to reach. In her presence, nothing mattered but my desire.

She wanted to meet, said she had something urgent to discuss. She sounded desperate and I gave in without much of a fight. We picked a spot halfway from where we both were and in less than a half hour, the two of us were together over coffee at the Northlake mall. What can I say, I'm weak.

"Hi, doll," I said when I first saw her, channeling Robert Mitchum.

"Not feeling like a doll today. It's your fault really. I was content with things the way they were. I accepted the reality of my marriage. But you used a word that I'd never thought about before."

What the hell have I gotten myself into with my big mouth? Helping Davis didn't mean I had to drive to Hilton Head for an assignation with a married woman. I was trying to kill two birds with one stone, satisfying my lust while avenging a friend. Right now, neither was going well.

I waited for her to elaborate but when she didn't, I had to respond. "And what word was that, Charlene?"

"Criminal," she said. "I suppose I always knew that successful businessmen break a few rules along the way, tell a few white lies. But I never believed that Johnny was anything more than a low rent kid from Brooklyn who'd climbed up the ladder."

I wasn't sure if Charlene's misgivings would be helpful to lowering the threat level. They might just put Serpente on higher alert, and therefore make him more dangerous. Or perhaps some calming words might make their way to her husband, and cool things down.

"Charlene, it was wrong of me to imply anything about your husband. I've never met the man. I'm sure he's no better or worse than anyone else."

"Riley. Don't try to shine me on. You said he was capable of having your friend beat on just to teach me a lesson. So don't tell me he's just an average Joe."

"Charlene, you were burned by your naiveté about the music biz. Screwed around by a bunch of guys. So the first fairly nice guy who treated you with a little respect seemed like a good deal for you. You thought that Boris Badinov or whatever the hell his Russian name is, was good enough for you."

"When I first met Johnny, I was a mess. A burnt out, self medicated, dumb blonde."

"Now who's shining who on? I mean, I have a one forty IQ and you're way smarter than me."

I have no idea what my IQ is, but 140 sounds good.

"I taught myself a lot after I got married. I had nothing to do, I was bored. I felt my mind turning to mush. First thing I did was go to the library and read the books that I read as Classic Comics to fake my way through class. I started watching the Discovery and History channels. I learned a bunch about pop culture in the twentieth century, and there's nothing you could ask me about modern music that I won't know about. I'm not the same girl I was when I met Johnny. And he let me do it, maybe for the wrong reasons but he let me grow."

"Benign neglect on his part. So you've outgrown him. Sounds like it's time to get out."

"I don't know what he'd do if I did. He's never been violent toward me in the past, but I saw a side of him that I'd never really picked up on before. There was a total lack of caring about anyone. Like as long as he was in a safe place, the world could be on fire and he couldn't care less."

Over the last five years, there were two women who had come to me for help and protection. Both were dead now. In my more troubled moments, late at night when I couldn't sleep, I replayed the days leading up to their final hours. I second guessed every move. If I had been just a little smarter, a little better at my job, they both might be alive today. Was I willing to take that chance with Charlene?

This started as a simple affair. My good friend had been assaulted and I wanted to find out who was responsible. Once I was sure of that, how did I plan to retaliate? I firmly was convinced that Johnny Serpente was a bad man. But if everything Randee and Derek were uncovering could be laid directly at his doorstep, the beating was the least of his sins. Even if he cared, sleeping with his wife didn't even start to even to score for thousands dying of cancer due to his corrupt building practices.

But the beautiful woman across from me had urgent matters of her own to deal with. Could I help her *and* nail Johnny in one fell swoop?

"Charlene, why are you scared of him now? Did something happen?"

"Just that very revealing conversation. I suppose I've been thinking about leaving for a while now, but after last night, I made up my mind."

# Thirty Seven

## Johnny Serpente

Johnny Serpente figured he had bigger problems to deal with than a suddenly insolent and ungrateful spouse. The day before their argument, one of his friends had approached him with a problem that couldn't be dealt with by telling him to boff a contractor.

"Serpy, a word please." The man hadn't exactly whispered, but he kept his voice low and glanced around the posh locker room to be sure no one could overhear.

"Sure, councilman, what's up?"

He lightly took Serpente's elbow and guided him to a vacant corner, out of earshot of a group of guests, who were loudly recounting their heroics and dressing for the post tournament awards dinner. "That plumbing inspector. The situation is getting out of hand."

"Yeah. I was meaning to talk to you about that. He didn't exactly get it when I hinted that it might be in his best interests to look the other way on some things."

"You call a thousand dollars in an envelope taped to his dashboard a hint?"

Johnny was already unhappy after losing the tournament because his playing partner had choked on the last hole. Winning would have meant that his name would have been inscribed on the massive plaque that adorned the club's lobby. The list of winners of the member-guest, club championship and handicap scramble dated back to the institution's inception. It would have been the final validation of his acceptance into this rarified atmosphere of Southern gentry.

"Look, councilman, I never ask you to get your hands dirty. I always insulate you guys from anything that might blow back. But you blew it with this gavone. Nobody told him upfront how things work here and this fucking boy scout doesn't want to play ball."

"Well, it's reached the point where he went to his boss and reported the bribe. Even gave him the envelope and all the money as evidence."

"Lucky we got his boss on the payroll, eh? Like Harry Truman said, *the fucking buck stops there*."

His friend ignored the mangled quote and continued. "It may not be that simple. Sure, we can suppress it for a while, but it may not be over. This boy scout, as you call him, might bump it up the ladder if he doesn't see results. Might even go public with it. He insinuated as much."

"How the hell did this guy get hired in the first place?" Serpente was getting more irritated with this swell as the conversation went on. He was tired of cleaning up other people's messes. He had enough shit of his own to cope with.

"The department was undermanned and they hired this jerk as a temp without vetting him fully. It happens."

"So what do you want me to do?"

"Clearly, this man needs some incentive to drop this matter immediately or it could affect all of us."

"So you want I should..."

"Stop right there, Serpy. I don't want to know *how* you handle it. Just handle it."

"And if he doesn't respond to reason, then what?"

"Speak to me before you do anything drastic. Understood?"

Johnny just nodded. The councilman squeezed his skinny bicep and stole away.

The councilman glad-handed a couple of guests, suggesting they retreat for drinks in the ballroom. He pointed them toward the elegantly appointed space and said that he'd follow momentarily.

Waiting for him around the corner was Moses Ginn. The councilman motioned the locker room attendant into a quiet hallway and quickly got to the point. "You heard?"

"I did," Moses said.

"I'm not convinced he'll get this done. He's let it drift too far already. We'll we have to take matters into our own hands."

"I would agree, sir. You need to stay on top of this."

The councilman said, "I hate to take such extreme measures, Moses. Thank God we haven't had to go that far in the past, but we have to contain this. Johnny could become a liability."

Another gaggle of guests approached and Ginn's posture and tone changed dramatically as he slipped back into his role.

"Yessir. I'll make sure them towels be where they belongs at right away, sir."

# Thirty Eight

## Derek Davis

Derek Davis' Monday was coming to a crashing conclusion. He sat opposite Kim Carson, a man he had known or thought he had known for a decade. In the past, the gawky, sandy haired banker had always been quick with a smile and a loan approval. Today, there were no smiles.

"How long have I been dealing with this bank? Twenty years?"

"And we appreciate your business over the years, Mr. Davis. If it were up to me, none of this would be happening."

"I vas only followink orderss!! Achtung, baby." Although he never liked it when others used Nazi references to describe their smaller problems, he couldn't help himself.

"Excuse me?"

"I don't understand how this could be happening. I did business with your bank because you were small and locally owned. I could have gotten better terms elsewhere but I stayed loyal. And this is how you repay me?"

Carson sighed in frustration. The banker was uncomfortable and wanted to get this over. He glanced around the small glass enclosed office as if he expected the cavalry to charge in at any moment and rescue him from this awkward moment. But no reinforcements appeared and he was left to deal with the situation on his own, something that was occurring with increasing regularity.

"Mr. Davis, you have to understand. We were purchased by a bigger institution last year. Because of that, we don't control your mortgage. It was bundled along with most of our others before the sale. Given that it was worth less than we had into it, it was considered a liability rather than an asset. We control the loan in name only. The government has imposed new guidelines and in order to receive bailout money, our parent company agreed to abide by them retroactively."

"Blah, blah, blah," Davis said."Bottom line is, I've got to come up with the entire amount within sixty days or you'll foreclose."

"I'm afraid so. I should have told you at the time when you applied for refinancing that this could kick in, but I had no idea that your income had taken such a dramatic hit."

"What about my assets? I still have a CD with your bank. My money market account could keep the loan afloat."

"Irrelevant under the new guidelines. Your income is submerged below acceptable levels and debt to income ratio is over a hundred. Your application triggered all of this. Otherwise, it could have been some time before anyone noticed. I'm sorry. I'm just learning all the new rules myself."

Davis' looked about the place. The bank's physical structure hadn't changed in the last three years. It had the same rich wood paneled walls, polished terrazzo floor and windowed perimeter offices that he had seen hundreds of times when going about his business. But instead of warm and welcoming, the surroundings now seemed cold and institutional. He'd had many happy closings there, depositing six figure checks thereafter. He'd even brought breakfast sandwiches for Carson on occasion when they had a morning conference or closing scheduled. He considered the man his personal banker. Now he was destroying the last vestige of hope to create his dream village. All it took was a phone call and quick dismissal.

Carson shuffled some papers on the desk. "There is one alternative I can think of offhand. You could consider a short sale. Heck, you may get some big shot Yankee thinking he's going to fleece one of his dumb Southern brethren and you could make out better than a straight sale."

A true rube might have bought that argument. But Derek knew the truth to be more complicated. If he allowed the bank to foreclose, he could walk away owing nothing and leave them trying to sell a distressed property for a loss. But if he sold short, he might have to bring additional money to the table, perhaps taking away most of what he still held. He figured his credit rating would be damaged less but he didn't even know that for sure. Either way, given his paltry earnings, he wasn't going to qualify for a bank loan anytime soon.

"I'll discuss it with my realtor. That's your only idea to get me out of this quagmire?" Davis asked.

"I'm afraid so. Again, I'm sorry. The regs are changing so fast that it's hard to keep up with them, but I should have advised you not to try to re-apply. Once I saw your application however, it was my fiduciary duty to report it."

*Thanks for nothing*, Davis thought. *You could have torn up the application and no one would be the wiser. I could have continued to make payments until the market improved and the bank would have made their interest and I could save my project.*

But the more he turned it over in his mind, maybe Carson was acting in his best interests. Stringing himself along about New Hope was slowly destroying his life. All those interest payments were draining his capital and if things didn't radically improve within the next year or so, all it would amount to was throwing good money after bad.

One of the hardest things a businessman is faced with is admitting a major mistake and accepting the financial consequences. Derek had never suffered a loss while building houses. He had some close calls --- some near break-evens that he had to sweat out. A couple of times this had occurred when the market sagged shortly after starting construction on a spec home. But he just tightened his belt and found a way to make it work.

He never really sympathized much when follow builders overextended themselves and declared bankruptcy. When asked for advice, he counseled them against trying to borrow more to salvage a project when cutting their losses was the most prudent course of action. Most hadn't listened.

Now he knew why. He never wanted to be a quitter. He always believed in his ability to rise Phoenix-like from the ashes of defeat and turn it into victory. But this time, the fates had gotten the best of him. He'd allowed himself to dream, and his emotions had overtaken his business sense.

There was a price to be paid. But while he was still alive and still had his wits about him, he'd find another way. He had no idea what that was.

"Excuse me, Mr. Davis. I have another appointment waiting. Again, I'm sorry to put you through this. Good luck to you, sir."

"Well, Carson. Man's gotta do what a man's gotta do," was the wittiest reply he could come up with before he turned and walked out the door, hoping never to return to this heartless edifice.

# Thirty Nine

After hearing Charlene's story, I was beginning to form a better picture of the type of man her husband was. I'd dealt with violent types before and certainly the kind of challenges Charlene had issued would have provoked a physical response in a man prone to spousal abuse. The fact that Serpente had used hurtful words but hadn't raised a hand was reassuring in a way. But I wasn't willing to take any chances, given my history. I told her that I would provide her safe harbor and that she should plan on moving in with me as soon as she could get her things together. No strings attached.

There was another aspect of Charlene to consider, loathsome as it was. Could she be a double agent, spying on us on behalf of her husband? If this was the case, she had done it skillfully. I couldn't be sure that her best interests didn't lay in protecting Serpente given all the comfort he provided for her.

I decided to concentrate on the smaller matter, hoping I might be able to find a side door entrance into Serpente's vulnerability. If I could prove he ordered Derek's beating, it might be like nailing Al Capone on tax evasion, opening the door to a wider investigation by the authorities.

There was still one untraced lead on the beating. I'd tried not to go that route in sympathy for a confused kid, but now I saw no alternative. Corey Wade could deny his involvement all he wanted to Julie Monahan, but I knew he was hiding something. I'd shown Corey's picture in the press guide to Randee Blankenship and the sharp eyed lady had no doubts that he was the lad she had seen hanging out with Derek's attackers.

Davis' recollection was foggy but he allowed that Wade did look like the kid who had helped him.

I made my way to the Davidson field house and quickly ascertained where the players' entrance was. I waited until practice was over. It was just getting dark.

He emerged with two other boys. Wade was a small forward, listed at six seven. He had yet to fill out and appeared more sinewy than muscular.

*Damn. He's not alone. A complication.* Following the three across campus, I stayed a safe distance behind, not that they would have noticed. The other two were chattering away about girls, hoops and food. Corey seemed subdued, as if preoccupied with something. Maybe he was just a shy kid, but big time basketball stars nowadays talk trash from the cradle.

The group split when they got to a dorm on the north side of the campus. Wade absent mindedly high-fived his mates and took off on his own. I picked up the pace and soon was almost astride the big kid, who still seemed lost in thought. A hundred feet ahead, I spotted a small alleyway between buildings. It would do.

As Wade and I neared the alley, I coughed loudly. The unexpected sound caused him to break stride. "Don't sound good, man," he said.

I lowered my shoulder and body blocked him into the darkness. He lost his balance as I drove him further in, pinning against the rough textured brick, my forearm pressuring the kid's throat. His eyes widened in fear.

"I'm here for Derek Davis," I said.

"I don't know who that is," he tried to yell, but the voice was pinched.

"He's the guy you beat up last week. Or do you do so many you can't remember their names?"

"Don't know what you're talking about man. Don't know no Davis."

I tightened the hold. Although the lad was taller and plenty strong, I had leverage and knew how to use it. "I didn't say you knew him. Just that you beat him up."

"What you talking about? I didn't beat nobody."

"Let me phrase it another way. You shoot your jumper righty, no?"

"What's that got to do with shit, man?"

"I'm thinking a broken pinky and ring finger might throw your shot off for a few weeks. Maybe even until the end of the season."

"Man, you crazy. Why you threatening me? Who are you anyway?"

"Your worst nightmare. I want some answers and I want them now. If I don't get them, Davidson will be minus a small forward for a while." I pushed harder into the kid's Adam's apple. "The man I represent got beat up last week. You were there."

His reply was choked and I let up a bit so I could make out what he was saying. "Man, whatever you do ain't nothing to what's waiting for me if I snitch."

"Here's the deal. I don't think you were a willing part of this. Your rep is that you're a good kid that came up under some tough circumstances and you're rising above it. Am I right? Just nod."

He did.

"Cool. Now the man you saw beat up and drove to the hospital, he was a pretty powerful dude. He could just snap his fingers and send someone to blow you away. You'd be a fly on his butt. Now me, I'm a negotiator. I'm not a violent man. I like to talk, not inflict pain if I can help it."

"Shit."

"Shut up. You think this is hurting? You should see the guys my partner sends when he really wants someone hurt. Not pretty. So I'm going to make you a one-time offer. I'm going to let you walk away from here, nothing hurt but your pride and all you have to do is tell me who hired you. That's all. Name of your boss. Then I develop amnesia. I don't know where I got his name. I don't know anybody named C-Wade. Coach doesn't know one of his star players was involved in something dirty. Everybody wins."

"You going after the brothers I know it's going to take more than a forearm shiver, man."

"Thanks for the advice. I'll make sure to tell the real muscle of the family."

The kid convulsed with fear.

"Oops, did I say family? I let that slip. Forget you heard it. Anyway, name and address. That's it. You give me that and this never happened."

"What's stopping me from warning them off, man?"

"Nothing, except then they'll know that you were the one who tipped me off and I don't know, they might object to that. But hey, if I were you, I'd pick my sides carefully. A couple of low rent gang bangers versus what I have backing me. I report, you decide. Like you want LeBron on your side or playing against you. Hey, I'm the nicest guy you'll meet from our little *familia*. The others wouldn't be talking to you this long."

"How I know you won't ding me right here after you get what you want?"

"You don't. Just my word. Actually, I tell my boss that you cooperated, he might want to send a little reward your way. After all, seems like you had a little twinge of conscience and drove him to the hospital."

"Listen. man. Loosen up on my neck and I'll tell you what you need."

I complied, ready to tighten at a second's notice if the kid cried out.

He said, "Two guys I know from the neighborhood call. They say they got business up Davidson way. They landscapers but they sell a little weed on the side. I tell them that's cool but I'm not down with that business no more. They say that they just coming out to discuss a deal with someone, that they need someone knows the lay of the land. They say there be a Jackson Five in it for me if I just drive them to this place where they're meeting this dude. Easy money and nothing bad happens to anyone. Just want me to help a brother out."

"And you bought that? A hundred bucks just to drive them to a place they could find with a GPS."

"Their whip ain't got no nav system. They not familiar with the turf here. Might get lost on the way out if they need to split in a hurry."

"What did you think this 'business' was?"

"I thought they just be moving some weed or something. Worst thing. And these dudes know shit about me I don't want out there, stuff I done when I didn't know better. But when I saw what they was doing to your boss, I ran. I wasn't driving no getaway car. Never got my Benjamin. Don't want it."

"So you came back and took the boss to the hospital in his car. I suppose he had his keys on him. How'd you get home?"

"Bus. Waited for forty five minutes. That's what happened, I swear. Your boss mess me up? For real? I help him best as I could."

"See, a man like that, he needs respect. It gets out a couple of punks can jump him at any time, well his rivals will see that as a sign of weakness. Usually up here, he doesn't need to travel with muscle. Now he does."

"What he doing coming out of that shit hole apartment anyway? He such a powerful man, why his crib not nicer? And what's with that beat up ride he got?"

"Visiting one of his girls. Occasionally has to sample the wares to maintain quality assurance. Get where I'm coming from?"

"Dude! I got no choice."

"Corey, I promise I'll make it right with the man. You'll have nothing to worry about. Matter of fact, he probably could make those problems with your past just go away. Files get misplaced all the time downtown. Now just give me the name and address and you'll never see me again."

"You be sure you don't tell them where it come from. Sound like they not in your boss's weight class, but they be plenty tough." He told me what I wanted to know.

I released him and brushed off his jacket with a flick of the wrist. "Later, Corey. Keep that sweet jumper, eh?"

The boy tore off quicker than if he saw an undefended lane on a fast break. I'd portrayed the mild mannered Davis as a Mafia king running drugs and string of call girls. Somewhere in my ruminations about Serpente, the idea of a fake don struck me as one I could use myself to intimidate. Later, when Wade had time to think about it, he could poke a hundred holes in the story. Chances are, he would bury the last five minutes deep within himself, surfacing only in nightmares or psychotherapy in twenty years.

I wasn't proud what I had done --- intimidating a young student who was trying to do the right thing. In Corey Wade, I saw echoes of myself thirty years ago, a modestly talented kid with hoop dreams. I'd gotten physical with bad guy suspects before, but never a teenage college student who had stumbled into a bad situation. The kid had tried to do the right thing to make up for his mistake by rushing the victim to the hospital and calling me for help as Davis had requested.

The story rang true. Through a mixture of fear and a little bit of greed, he'd been hoodwinked into participating in a felony. Between his fear of my fictional boss and the reprisals he would risk if his cohorts knew that he had snitched, there was little chance of him sharing his story with anyone. It explained why he wouldn't even admit to Julie Monahan that he helped Davis.

But unless I find the names given to be patently false, I see no need to push the boy any further. Maybe this experience will be instructive about being more cautious when it comes to doing favors for old friends. But try as I might to rationalize what I have just done, I have a sour taste in my mouth that won't go away. Were the means I had just used to send a message any holier than Serpente's?

# Forty

### Derek Davis

"I'm surprised you haven't delegated this to some intern, Mags," Derek said. He was sitting on a Frontgate barstool in a home that he couldn't afford, even at the peak of his earnings.

"Multi-million dollar clients can be demanding. They don't understand the vagaries of the market like we do, Derek," she answered. She reached over the blue pearl granite to a bottle of white wine she had brought for prospective buyers. "End of the day. Let's not let good wine go to waste."

Derek weighed her offer versus the doctor's advice to go easy on the booze while taking painkillers. He had moved from the strong stuff to Advil over the weekend and despite the warning labels, he decided that a nice chardonnay might be just what he needed to mellow out. After his encounter at the bank, he dialed Maggie's cell phone and she invited him to join her at the open house she was tending.

"Pour me just a splash, Mags. Can't let you drink alone." He looked around the spacious kitchen into the great room. This house was impressive. It went on and on. Nine thousand square feet of heated living space, the brochures declared. And what living space it was.

There were polished limestone floors in the kitchen and breakfast area where they currently sat. Each of the six bedrooms had a private bath, elegantly decked out with granite counters and top of the line fixtures. The builder had cut no corners here. Every room was wired to the gills for every conceivable electronic marvel yet to be invented.

It had a theatre on the upper level that could accommodate sixteen neighbors on reclining leather seats. The projector beamed high definition images onto an eleven foot diagonal screen.

"What are they asking for this place, Mags? Just out of curiosity."

"Four mil. They'll be lucky to get two and a half."

"Wait a minute. There's at least that much in the building alone. This lot with a main channel view of the lake had to cost over a million."

"You're forgetting the exterior. There's a saltwater infinity pool. Built-in outdoor kitchen, complete with gas fireplace. Refrigerator, grill and oh by the way, weatherproof flat screen. I take it you never came to a party here."

"Can't say that I have. Who owns it?"

"Hedge fund guy. Builder was that British gent, builds houses to look like castles."

"I know the one. Peter something. I must say, the work is impeccable. He was always a cut above me when it came to that. I mean, there's high end and then there's high end. But two million five? That's a steal."

"Derek, I said they'd be *lucky* to get two and a half. Even then, there would be resistance, since the property taxes are so steep."

He stood up and walked toward the great room. The ceilings were twenty feet high, beamed with hand hewn cedar, and faux painted to resemble leather. There was a cherry paneled study, lined to its thirteen foot peak with lawyers' bookcases. He returned to the kitchen shaking his head. "I take back my earlier estimate. There's two nine in the building alone."

"You might be right. But it doesn't matter. There are so many foreclosures at this level that no one is buying unless it's a complete steal. I agree you couldn't duplicate this place for much under four, but unless you lure in someone who doesn't know the territory, nobody would even look at it at that price point. Hey, you're the only one who came to the open house today and I sense it isn't because you want to buy this shack."

"So why are you listing it for four?"

"I've known the Calleys' for years. I told them what I told you, but he's not willing to let it go at a loss. But until I get this down to the right price, I lose money every day I have the listing. Advertising, MLS fees, payroll."

"So why take the listing at all? Just because you like them?"

"That's a factor. But first, they're the type that'll buy and sell many houses over the years so if I don't make out on this one, there will probably be others. Plus, anybody who is looking at this has enough money to check out my other listings. If they think this one is overpriced, it makes the others look like a bargain."

Derek's attention drifted to the appliances. Sub-zero, Wolf, AGA, Bosch. There had to be forty five grand in appliances. "But don't you run the risk of losing these clients anyway? If this doesn't get offers, might they blame you and go to another realtor who promises them the moon?"

"Could be. I told them the hard truth about price --- hopefully they'll appreciate that and will come back to me later when I'm proven correct. But heck, if somebody else can get them four for this place, more power to them. That's when I retire to Jamaica." She took a sip of wine, a gentle grin crossing her features. This was one savvy broker, and Davis trusted her judgment implicitly. "But Derek, you said we needed to talk."

"Yeah, well it's about New Hope."

"That's what I figured. Now what?"

"The bank is calling my note. I've got sixty days to sell or they'll start foreclosure proceedings."

Maggie Holmes bit her lip and looked at the floor. "You want my honest opinion?"

"Always."

"Let them. Let the bank take it. Now --- you have a million dollar note on it, correct?"

"But I paid 2.5."

"Haven't you been listening? The Calleys paid close to four for this place. They'll lose close to two million if they want to sell it today. Why should you be immune to the market?"

He really wasn't prepared for Maggie's brutal honesty, as much as he thought he would be. "But that land is prime. Once the economy comes back, it'll be worth double what I paid."

"And when exactly will that be, Derek? Got a crystal ball? You say your land is prime. And this place isn't? Fact is, it doesn't matter what you paid. It's what someone is willing to pay now. And that's seven fifty, give or take. Cut your losses."

"But I put a million five down. Where does that go?"

"Gone with the wind, my boy. And don't worry about your credit rating. They're not lending money now anyway no matter how credit worthy you are."

Davis felt his windpipe thicken. "Maggie, all my life I've tried to do things the right way. This development was going to be my legacy. My contribution. Now you're telling me that not only is my dream dead, but it's taken my life savings with it."

Maggie Holmes couldn't afford to be sentimental. She was a businesswoman who could stand toe to toe with the toughest pricks on the planet. She had to tell sellers that their houses, their nest eggs, were worthless now. She had to tell buyers that the banks wouldn't give them mortgages when a few years prior, they were handing them out like complimentary toasters for new accounts. *No credit check, no income verification.*

She had to avoid his eyes. She felt awful about this but there was little she could do to ease his pain. He was a good man who had worked hard his entire career, but now he had no pension, health insurance, or future earning power.

She said, "Derek, give me the listing. I'll scour the state, damn, I'll scour the world for buyers for you. But you need to face reality, I have no chance of finding someone who can get you out of this whole. I'll sacrifice my commission to help you out. But understand, foreclosure is coming. Prepare for it. Talk to your accountant or whoever gives you advice on money matters."

"Damn Mags, I'm having a hard time coming to grips with this. Everything I grew up believing just seems to be so much bullshit now. *The American dream of home ownership*. Now it feels like nothing more than a scheme to enrich the banks and corporations who kept upping the ante. And I bought into it. In fact, I aided and abetted. We couldn't let people be satisfied with what they had. It always had to be more."

"Hey, I was part of that game, too. I guess I still am. I know that."

"But that's just it, Maggie. Yeah nowadays, the average house is double the size it was when I started building, and around here even that's considered tiny. Kitchens have computers, microwaves, granite, stainless steel. You're considered underprivileged if you don't have those things. But are we really happier with all these conveniences? I mean, we used to call them labor saving devices. Like it was somehow wrong to labor over something you take pride in."

He rubbed his eyes and took another sip.

Maggie said, "Let the bank foreclose, Derek. Stop making payments and walk away. They'll take a hit, too. You've made them a lot of money over the years, sending mortgage customers their way, paying interest on your note."

"Thanks for caring, Mags. But I don't think I can just skip out. I signed a contract. The measure of a man is not what you do when times are good. It's when times are tough that really counts."

He shook his head and began to pack up. Just over a week before, Derek Davis was in a hospital bed, warding off pain from a big time beating. Things looked rosier then.

# Forty One

## Derek Davis

After his heart to heart with Maggie, Davis waited for King at the bar of 131 Main, a restaurant they both liked in Cornelius, the next village south of Davidson. Sipping a club soda, he checked his watch every two minutes, wondering what had kept his friend. Although King's profession rarely led him into peril these days, Derek hoped that his own problem hadn't led his friend in danger. It was 6:45, and King was due fifteen minutes ago. It wasn't like him to be tardy and he always called when he was running even just a few minutes late. Between that and his meetings today, he was a bundle of nerves. He wished that he could order wine, beer, scotch or whatever might calm him, but he was mindful of his doctor's warnings.

His cell vibrated. *Good, King calling with an excuse*. But although the number was familiar, it didn't belong to King.

"Derek. It's Liz."

His stress level went up ten notches. "Liz. Wow. Didn't expect to hear from you. Still in Europe?"

"No. Got in this morning. I can barely hear you. Are you at a party? Is this a bad time?"

He wanted to say that her call couldn't have come at a worse moment. He was up to his neck in problems. With everything on his plate already, he wasn't sure he could handle this now. But he couldn't let the opportunity pass, if indeed it was an opportunity.

"No, I'm waiting for Riley at 131 Main. Let me go outside where it's quieter." He motioned to the bartender to save his drink and headed to the parking lot. It was chilly but he didn't notice.

"Okay, that's better. God, I miss you. How was France?"

"Uh, it was all right, I guess. I was laid up for a bit, so I didn't really travel much."

What exactly did laid up mean? "Are you okay now? Anything I can do?"

"No, I'm fine, I guess. I just wanted to hear your voice."

She didn't sound right. Maybe it was jet lag, but she sounded weak, uncertain. All the "I guesses" were uncharacteristic. He took comfort in the fact that she had called the day of her arrival to hear his voice.

"When can I see you? I imagine you're tired from the flight. Is tomorrow good for lunch maybe?" he said.

"I'd like that. We need to talk. I need to apologize to you. I haven't been very honest with you since we agreed to take a break in our relationship. There are some things I need to get out."

Todd Weller, no doubt, was one of those "things". He'd already come to grips with that, not that he liked it. But where did it stand with Todd? Did she plan to announce that Todd was her new man and that she wanted him to hear it firsthand out of respect for once they once were?

"Yeah, I understand. I have some things to tell you as well. How about the Mimosa Grill at noon?" The restaurant was pricey but at this point, a fifty dollar lunch wouldn't affect his diminishing bank account.

"That sounds nice. We went there to celebrate the first anniversary of our meeting. Remember?"

It was a night he'd never forget. For many reasons.

He said, "Of course. I'll see you then. Love you."

"Me, too."

He hadn't intended to use the L word. It slipped out. But she sort of said it too, hadn't she?

He stood outside for a moment longer, the cold finally starting to sink in. Things come in threes. The beating, the bank, and now Liz. Was she the third act of a tragedy?

# Forty Two

I waved as I pulled up to where Davis was standing. I shouldn't have been driving in my condition, but I was being overly cautious in case some cop with nothing better to do pulls out a Breathalyzer.

I yelled to Derek, who looked as out of it as I felt. "Sorry, I'm late. What are you doing out here in the parking lot? Let me park the car. Order me a Molson and I'll meet you at the bar."

The bartender was just sliding my beer across the bar when I walked in. "Timing is everything. Thanks. How are you, my sullen friend?" I said, trying to muster up bonhomie and good cheer that I didn't feel.

"What the hell are you so merry about, Riles? Panthers pick up Peyton Manning on waivers or something?" No doubt Davis could smell the alcohol on my breath and sensed that my jovial mood was forced.

"Ah, would that they could. No reason in particular. Just trying to inject a little joy into the room."

Davis relayed his conversation with Maggie and the dread options that awaited him. He said in conclusion, "So it may be a new beginning in the sense that I start over with nothing and over a mill in losses, but I'm missing the joy in the situation."

I said, "You and I have had this conversation before. Honestly, I think that land was an albatross and you'll be well rid of it. Hey look, I have a big empty house. Why not stay with me for a while? I'd enjoy the company. You want to pay rent, we'll run a tab and someday you can pay me when things get better.

And you can work some of it off. Not just house stuff but you're pretty handy with a computer. I might be able to put you onto a couple of P.I. things that you can check out for me."

"Riles, working for friends is a bad idea. You have to be prepared to lose the job or the friend. I'm not willing to take that risk."

"Maybe, I'm not putting this the right way. Oh, hello, mister. Can I help you?"

A large man stood behind Davis, his bulk imposing. He had to stand at least six five. He might have been sixty five, seventy. Bald, with craggy skin lined from outdoor labor. His features reminded me of Dean Jagger in *White Christmas*. The guy had the bearing of high ranking ex-military.

Davis said, "Hey, Paul. Haven't seen you since forever. Riley, Paul Larsen was one of the best builders in Charlotte for a lot of years. How's it going, colonel? Meet Riley King. He's a good friend of mine. "

Paul Larsen had spent a lot more time at happy hour than Davis, and club soda was not his beverage of preference. There was a heavy scent of bourbon on his breath as he shook my hand, ignoring Davis. Drunk as I was, I was not prepared for the hydraulic pressure the big man's hand exerted.

"Firm grip, King," Larsen said. "I like that."

"Not a slouch yourself, Mr. Larsen. Colonel?"

"Air Force. Flew sorties over 'Nam. Been building houses now for over thirty years. Up until two years ago, that is. Did a lot of the work by hand. Got the scars to show it," he said. "What the hell happened to you Davis? Look like you been in a train wreck."

"A little misunderstanding with a two by four," Davis said. "It's been tough for us all. I haven't built anything in a while either."

The faint smile faded from Larsen's rugged features. "My house is in foreclosure."

"I'm sorry to hear that," I said.

"Ask your friend why that is." Larsen hadn't looked directly at Davis the whole time. His gaze was fixed on me, as if measuring me up as an opponent. "Come on Davis, tell your friend how you screwed me out of house and home. I'm interested in hearing your excuse."

I stepped between them, although still shaky on my feet. "Now look, Colonel Larsen, it's pretty apparent you've been drinking a bit. It's never a good idea to get into an argument with friends when you've had a couple too many."

"You should talk. You reek of liquor, pal." He exhaled directly in my face, as an exclamation point. "Friends? Hah. I thought this guy was friend. Go ahead, tell the man what you did. Or are you too chicken shit to fess up."

I was forced into battle mode now. "Okay, that's enough, Gunny. Leave the man alone."

The big man was older, slower, and sported a bit of belly. He looked tough as nails, but whatever skills he had honed in the service were distant memories by now. Still, with his size advantage, he'd be hard to bring down quickly in a crowded room. I'd already gotten tough today with Wade and after a few drinks to wash away the guilt, I didn't relish another confrontation in my compromised state.

Derek interceded. "It's all right Riley. He's got a right to hear the truth. What Colonel Larsen is referring to is my role in appraising his house. A few months ago, I did a favor for a realtor I know. The banks didn't have enough appraisers under contract given the glut of foreclosures, so I agreed to help out. I never saw the final tally they accepted, but I imagine it was less than you figured. I'm sorry Paul, I was just being honest."

Larsen was unimpressed by the excuse. "Well, I did see the numbers. I had a million and a half into that place and your report said I couldn't sell it for 800 thousand. Do you know that there's thirty six inch footings under that foundation. Poured concrete walls a foot thick?"

Derek said, "Come on, Paul. You're a builder. You know people don't pay extra for that. They assume the foundation is adequate. You overbuilt it. If we ever had a 9.0 quake, your place would be the only one standing. But folks who will appreciate that are few and far between."

The old man snorted. "And did you know there's no face stone in the building? All the fireplaces are solid rock. The beams --- I cut the cedar trees off the property and milled them myself. The wood floors in the bedrooms are koa, imported from Hawaii. Triple glazed windows, hurricane rated. "

Davis had to feel sorry for the old man. He was now essentially repeating his earlier conversation with Maggie, this time with the roles reversed. It couldn't feel any better. The man had poured his heart and soul into a place that he thought he'd live in forever. He'd built a veritable fortress that no natural disaster could destroy, but he'd made some basic mistakes.

Derek said, "Paul, other builders will see what you've done and admire it. The craftsmanship was superb. Some of the best I've seen. But I checked out the comps and eight hundred was generous given the square footage. You made the kitchen too small. The master bedroom is tiny by today's standards. And the bathrooms. Not enough of them and very utilitarian for a house in that price range."

"You sound like them real estate whores now. They don't know nothing about the way houses should be built. You think these rich bitches cook anymore? Why do they need a big kitchen with all those fancy European appliances. To heat up their take-out? And why give more space to the shitter than necessary?"

Either Larsen was inebriated past the point of reason or had truly gone off the deep end in his despair over the market.

Davis said, "Paul, you might be right about some things, but you were a builder, you *know*. You have to give people what they want. And they want big kitchens with granite and high end appliances. Roomy baths, like spas. I saw a place today, the seller had almost four million into it and right now the best offer he's going to get is half that. And it has all the bells and whistles. The market sucks, man. The trick is knowing when to get out and you and I both held out too long."

Larsen's imposing presence shrunk by half and he seemed on the verge of a breakdown. "Damn, man. What do I do now? Building houses is all I know how to do. What do I do with myself? I'm sixty nine years old. Got an inner ear problem so I can't climb ladders. Self employed all my life so I have no pension. We had to let our help go yesterday, I'm maintaining all the landscaping myself. My arthritis is flaring up worse than ever. But the worst thing is what's happened to my wife. Jeanette went from a sweet and gorgeous Southern Belle to a bitter old crank. Look at her over there. She must have put on fifty pounds. She wakes up crabby and gets worse as the day goes on."

He nodded toward the table where his wife was sitting. She was a heavy-set, sour faced woman, alternating between staring daggers at our grouping and downing swigs of an amber liquid. She looked more mean and hostile than her husband.

"My kids are grown and living out West. They're struggling too and I can't help them out. Yesterday, I applied for a job as a greeter at Wal-Mart. Waiting to hear back. Pays three hundred a week. Maybe a touch more if I can get overtime. "

He dropped his head and stared blankly at the floor. I had wanted to like Larsen from the start. His proud military bearing, his strength and dignity, now sagged. And I couldn't fault the man for striking out at someone who had once been a friend that he now perceived as disloyal.

This was heartbreaking. I'll never look at a Wal-Mart greeter again and not wonder why he had to work well past the time he should be enjoying retirement.

"Life sucks and then you die, eh? Some of us not soon enough." Larsen shook his head and slowly went back to his spouse.

Davis watched the old man's unsteady gait as he moved away. From my vantage point, it seemed as if he saw himself in ten years and didn't like the picture.

# Forty Three

I slipped the holster over my neck and tightened the cinch. I've lost a few pounds since I wore it last. My black leather jacket was loose enough to conceal the gun to the untrained eye.

I was pleasantly surprised at the lack of a hangover. Maybe high end single malt didn't have sulfites or any other shit the cheap stuff contained that gave you a bad morning. I was headed for an area of Charlotte that I haven't visited lately and frankly would have preferred to keep it that way. It housed the denizens of the city --- gangs ruled, and if you weren't a member, your life didn't count for much. I'd cultivated some sources there when I first hit town but since then, my clientele have become more white collar. There was something unsettling about returning to the area where I had first made my bones in the New South. I much preferred the suburbs where the greatest threat to my peace of mind are the scornful looks I get from neighbors if I pull out of my driveway too fast and almost hit their dog. Maybe I'm growing soft. Maybe there's no maybe about it.

I didn't really have a plan: it wouldn't do me much good in this locale. I'd done some background work on the computer prior to setting out. The address and men in question belonged to a small landscaping team. They had been in business for a few years, no assets other than an old truck, a trailer and several John Deere mowers, tractors and weed whackers. From the sky, the house the men lived in looked ill kept and the front was mostly garage. But I had long since learned that Google Earth pictures often bear no resemblance to what currently occupies a space.

Landscapers of this ilk generally get out just after dawn. Their bank account depends on the volume of work they can accomplish. Bad weather is an enemy. Most of the machines they operate are not engineered to function well when wet, and even morning dew can cause a mower to overturn on a mild grade. Most go ahead anyway, damn the risk. The upside was that it pays good money for outdoor work and the machines do most of the heavy lifting. I worked with a crew like this over three summers while at Georgetown. I was fortunate to have other options after graduation. These guys didn't have that luxury.

I figured I'd scout out the address right before sunrise, when the faint orange glow from the east is just enough to illuminate my view. The house and shop looked pretty much as the computer image had shown ---- a one story ranch, just a grade above a double wide. The white vinyl siding was thin and stained with mildew and moss. The windows were small and grimy. The driveway leading up to the garage was unpaved, the crushed stone escaping its boundaries to litter what could charitably be called a lawn, spouting more weeds and clover than fescue. Landscapers, eh? I recalled Davis's adage about carpenters, that the last house they get around to fixing is their own. An old Ford truck was parked outside the front entry, already hitched to a beat up trailer.

I parked three doors down and sipped Dunkin Donuts coffee, rationing it through two old fashioned doughnuts that would serve as breakfast this morning. Almost on cue as the sun's first rays peeked over the trees, two large black men emerged from the house --- yawning, stretching and scratching. They were quiet and purposeful --- one of them started the truck, slowly pulling it toward the garage bay while the other raised the door to reveal their equipment. They probably repeated this rite three hundred times a year and could go through these motions while half asleep, as they now seemed to be.

There was barely enough light for pictures, but my powerful zoom lens was able to capture their images with decent quality. If Blankenship could confirm that these were the men who attacked Davis, so much the better. Her testimony would never hold up in court --- any defense lawyer worth his fee would eviscerate the memory of an older woman peering down at two black men from a distance in shadowy light. But her word would suffice for my purposes.

I was of two minds on how to proceed next. My usual bent was the direct approach: isolate the man whose name Wade had provided, intimidate him at gunpoint and see if he'd give up the next rung on the food chain. Crude but effective.

The other was role-play --- pretend to be a fellow scum and intimate that I might have some dirty work for him. In this line of gainful employment, references aren't freely given, but over a beer or a joint, muscle heads tend to brag about their successes. This involved undercover work which would take more time and hold more risk.

I chose option number one. My state of mind had a lot to do with my choice.

I didn't want to take on both of them at once, so it was best to follow them until I could isolate the target. They piled into the cab after loading and securing their equipment. The truck pulled out of the driveway, dispersing even more gravel onto the greenery.

So they cut some grass, sold some grass, and provided some muscle on the side. Amateurs. No wonder I hadn't known of them. I wondered what their business cards would look like. **Langston's Landscaping and Thuggery. No Job 2 Small. Beat-downs While U Wait.**

I followed a safe distance back but the two seemed to be in an animated conversation and unmindful of any tail. They stopped at the same Dunkin Donuts that I had visited. At least they had good taste in fine breakfast cuisine.

From there, the rusted truck moved south toward the state line, briefly jumping onto I-77 just before its junction with the 485 Beltway. They crossed into South Carolina, heading southeast toward Indian Land. I wondered if they were licensed to do landscape work in South Carolina. Maybe that state didn't bother with such legalities, or as its residents might say, *intrusions on their freedom*. The passed a number of gated subdivisions in Fort Mill until the country widened out again, into horse farms and the occasional manor on a hill.

I had a feeling of déjà vu, as if I'd been here before. This big sky land was far from my usual haunts and I couldn't recall exactly when I'd seen it last. The truck turned onto a private road and headed up the winding path toward a large white estate with square pillars adorning the front, a quarter of a mile off the main track. The drive was lined with white rail fencing, the type employed to restrain horses. Indeed, several were grazing in a meadow to the side of the property. I could barely make out a small red barn over the rise, housing paddocks where the animals spent the night.

I drove past the entrance until I came upon a small copse of pines where I could safely pull in and shelter the car. I'd approach the house from the side, carrying only a pair of binoculars and the gun. It took ten minutes to find a comfortable vantage point where I could observe what was happening without fear of detection. Places this grand generally had security of some sort, sometimes the four legged kind. I didn't fancy trying to outrun a pack of Dobermans or having to shoot a dog who was just doing what he was trained for.

I trained the binoculars on the front portico, where the men had parked and were finishing the unloading ritual. A white haired man came out onto the front porch, clad in high laced boots and brown woolen pants, topped by a bulky red sweater.

My God. I have been here before. Only once, a year ago. I know that man.

It came to me as suddenly as a cloudburst on a spring day. There was no further point in following the landscaper/thugs. I now knew the answer as to who had ordered the beating of my friend.

The tougher question was --- should I tell Derek?

# Forty Four

## Derek Davis

Liz called Derek's cell. She had decided against the restaurant and instead felt it better that they meet at her apartment. Home turf. He didn't argue.

He'd been out earlier to Belk, the big department store chain in North Carolina and picked up the closest approximation he could find to her original Pashmina scarf. He rehearsed his speech on the drive. Revised it a dozen times but it never sounded quite right. Over the last week, he had begun to doubt what he was sure of.

He parked at a meter a couple of blocks away from the high rise and shivered against the November chill until he reached the warmth of its lobby. The doorman greeted him with mild surprise, even though he was expected. These guys know more about the tenants than their immediate family, and the good ones keep it to themselves.

Her "we need to talk" invitation sounded like a doctor calling with less than favorable test results. He tried to take the optimistic view that he had nothing to lose. They hadn't been together for almost six months, so little would change if this was indeed the last goodbye, other than the abandonment of hope. And with Derek Davis, hope was in short supply these days.

It wasn't until he reached her floor that he realized he'd been so preoccupied with what he was going to say that he had left the scarf in the car. She came to the door dressed casually--- plaid shorts, navy sleeveless tee. Barefoot. She kissed his cheek briskly like politicians do in foreign countries, no real affection.

"I ordered out. I hope you still like the turkey club on whole wheat toast from Zoe's. Diet peach Snapple." Her tone was colorless, as if ordering the food all over again. "It's in the kitchen." She walked away, expecting him to follow.

He was struck by how bad she looked. He wondered if it was just that she paled in comparison to Charlene Serpente, the last woman other than Randee that he'd had regular contact with. But no, Liz looked haggard, tired, almost as if she'd been ill. She hadn't smiled, not even a glimmer when he'd arrived

"My God, Derek, what happened to you?" In the light filled kitchen, she noticed his face for the first time. He had expected the reaction as soon as she opened the door, but she hadn't looked directly at him then.

He explained.

"Do the police have any idea who did this?' she asked.

"King's looking into it. It's too small potatoes to get the cops involved. It looks worse than it is. Hurt like hell at first and the work to straighten out my beak was no walk in the park, but it's not so bad now."

"Oh, you poor man."

In the past, when he'd suffered minor injuries on the job, he remembered how solicitous she had been, how it was "my poor darling or poor baby." Now it was, "poor man", as if they were passing a homeless person on the street. They had grown that far apart. It made what he wanted to say all that much harder.

"I'll live. So, how was Europe?"

"Well, that's why I wanted to talk to you. I need to be honest with you about why I went. I spent a lot of time thinking about you while I was there. About us."

She unfolded the wrapping around their sandwiches and served them on small white china plates. She opened her Dasani water and his Snapple and poured them into tall clear glasses. The silence was awkward.

He felt the need to say something. "I've been doing some thinking, too. Regardless of what you're going to say, I want you to know something. While you were gone, I missed you a lot. I got a taste of life without you and I didn't like it. "

She grimaced a tight smile. "You may not feel that way when you hear what I have to tell you."

He interrupted before she could get her next thought out. "Liz, I don't care. I feel the way I do about you and nothing can change it. "

"Wow. Is this Derek Davis or some kind of perfect replica? You never said stuff like this before. If someone in a movie said what you just did, you'd snort in disgust at the bad writing. 'Men don't talk like that', you'd say."

"I vaguely remember that quote. Well, I guess I took things for granted after a while. I didn't think I needed to say certain things, that you just knew how it was with us."

Her sad eyes were fixed on him now. "I knew that your dream of building that development was more important to you than I was. You may have cared for me, but you cared a lot more about building that place."

"That's not fair. You're a person, that was an idea."

"You had a choice. You could have married me. You could have worked for daddy or done something else until building picked up again but you choose to hang onto that land."

"Well, that's all academic now. The land is gone, or will be soon." He told her about the bank and his subsequent conversation with Maggie. "So your competition is dead. Whatever I do from now on, I want it to be with you."

"So I'm the consolation prize. Plan B? New Hope is over, so you'll settle for life with old Liz, is that it?"

This wasn't going the way he'd practiced it. "Liz, can we start this over? I didn't come here to argue with you over the past. I wanted to talk about the future."

"But they're linked, don't you see? You could have given up a year ago. Kept the house. Sold the land then, maybe break even. But you held on. You saw what it was doing to us. But it was more important than me. You can't acknowledge that?"

He stared out the window at the gleaming city beneath. "After this, I'll be down to almost nothing. I'll figure something out. The point is without you, none of it matters."

She was slowly shaking her head through tears. "Why couldn't you have said that months ago?"

"Because I was caught up in bullshit. Ego. I know your daddy gave you everything you wanted when you grew up. I didn't want you to have to do without. I didn't think you could take it. I wanted to be the big provider, keep you in the style you'd become accustomed to. I thought you'd resent me if we had to live on the cheap."

"That's the problem. You thought I was shallow. That I couldn't put aside these little petty luxuries to be with the man I loved. That hurt more than anything."

"But I know now it was me. Maybe I'm some kind of relic, but I wanted to be the breadwinner. Give you the freedom to do whatever you wanted and not worry about finances. Do charity or be a lady who lunches. Whatever. And I couldn't give it to you. I felt like I was a failure. I felt that you'd be better off with someone who could take care of you. That's what I felt."

She dabbed away tears. His voice was becoming hoarse with emotion. He took a long gulp of his tea. "Liz, I want you. That's all that matters."

She didn't answer.

He backed off and said, "Okay. If that's how you feel, I'll respect that. I messed up. I have to live with it."

"Derek, I went to Europe for a reason. I need to tell you why. I went because I thought I was pregnant."

The words resonated like a flash/bang in a confined space. They took him completely by surprise. He had no idea what to say or how it made him feel. He had never come close to being a father before. She was right, his career had always come first. And this would have been a lousy time to start a family. He didn't know what he would have done or what she would have allowed him to do had he known, *but didn't she owe him that*?

"You thought you were pregnant?" he said, almost to himself. "We were careful, weren't we?

"We were. Derek, I went to Europe, not sure what I was going to do. I missed a couple of periods. I thought I might have an abortion there and no one would have been the wiser."

"And didn't I deserve some say in this?"

"Here's the hard part, the one you won't like. I met someone and made a stupid mistake. Just once. I was with another man. No protection. That's it. That's what I did."

He swallowed hard. He'd accepted that Liz had been with Todd, and had told himself that he could live with the image. But hearing her say it reopened the fresh wound.

"Derek, I never gave up on us. All the time I was in Europe my biggest fear was how you would react to what I just told you. I'm still afraid that when you've had time to think about this, you might not feel the same way."

"But you *thought* you were pregnant? You didn't take one of those tests they sell in the drug stores? Does that mean you weren't?"

"I told you shortly after we met, that I miscarried once during my first marriage. This felt the exact same way. Morning sickness, feeling nauseous all the time.

Maybe I was so guilty about how I got pregnant that I wasn't thinking clearly. But I'd been through it before and I knew all the signs."

She paused, gathering courage. "It turned out to be a tumor. More than one actually. While I was in France, they removed both ovaries. They thought it could be cancer, but the biopsies came back benign. I was lucky. This means no children, but it could have been much worse."

"I wish you had told me. I wish I could have been there for you. But Liz, the fact is, you weren't pregnant. You didn't need to tell me about that one-nighter. Why did you?"

"Because I don't want there to be any secrets between us. What I did was wrong; there was no love involved or even respect for that matter. It was someone you know but I don't see any purpose in telling you who it was unless you feel you really need to hear it. Bottom line is --- I think I did it to punish you. For not trusting that I didn't care about the money or any of that other stuff. I just cared about you."

She let that sink in for a few seconds and then said, "I realize this is a lot for you to process. I don't expect you to say anything now. Take all the time you need. I just thought I owed you the truth."

"I don't need any more time. Liz, I want you to marry me. Not in a year, or a month, but now."

She said, "Oh my God. Let's get married as soon as we can. I don't want either us to have time to re-consider it. I love you."

They held each other close. It felt right. Derek felt truly happy for the first time in months.

They rushed through the details. Just a quick civil ceremony. No best man or maid of honor. No guests, witnessed by whoever was there at the time. No pictures or gift registry. The main expense would be whatever the county charged for a license.

They would tell no one in her family, until Liz had a chance the smooth things over, if indeed that was possible. Her father exploded when his dementia ridden wife told him that Liz had actually did have an abortion. He refused to listen when his daughter swore to him that she hadn't. He made noises about his will and how he never wanted to lay eyes on her again. Although they had their falling-outs before, never had his reaction been this extreme.

But to Davis, none of that mattered at the moment. Her dad had never really liked him and Derek wouldn't have accepted his money under any circumstances. C'est la vie.

# Forty Five

Back at the condo, Randee Blankenship was hard at work over her computer. She had the videos of the slipshod work Serpente was doing and was compiling the clips into a short film. As I walked in, she was cursing the latest edit which had caused a choppy transition.

"Those words coming out of that mouth! Randee, I'm shocked," I said. "Sounds like you taught in the Bronx, not the upper West Side."

"And hello to you, Riley."

"How's the video going?"

"It needs a narration. Didn't you once mention he knew someone in radio down here?"

Stone was too far away and the thought of asking Patrick Henry for help was unappealing but he did have great pipes and had done documentary work before. "I'll leave you his number but I'm not sure if he's the right man for the job. You're sure the internet is the way to go on this?"

"I called the papers. I tried TV and radio. They're not interested. They're feeling the pinch too and they don't have the resources to send reporters to follow through on this. I'm trying to get my plumbing inspector contact to go public, but he's suddenly gone incommunicado. I think someone may have gotten to him. It takes balls to be a whistleblower. The mainstream media outlets aren't buying it, no matter what I show them I have. They think I'm some conspiracy theory crank. Builders cut corners every day, one guy told me. It's like telling the public that used car dealers can be sleazy. What else is new?"

I said, "Unbelievable. If car dealers were intentionally selling cars with faulty brakes, *that* is an important story. VW lost billions because they faked emissions tests. And that's the same thing that's happening here. Asbestos causes cancer. Bad wiring causes fires. Poor workmanship can cause mold. This stuff is a public health hazard. They don't care about that?'

"You're preaching to the choir. I've done more research and I know how it works. He hires immigrants from Central America, many of whom are here illegally, at less than the minimum wage. They scavenge condemned old buildings and toxic waste sites all over the state and remove pipes, wiring, arsenic treated wood, whatever they can salvage. Then he re-uses it in his buildings instead of new material. The irony is that a lot of his workers live in this same public housing with relatives, so they're doubly exposed to this crap."

"That's rotten, screwing the poor workers and their families. But the other stuff sounds like that *Salvage Dawgs* show on TV. Isn't that kind of a good thing, recycling usable material rather than dumping the stuff in landfills?"

"If it was high quality reclaimed product like on that show, I'd agree. But this is stuff that was banned years ago because it's toxic or in the case of the wiring, flimsy and dangerous. Pipes have lead in them that will leech into the water supply. And he has no regard for the safety of his workers. Pays them by tonnage."

"Good work. This bastard will have his day. But I'm afraid now we've got even more shit to deal with. I found out something about the attack that I haven't told Derek yet. It wasn't Serpente who ordered it. It's someone he knows and it's actually worse."

"I hope it's not anything that would spoil the wedding."

"The wedding?"

"I thought you two talked all the time. He asked that Deveraux girl to marry him. He didn't tell you?"

I had postponed telling Derek what I had discovered about his attackers. Now I had an even stronger reason to keep it hidden. The man I had seen with the landscapers in South Carolina was none other than Jack Deveraux, Derek's future father-in-law. Although my friend was becoming quite the pacifist, I couldn't imagine this latest information going over very well. I needed tell Derek in person when the time was right, if it ever was. The last person I could trust with this was the woman in the room with me now: Randee was lousy at keeping secrets.

I tried to greet the wedding news casually. "We've both been chasing our tails lately. Well, great, I'm happy for him. But back to the matter at hand, you need to hold off on that video until we get our ducks lined up."

"This is a powder keg, Riley. It can't wait much longer. But wait a minute, I thought you were sure Serpente was behind what happened to Derek. What changed your mind? And what about my cat?"

I laid it out for her, soft pedaling my muscular handling of Corey Wade. It was reduced to a serious conversation with the young collegian.

"Look, Randee, I'm sorry about your cat but we have no proof Serpente had anything to do with that either. I promise, I will follow through on that but I need some time."

"Riley, my cat and Derek's woes aren't the issue anymore. You must realize that by now. Derek's beating caused you to investigate Serpente initially, but what I've uncovered is a lot more serious."

She was right about that and there was no diverting this woman once she set her mind onto something. "Randee, I want to bring this guy down too. I've been in contact with his wife. She says she's about to leave him. If she's really on our side, I might be able to convince her to grab some documents or something that would be a smoking gun against him that no media person could resist. But her leaving is going to set a lot of things in motion. If he becomes unhinged by this, he could resort to desperate measures. Against you, Derek and God knows who else. Let's work together here and try to release all the pieces with a clear timetable in mind. Then we'll have a greater chance of winning."

"Some of my former students are computer programmers. I ran the idea by a couple of them and they agreed to help. If they can get this video to go viral, then the big media outlets will take notice. It won't matter if he tries to come after us, he'll be running for his life."

"Maybe. But still, please I'm begging you, wait. Let's coordinate all of this. Will you do that for me?"

She was about to disagree, but the look in my eyes convinced her. "All right, I'll hold off. But not forever. I'm going to nail this bastard. With or without you. Don't make me wait too long."

# Forty Six

## Derek Davis

Davis was in the conference room of Magnolia Holmes' real estate office, responding to her terse but excited message that she had further news on his property.

"Derek, sorry I made you come into the office but I like to present offers in person. You know as a broker, I'm obligated to present all offers, whether I consider them acceptable or not." Maggie Holmes rattled off the boilerplate by rote, Mirandizing Davis for what was to come.

"I'm just surprised you got interest so quickly, Mags."

"You may not be when you hear the offer. I told you I have ties to some investors. That's the good news *and* the bad news. They're like sharks sensing blood in the water. They're looking for undervalued properties and sellers who are desperate. They have cash that isn't getting them much return through traditional channels."

Although Maggie Holmes ran one of the most successful real estate firms in the state, the recession had hit her interests hard. Listings that she wouldn't have considered taking five years ago were her life blood now. Her tastefully decorated office showed signs of deferred maintenance. The once daily cleaning crew now came once a week and her agents were expected to maintain their own cubicles. In their heyday, every booth was occupied. Now only two or three were in the office at any given time. The dry erase board indicating where each broker could be located had been filled to overflowing; presently, it was mostly white space. Formerly hot agents now worked part time from home or had found other means of support.

"I'm acting as a dual agent here, Derek. I have your listing and I also represent the buyers. That basically means I can't tip either party off on where the other is headed pricewise. Having said that, the buyers have authorized me to inform you that this is their best and final offer. Now since we've always operated on trust, you're perfectly free to find another agent to represent you and it won't affect our relationship."

"I trust you, Mags. But you're sure they're telling you the truth? They'll walk away if I don't meet their price?"

"So they say. I can tell you that they are all business. They structure deals that work for them. They don't really care what you paid or what you owe.

They come up with a number that they feel meets their profit expectations. In the past, yes, they have walked away. There are lots of attractive deals out there and they don't feel they have to compromise."

"I see. Well, let's not drag this out any longer. What's the figure?"

"Eight. They wanted to start at seven fifty and it took all my powers to get them to go to eight. "

"You know I still owe a million on it."

"Like I said, that doesn't matter to them. The problem is that buyers are not patient these days. They want a deal done now and have said they will move onto something else if they don't get it. Or like we talked about before, you can let them foreclose. It's possible that my buyers would come back at a foreclosure sale or someone else might come along."

"So if I accept this offer, you understand, this would just about wipe me out."

"I'm sorry, Derek. I wish I could help. Since this is a quick in-house deal and I love you dearly, I'll forego my commission. You know the old axiom that the first offer is usually the best offer. I don't think that you'll do any better if you wait. I don't want to rush you, but the buyers have also stipulated that the offer is good for forty eight hours, then they move on. They must have an in at the bank, since this is technically a short sale and they normally take a lot of time because the bank has to approve. Again, my advice is to talk to your financial adviser and make a decision. You know what I think."

"Yeah, I do. Thanks, Mags. I know you're trying to do the right thing. Can you at least tell me who these guys are and what their plans are for the land?"

"I was afraid you'd still care about that. It's the Silver Brothers, the tract builders. They haven't shared their plans with me specifically, but you and I both know what they do. They build fast and cheap. They'll subdivide the property into as many lots as the county will allow and my guess is they'll sell in the current sweet spot, the three to four hundred range."

"So they have no interest in my master plan. No New Hope. No progressive development. No new American lifestyle?"

"Fast and cheap, Derek. It's what they do." She tried to inject a positive note to close the conversation. "Hey, Derek, I meant to tell you when you came in. You look a whole lot better than a couple days ago. You're healing fast. Getting those dashing good looks back and then some. Chin up."

They hugged and he walked out of the office, dazed and confused. He'd feared that this was coming and had replayed alternatives in his mind over and over, always coming to the same conclusion. As much as he hated the fact that the bank was unwilling to work with him despite the many years of profitable business he had given them, he did owe them money and they were free to recoup as much of it as they could.

Liz would be with him, even if he had no money of his own. That much he was sure of now.

The dream of New Hope was over.

But there would be other land that would suit his purposes, somewhere. He'd re-invent himself somehow. He was in good health, minus the recent damage, and still had his wits about him. He would have a few grand left after liquidating his remaining assets, no debt, and a good woman willing to work with him to rebuild the business. The idea of starting over clean actually was liberating, and despite all his recent misfortune, it raised his spirits.

# Forty Seven

## Derek Davis

Davis was at Liz's, absent mindedly thumbing through the mail he'd picked up at the condo. He paused at a shiny piece of thick stock that initially appeared to be junk. "Hey, Liz, this is interesting. Charlotte realtors are doing a seminar tomorrow with some area builders. Typical, they send this out at the last minute, too late if people already have plans. They're trying to drum up interest in new building, which is dead at the moment. *Morning session with coffee and some of the area's top builders.* Makes sense, most of them don't have anything else to do these days. Surprised they didn't call me. But check this out --- one of them is Johnny Serpente. I think maybe it's time I actually meet the man that's causing all this grief."

"Take Riley with you. This guy could be dangerous, especially if he comes with a posse."

"No, I need to do this on my own. I'm not sure how I'm going to play it yet. Maybe I just observe. Try to get a read on the guy. I won't get confrontational.

I'll be careful if he has any muscle with him, although I would think in this kind of setting, he wouldn't think he'd need to bring the troops."

Derek lay awake most of that night. He had changed his mind about a dozen times on how to deal with Serpente. Serpente was the last bit of old business he wanted to clean up before embarking on his new endeavor, whatever that was to be. He contemplated asking King's advice, but he knew his friend would try to dissuade him from going alone. He needed to summon up the courage to take care of this himself.

Ironically, the loss of New Hope empowered him. It was time to move forward with his woman and start fresh.

Today, by confronting his adversary successfully, it could go a long way toward restoring his self esteem, which had taken a beating worse than the ones that Serpente's goons had dealt.

He showered and wrapped a towel around his waist. The face that peered back at him as he shaved was only slightly different from the one he was used to seeing, but he had to admit, the new nose and tighter jaw line was an upgrade. He'd never believed in plastic surgery since the inner man stayed the same. The endless pursuit of beauty would only leave one endlessly dissatisfied. Whatever demons of self doubt that motivated people to cut into their skin in hopes of looking younger or smarter or prettier, would remain long after the scars had healed.

But since this accidental improvement, he did feel different. He wouldn't go so far as to call it a re-birth, but his life was about to undergo a big change. And the new face looking back at him was symbolic of the transformation.

So today, he would deal with the last vestige of his previous life, and finally come to grips with the nightmare personified by Johnny the Snake. While lying sleepless, he'd rehearsed different approaches but none of them rang true. Whatever happened today would be spontaneous, or he'd only use one or two of the lines that had come to him overnight.

Davis entered the lobby of the motel where the seminar was to take place and followed the computer printed signs to a modestly proportioned ballroom. The motel was part of a chain that specialized in accommodations for business travelers. No one was staffing the entry desk --- on it were blank name badges next to a sign-in sheet instructing participants to create their own identification and to enjoy the seminar. Just inside the room was a folding table adorned by a plain white tablecloth, on which lay three open boxes of Krispy Kreme doughnuts and a silver coffee urn, paper cups, packets of sugar, artificial sweetener and individual portions of half and half. Davis resisted the temptation to swipe a few of the sweeteners and proceeded to pour himself a cup of the weak brew masquerading as java.

Again he was struck by how the recession had affected the industry. Past seminars were held at a prestigious Uptown Charlotte hotel. The food table had been laden with pancakes, French toast, bacon, sausages and an omelet station manned by two chefs. Rarely attended by fewer than a hundred realtors and builders, these events had been open only to high achieving  practitioners. Now, just minutes before the first speaker, there were perhaps three dozen people, most of whom didn't appear too prosperous. They huddled together on cheap folding chairs in front of a makeshift platform.

Derek sat in the back row, not more than thirty feet from the dais. There was a laminate veneered lectern in the middle of the platform, flanked by two tables. On the left sat Serpente, looking uneasy in front of the small crowd. He was chatting with four others Derek didn't recognize, but who he assumed were sponsors of the event.

Davis dutifully sat through the pro forma introductions and the clichéd homilies to the industry. Any statistic that showed the slightest bit of optimism was trumpeted loudly. Any trend that reflected what was really going on was either ignored or rationalized away. All the forecasts pointed to a better year than last, and with rates at historic lows and inventory high, this was a great time to invest in real estate. The message fell just short of late night infomercials that herald new ways to make a fortune with little effort and no money down.

All the while, Davis was evaluating Serpente. As advertised, the man was small. He had a weak chin, prominent white teeth, thinning gray hair and an unfortunate complexion. The only feature that seemed out of place was his too perfect nose, leading Derek too deduce that once upon a time, Serpente had availed himself of the services of one of Shamaylan's colleagues.

But the spindly form was dressed tastefully, in a dark blue suit, pale pink shirt and narrow yellow silk tie, cufflinks and collar pin. He and one other man were the only ones in the group dressed so formally--- the others on stage ranged from company logoed blazers to long sleeved polo shirts more suited to a day in the country. No one else wore a tie. Derek suspected that Charlene had dressed him that morning.

He did project an oily presence, as if he were the most important person in attendance and was accustomed to a much grander setting. When it was time for him to speak, Serpente got up and rattled on about the virtues of hard work, how the tough got going in tough times and how opportunities were calling out for the bold to take advantage. Although he carried note cards to the lectern, he rarely consulted them as he riffed on well worn platitudes. He closed by emphatically stating that even though times were hard, we owed it to the community to give something back, and that we should be grateful for our success and mindful of those less fortunate.

What Serpente had said was perfectly in tune with Derek's own philosophy, but words were cheap, deeds less so. Although his voice was high pitched and nasal, he spoke clearly and few vestiges of his Brooklyn accent were apparent. The moderator opened the floor for questions. None of the queries from the floor were challenging --- most were designed to showcase the questioners' expertise as opposed to seeking any real insight from their subject.

Serpente was the penultimate speaker, followed by a well dressed chap from Mexico, extolling the virtues of selling internationally. He was even more optimistic than the others, praising the cooperative government and suggesting that real estate investors could make double digit returns selling to American ex-pats who desired a warmer climate and laid back lifestyle. Mercifully, the entire exercise was over in just under ninety minutes, and the patrons either scurried out or clustered into small groups, hoping to get private answers to vexing questions they didn't want to share with the larger group. Davis waited for the group around Serpente to disperse before approaching him. He used the time to speak with the Mexican standing nearby, who the others avoided as if he had snuck over the border illegally.

"So, money to be made south of the border, eh? I'm a custom builder. Derek Davis. I imagine there's work for people like me down there as well."

"Oh yes. In fact, this may be a fortuitous moment for us both." The man's very nature exuded optimism.

Davis kept one eye on Serpente. "Oh, how so?"

"I represent a project in San Miguel de Allende. Beautiful village in the Central Mountains. We are about ninety per cent sold, and we can't build the haciendas quickly enough. We need a supervisor for the final phase."

"Interesting. I'm not all that busy at the moment, with the recession and all. Not a lot of spec building going on here."

"Do you have a resume or list of projects you've been involved with?"

The group around Serpente was breaking up and Derek couldn't let him leave without confronting him. He wasn't interested in leaving the country for work, and he needed to blow this guy off, politely if possible.

"Tell you what. Give me your card and email address and I'll shoot you some stuff about myself."

"With pleasure, sir. Very nice to make your acquaintance." He handed Derek an embossed business card, bowed slightly and waltzed away.

Davis was impressed by the Mexican's charm and politesse. He accepted the gentleman's card and edged toward Johnny Serpente. He imagined his next little chat would be somewhat less gracious.

"Mr. Serpente?" he said, extending his hand.

Strictly as reflex, Serpente reciprocated. His grip was moist and weak.

"I'm Derek Davis. I just wanted to let you know that I got your message. Loud and clear."

Serpente eyes flashed about the room, looking for a security guard or anyone who could bail him out of this prickly mess. Davis had him by a half a foot and thirty pounds. Although Derek tried to appear non-threatening, the smaller man's trepidation was obvious.

Davis gave a weak smile, hoping to allay the man's worries "Sorry things didn't work out with your bathroom. I don't know if your wife told you, but I was in the hospital for a few days. Fact is, I missed your calls and by the time I got out, you had moved on without me."

Poker face. Still nothing. Serpente wanted to end this as quickly as possible. But it wouldn't look good to anyone observing if he appeared cowardly in the face of a threat.

"My wife did mention that. No permanent damage, I hope."

Davis elaborated, hoping to draw a more definitive reaction.

"A couple of big goons beat me up. Broke my nose, bruised some ribs. They were afraid that I had a punctured lung, but turns out I didn't. Hurt like hell, though."

A shadow crossed Serpente's face. An indication of empathy or regret? "Hey, I'm sorry to hear that. Tough luck there. I thought you had just taken off with our money and weren't showing up. That happens with subs a lot, as I'm sure you know."

It seemed clear that Davis had not come to exact retribution with physical violence. Serpente was relieved and his bravado returned. "But with me, it only happens once."

"I'm not sure I take your meaning," Davis said.

"As a fellow builder, let me give you some friendly advice. Somebody messes with you, fire him on the spot. And don't be shy about letting his fellow workers see it. Make it clear to them that you fuck me over once, that's it. I ain't hiring you again."

"And you thought I messed with you, is that it?"

"Hey, *stronzo*," Serpente said, employing a term that wouldn't pass easily in Brooklyn but convinced the country clubbers that he was authentic. "How was I supposed to know? Shit happens. I know how long a bathroom remodel should take with a decent sized crew. I let Charlene handle this hoping she'd learn a couple of things---that what I do for a living ain't that easy. Not like buildings go up themselves. You need to run a tight ship. There's lots of clowns in this business. They think that because I'm not a Joe College type, that I ain't smart and they can take advantage."

Davis had not expected Serpente's insecurities to come pouring out to a virtual stranger. He pressed further, hoping the man might slip into an admission of guilt. Davis said, "I wasn't trying to take advantage of anyone. I assume you saw the numbers and checked out the work I did. I was giving you good value, or I should say giving it to your wife."

The double entendre was intentional.

Serpente didn't take the bait. "Must be tough, cutting things so close, just to make a buck. Getting your hands dirty. You were a hot shit builder at one time. See, I did my homework."

Serpente had undergone a transformation as the confrontation evolved. Once he was satisfied that Davis posed no physical threat, the little man seemed to grow in stature. Whereas his initial bearing indicated a tinge of fear, he now radiated authority. Even the implication that his wife might be attracted to another man didn't seem to faze him. He wasn't above using it to his benefit, in a cold, reptilian fashion.

"Lot of folks take me for Fredo, because I'm not the biggest guy on the block. What they don't know is they're really dealing with Sonny."

"You going to smack me in the head with the nearest garbage can, Serpente?"

"Look, Davis, I'm sorry you got beat up. But bottom line, gavone, is that one guy doing all this work himself, was going to take a lot longer than if I brought in a crew to knock it out. I was willing to put up with it since your price was pretty good, but once you didn't show up, I wasn't going to fuck around with it anymore. Tripping over a two by four when I need to take a piss in the middle of the night gets old fast."

Serpente had a self satisfied leer on his face. He'd taken this big handsome guy down a peg --- this guy who built houses for rich snobs at premium prices. A guy who probably thought he was slumming doing a master bath remodel, hoping to bang his wife in the process.

Davis faked the biggest smile he could muster. "You know, it's funny Johnny, can I call you Johnny? Word is floating around out there that you might have been behind the guys who beat me up. Maybe because your wife *was* teaching you a lesson, that she could run a job better than you."

He let that hang.

He could feel the anger rising in the little man. Serpente said, "People can say whatever they want. I'm not sure I even believe this little fairy tale that some big bad boys beat you up. You don't look so bad to me. You think a guy like me is pussy-whipped, because I indulge my beautiful wife from time to time.

Trust me, shithead, when it comes down to it, she knows who's boss."

As quickly as the man's voice rose in irritation, it cascaded down to a modulated cool.

He said, "Davis, Far as I'm concerned, our business is finished. Too bad you're such an arrogant cocksucker, your work is actually decent. I might have had a spot for you on one of my crews. Installing shitters."

His lips curled into a sneer and he walked away. At that moment, Davis would have liked nothing more than to slug the little bastard for his condescending attitude. But he suppressed the urge.

The man wasn't likeable on any level, but whatever others may have said about him, he had an enormous amount of self control. Davis had hit his hot button when he brought up Charlene, but after a moment's flare-up, the man retreated to a more sensible position. This wasn't a man who operated on raw emotion.

He might resort to violence if pushed too hard. He knew what his wife was, and accepted it as part of life's rich pageant. Blankenship's crusade would be satisfying if it nailed this arrogant prick, but as far as seeking final answers about his beating, Derek had only created more questions.

# Forty Eight

I'm normally out of bed by seven; on alternate days I run three miles along the lake shore and this was one of those days. It was cold this morning --- overnight temperatures had plummeted into the low thirties and the bed was warm and inviting. But it was time to start the coffee and after a slow run, I mapped out my day.

I wanted to talk to Rick Stone. Although the guy had been a sports talk show host for many years now, he was former military and tough as they come. One of the hardest things about moving south was missing my friend's constant presence.

There was another reason I couldn't sleep in. It was still in the guest room, dozing angelically. Charlene Serpente had spent the last few nights with me. Her nocturnal talents had yet to be tested, partly because I was conflicted about Jaime, but also because I didn't fully trust her. She hadn't asked any probing questions about our campaign against her husband, but that didn't erase all my qualms. The double agent business is tricky, while she had admitted to me that her marriage is based on a lie, I'm not so arrogant to believe that she isn't capable of deceiving me too.

Charlene was married to a bad guy, but a bad guy I now knew had nothing to do with Derek's beating. There was no immediate reason for Johnny to come after anyone now if Randee played things the right way. The only one in danger might be Charlene, and I was keeping her close, in case she had been honest with me all along.

I hadn't spoken to Davis for a couple of days. Since our friendship began, it was rare for us to go this long without at least touching base. My problem how to handle the knowledge I now possessed about the attack. Was it better to let the thing appear unsolved? Davis had said he could move on with unanswered questions. But might he someday find out on his own and resent me for not telling him the truth? Then again, how would he know I knew unless I told him? Oops, Randee knew I knew. That meant he'd find out sooner or later.

I also couldn't go much longer hiding the fact from my girlfriend that I was harboring Charlene. And I although I wouldn't admit it to Jaime, I wasn't just sheltering Charlene out of altruism --- eventually something physical was bound to happen. I couldn't live with her in such close proximity and deny the attraction, especially after a couple of jolts.

As if it could read my thoughts, the cell phone sang out a jazz trumpet ringtone. Davis. Not Miles, but Derek.

"Hey, Riles, where ya been?"

I cleared my throat of the morning fog. "Busy. Business has picked up a bit. What's going on with you?"

Davis supplied more details about the offer on the land. I said, "That's good. I know you're disappointed that you have to sell with all the plans you made and all, but it's not like there won't be other opportunities."

"Well, I have help. Liz and I are back together. She's back from Europe. We've had a couple of long talks and we realized that no matter what, we belong together. We might even start a design/build business together. Or expand the company she started a while back but never really took too seriously."

He told me about her false pregnancy and the abortion that wasn't. His father-in-law-to-be was only a footnote. That would change when I confessed what I knew.

I said, "Hope I'm not spoiling the surprise, but Randee said that wedding bells are ringing?"

"That's the main reason I called. Buried the lede, eh? It's a done deal. I hope you approve."

"That's great. I've always liked Liz. I'm happy for you."

After accepting my congrats, he moved on to his meeting with Serpente and how the little man had reacted. He said, "Serpente may be a snake, but actually talking to him, I'm not so sure he was behind my beat down. Whatever. But along those lines, Blankenship's video is ready to launch. Her crusade to expose his shoddy building practices won't wait much longer."

"Derek, Randee is a tough cookie, no denying that. But one little old lady isn't equipped to destroy an empire that this dude took years to build. Even Pete Shabielski, who's afraid of nothing, backed off when I mentioned Serpente. Let's not push his buttons right now."

"That's not going to deter Randee. She's got a big plans. Hey, look what the internet did in Egypt. Took down a dictator through social networking. You can't tell me that Serpente is tougher than Mubarak."

"You don't have thousands demonstrating in the streets against Serpente either, pal. And more than a few died in those protests. One thing when it's halfway around the world, another when trouble is at your back door. Before you guys go forward on this, let me call a couple of my FBI buddies. Maybe they can lean on a couple of locals to apply some pressure. Or maybe a U.S. attorney. Let's make it a fair fight."

"Riles, you know I trust your judgment on things like this. Okay, I'll talk to her. But when she gets a bug in her system, look out."

"Do what you can. Let's hook up later."

We broke the connection. I was dragging my feet on telling him about Jack Deveraux, pretending to myself that there were other matters that required my more immediate attention. He was so happy about rekindling with Liz, I hadn't the heart to bring him down just yet. I dialed up Stone to run my dilemmas past some fresh ears.

"Ricky, my man, how's life?"

"Can't complain too much. New York teams suck at the moment which is actually good for us. Callers like to diss a lot more than they like to compliment. How's things in old Dixie?"

"Complicated. That's one reason I called." I related the entire story to Stone, including the ugly parts involving my behavior, which his tough guy approach to crime heartily endorsed.

He said, "Does Jaime know you've got this hot babe sleeping a few feet away from you?"

"Negative. I've talked to her a couple of times, just to check in. She has no idea."

I heard Stone exhale. "You could tell her you've been hiking the Appalachian Trail."

"Funny. I'm going to call her later and explain. But how do I tell Derek? The guy's about to get married, and it seems his future father in law sent two thugs out to kick his ass."

"You said that this Liz person went to Europe, thinking she needed an abortion. They don't have clinics down there in Dixie?"

I said, "I guess she didn't want it known and there are a lot of zealots down here picketing abortionists. They're photographing women who go in there and uploading them to Facebook. I'd imagine that someone in Liz's circle would catch on pretty quickly."

"So she'd naturally be afraid of her evangelical dad's reaction if he found out. Well, now we know what his reaction was."

"I don't want to break up the guy's wedding. Knowing her dad ordered the beating can't sit well with him."

Stone was firm. "Look, he already knows her father cut his daughter off over the abortion. How much worse can it get with the old man?"

"You have a point. Derek should know about Deveraux the Elder. I'll tell him today but he's got to decide if and when to tell *her* what her father did. I'll be glad not to be participating in that little tete-a-tete."

"Chicken."

I said, "Doctor Phil, I'm not. Hey, what are you doing over Thanksgiving? I might be able to hook us up for a round or two at Quail Hollow."

"Site of the 2017 PGA Championship? Say no more. I'm there. Between the holidays and the fact that I can do the show from anywhere with a strong ethernet connection, I might just stay for a few weeks, if you don't mind. Be good to get away."

"Best news I've had in a long time. Let's make it happen."

# Forty Nine

"What's going on, Riles? I'm the one who should be down in the dumps. You haven't lost your life savings." Davis playfully punched my shoulder.

"Why the long face, Secretary Kerry?" he said.

Derek had tried all sorts of zaniness to brighten my demeanor, but I was having none of it. We sat at Jason's Deli in Cornelius, which seemed like a neutral meeting place when I suggested that we needed to talk. At three in the afternoon, there were few patrons and the staff was under no pressure to clear tables. Other than the occasional trip to the beverage dispenser for refills, our conversation was uninterrupted.

"I have a little secret I've been hiding from you," I said. I had a plan to ease him into the bad news by explaining my own troubles first.

"Don't tell me you're finally coming out of the closet? I applaud your courage my friend, but I'm spoken for."

"Funny. No, my problem is quite the opposite. The past few nights Charlene Serpente has been staying at my place."

Davis didn't look surprised. "I should have known a hound like you wouldn't let go of the scent. What do you want me to say? Mazel tov?"

"You're a barrel of laughs today. If you'd like to lecture me about what a bad idea it is, I can give you two minutes."

Derek took a big gulp of his unsweetened tea and smacked his lips, like a cowboy finding satisfaction at a water hole in the desert. "I'll spare you the sermon. I'm living in sin myself these days. Spent the last several nights at Liz's."

I saw a natural segue to the next item on the docket, but I approached it circuitously. "And how is that going?"

"Great. I have some things to get over, but I'm dealing with it."

Maybe he already knew about Jack Deveraux's role in their little melodrama. That would alleviate the need for me to be the bearer of painful news. It could be I'd been churning over this for nothing. "I may not be a good role model, but I'm a good listener. You want to talk about it?"

"Riles, I trust you more than anyone on the planet. I can talk to you about things I could never talk to her about. So yeah, you and I will never be physically intimate, but I think you know me, the real me, better than Liz ever will. I guess that speaks volumes as to why I've never gotten married until now. Maybe deep down, I don't respect women as much as I do guys. Sounds kind of icky, but there it is."

I'm not good at listening to soul baring, even with best friends. I didn't know what to say.

Davis said, "I've come to an understanding about myself that I always needed to feel in control with women, that I had to have to have fifty one per cent of the leverage. If push comes to shove, I break the tie. I needed to feel just a wee bit superior in the relationship. The protector, the stronger one. I'm learning this stuff about myself now, maybe because those two guys beat the cockiness out of me. So I'm trying to break that pattern with Liz because I realize that she *is* strong. She's done things on her own that I don't know I could do. It's going to be fifty-fifty from now on with this woman who's going to be my wife."

"Derek, I came here to tell you a couple of things. Charlene was one of them. The other is that I know who ordered the attack on you. I've known it for a couple of days now. That's why I haven't been in touch. I didn't know how to tell you."

"The great Riley King afraid of the truth? I'm shocked, shocked."

"I tracked down the two guys who did this to you. Don't ask how, not my proudest moment. They're landscapers by day but both of them have a rap sheet dating back to their teens. To give them some credit, they seemed to have stayed out of major trouble for a couple of years now that their mowing business has grown. But I guess old habits die hard when there's good money involved. They work the whole area, from Concord all the way into South Carolina and they just happen to tend to a certain ranch in Rock Hill. I followed them there and they spent more time talking to Jack Deveraux than they would if he just needed some shrubbery trimmed. Jack, short for John. Johnny? Sorry to be the bearer of bad news."

Davis was gobsmacked. Already struggling with the image of his soon-to-be wife spending the night with Todd Weller, now he had to deal with the fact that her father had ordered a savage beating.

"Why would he do that?" Davis said, knowing the answer already.

"He assumed you were the one who impregnated his daughter and sent her off to get an abortion by herself."

"She confided in her mom. She must have confused reality with what Liz told her *might* happen. Her mom swore that she'd never tell anyone but the woman has early stage Alzheimer's."

"And who's he going to believe? I've seen it before, Derek. Lifelong partners are the last to admit to themselves that their spouse is losing it. They don't know how to cope with it so they stay in denial until the facts overwhelm them. It could be months, maybe years before Deveraux believes his daughter over his wife."

I could see my friend's mind racing as we sat speechless. I thought about the Paul Newman movie *Sweet Bird of Youth*. Hollywood wasn't very daring back then and had changed

Tennessee Williams' ending. The boy who messed with the southern patriarch's daughter was merely roughed up and disfigured in the final scene. The original play on Broadway was not so reserved. It ended with the wayward boyfriend's castration.

At least Jack Deveraux had drawn the line short of that.

# Fifty

Charlene had not told Johnny that she was leaving for good. She'd dashed off a short note saying that she was headed to Hilton Head for a few days to work on the condo.

Apparently, this was the way their arrangement worked. She's taken lengthier sabbaticals in the past to vacation with her perennials, and he had never questioned the absences. But this flimsy excuse wouldn't hold forever and there was no telling what Serpente's reaction would be when faced with losing her permanently.

Although no formal truce had been declared, the Russian hadn't escalated the war against Randee. Maybe he believed that poisoning her cat had made the old lady back off. If he only knew.

Although it was getting late in the day, I knew Jaime would still be in her office. The relationship with Charlene was still chaste, but I'm not made of stone and I hoped that by unburdening myself to my *real* woman, I could ease some of the tension. We had spoken a couple of times over the last days, but it was mainly small talk about Bosco and the few television series that we were both addicted to.

Charlene's presence at my home had not come up. That was all on me. I was fearful of her reaction. Maybe deep down, I felt that the relationship was hanging by a thread anyway and that this might be the thing that broke it.

After initial mumbled affections, I summoned up the nerve to broach the subject.

"Jaime, there's something I need to talk to you about."

"Uh oh."

"It's not an 'uh-oh'. At least I hope it's not."

"Well, I have something I need to talk to you about, too. Flip you for who goes first."

"I got heads. Ooops, it's tails. You go." She'd given me the opening to bail out and I'd walked through it. Some tough guy I am.

"Coward. Okay, here's the deal. I need to go away for a while. West Coast. Eastwood is thinking of letting his option expire on the Elton Spicer series. Feels he's a little too old for the part."

"An actor admitting he's too old. That's a first. But Spicer's an old fart anyway. Isn't that part of the charm?"

"The man has old school integrity, what can I say? As long as he's not talking to empty chairs. Anyway, word is that Harrison Ford is interested. But Eastwood directed the first two and he'd be perfect to continue as director, if not playing the character. So it's a complicated deal and it's probably going to take a month or so to hammer it out, especially if Eastwood doesn't want to direct."

"So let me guess, you want me to come out and muscle him into it?"

"Only as a last resort, tough guy. I'll try all my feminine wiles first."

"Hey, I'm broad minded but not so much that I'd let my girl sleep with a film legend, even if he is eighty something."

"Hey, whatever it takes. It's Hollywood. But seriously, that means I could be out there into the New Year. Hopefully not. I'd be staying with my dad in Holmby Hills."

"In John Peterson's sprawling mansion. Beats my little shack on Lake Norman."

"But it won't have you in it, sweetie. So I might just have to snuggle up to Clint or H."

"Oh, so he's H now. I guess this won't be your first contact with Han Solo."

"Only preliminaries. Don't get jealous. But see the problem is, I can't leave Bosco in New Jersey all that time. I mean, they love him at the office but I really don't trust anyone there to take care of him, especially over the holidays and you know he hates kennels. So I was hoping, since you're all set up down there, that you could take him."

I miss the dog and would love to have him around, but Bosco was one of the tangible commitments that Jaime had to me. We weren't engaged, there was nothing formal about the relationship, it just was. Every so often, she'd mention that the weather wasn't so bad in Jersey and that I should think about moving back or I'd tell her that she could work out of Charlotte and commute to New York for a week once a month, but neither of us have given in so far. Maybe we were just postponing the inevitable. If we really wanted to be together, we'd find a way.

"How would we get him here? I can't drive up now, I'm involved in something. And I wouldn't subject him to flying."

"Well, I was talking to Rick the other day and he said he was going to motor down to visit you soon. I'm sure he wouldn't mind taking Bosco for company."

"Funny, I talked to him earlier and he didn't mention Bosco. You two were planning this all along behind my back. Could you be persuaded to fly back from L.A. through Charlotte when you've wrapped Clint and H into a neat little bundle?"

"That was next on the agenda. Great minds think alike. I've got a couple other deals cooking out there but hopefully everyone will want to get things done before the holidays and we can spend Christmas together in Carolina."

"Great. I'll talk to Rick and firm up the dates. When do you need to leave?"

"Early next week. Tuesday, I think. Hey, there's a call I got to take. It's H. Love you."

"Me, too."

Bosco, Stone, Charlene and me under one roof. Thanksgiving dinner will be a riot.

While contemplating how to erase any trace of Charlene in the house by Christmas, I made another call, this one to a colleague in New York, a thirty year veteran of the Bureau who had risen faster and higher than I ever could. Dan Logan was a rough and tumble sort who had learned everything there was to know about bureau politics over the years. He knew all the right buttons to push to get things done. Any assistance he had given me in the past usually came with a price tag. Our relationship carried with it an unwritten balance sheet, which was presently tipped slightly in my favor.

"Dan, it's Riley. How the hell are you?"

Logan's voice was high pitched and raspy, unexpected coming from such a large man. The florid Irishman loved musical comedy, and I had always managed to come through with tickets for the man when he needed a favor, although since moving to Charlotte, my Broadway contacts were waning.

"Hey King, what's going on down in the land of cotton?" Logan treated Charlotte like it was Mississippi. He knew better, but enjoyed ribbing me about my migration.

"Seventy five degrees and sunny. The air is fresh and clean. No traffic to speak of," I said.

"Ah, the good life. Must be nice. In short there's simply not, a more congenial spot, for happy ever aftering." Fifties and Sixties musicals were his particular favorites and he quoted them whenever he thought it apropos, which talking to me, was always.

"Don't you find the pace in NY a little fast up there for a man of your particular tastes?"

"Nah, I was ready for it. I've lived all over the country." He had started in Florida, where his first wife had left him rather than subject her children to his transient lifestyle with the bureau.

Moved to Arizona, Iowa, Missouri. And then, a big terrorism bust landed him in New York.

"Met a nice girl, Riles, we're getting married in the spring. Ding dong, the bells are going to chime. Who'd a thunk it? Agent-in-charge in the Big Apple. All the shows I want. Better seats than you ever got me. Yankees. Giants tickets. I'm a happy man."

"Rex Ryan didn't turn you into a Jet fan? I guess there's no hope."

"Let that fat tub of shit win something first, then he can spout off about his squad. I'm glad his ass is in Buffalo now. Hope he freezes it off. But you didn't call me to talk football, did you?"

"Still sharp as ever. No wonder they promoted you. And I'll never tell what I know about the priest and the gangster who made your rep."

"Ah, yes, there is that. Riley King. Let me guess. Calling to settle accounts?"

I chuckled to myself. "Yeah, I do have something you could help me with. Got this kingpin down here, name of John Serpente, aka Johnny the Snake. Big time builder, does a lot of public housing. Corrupt as hell. Payoffs. Sub standard materials, sometimes hazardous. Get the idea?"

"Sure, but that's not my beat. Long as it doesn't cross state lines, sounds like a local matter. Not sure what I could do to help."

"I know that. But I'm looking for some background. You see, he moved down here thirty some years ago. From Brooklyn. Apparently he was a small fish in the Russian mob. I lost all touch with that group when I left New York, but I know you have C.I.s in Brighton Beach. His name was Dmitry Zubov back then. Ring a bell?"

"You're saying a Russian mafiya guy moved to North Carolina, and changed his name to, what was it? Serpentine? "

"We're not talking about Alan Arkin and *The In-Laws* here. It's Serpente. Yeah, I thought that was strange too. But the locals down here didn't know from Russians back then, but had a healthy fear of the Sicilians. I guess some of them needed a little prodding to let an outsider in on the good old boys' swag."

"And HBO finally made it to the hinterlands and they saw the Sopranos, too. You think he's sharing some of the take with the mob boys back home?"

"Maybe. That would cross state lines and make it a federal matter. Or maybe some federal housing subsidies make it of interest. But right now, I'm just trying to dig up whatever dirt I can find on him."

"The Russkies are into a lot of things, but public housing in Carolina doesn't seem like one of them. No offense, but they're into rubles, not rubes. They work internationally, mostly both coasts and some in southern Florida. This sounds like small change to me."

I explained Blankenship's plan to expose Zubov/Serpente on the internet.

Logan was skeptical. "I suppose it might work, but if this guy Zubov really is connected, your teacher friend would be sticking her neck way out. I'm not surprised this shit happens everywhere. You know we stung your ex-mayor down there on bribery and corruption. What have you got to back this up?"

"We have a video documenting the substandard materials and the word of an inspector who has since vanished. Randee's apartments are way past the statute of limitations, I know that."

He said, "The bureau has better things to do with their resources like *duh*, terrorism, to waste its time on something they consider inconsequential."

Charlene had broached the idea of using my contacts with the bureau to see if somehow federal charges might be in order. I wasn't sure if Logan would agree, and apparently he didn't. But it was worth a try.

I said, "I was just thinking if there was something this guy had done or was still doing up there, you might rattle some cages and cut off his support."

"Well, you ought to know Riley, short of murder, anything he might have done thirty years ago here is way off the books. All I can promise is that I'll ask around. I agree that something smells funny. I still have enough contacts in Brooklyn with the old guys to get some dirt but I can't say that it will lead anywhere. But I got to tell you, let this loose cannon teacher know that taking on the Russians isn't like going up against her local principal. Even though Sting thinks the Russians love their children too, they play rough and hold grudges."

"I know, but she's a stubborn old cookie. The greater the odds, the more determined she gets."

"Okay, you've been warned. Dmitry Zubov? Age? Got a picture you can Email me?"

"65ish. And you'll have the photo within a minute."

"That'll work. Wait a sec. Just thought of it. Got a guy who retired couple weeks back. Worked the Russkies back in the period you're talking about. Let me ring him up and call you back in a bit. I might have some answers for you"

"That would be great. Thanks Dan-o."

"I prefer, book 'em, Dan-o. Let's hope we can."

# Fifty One

The Brickhouse was nearly empty after ten p.m. when there was no Davidson game. Davis and I were glad for the lack of ambient noise and both of us were slightly in our cups.

"Hey, man, I know you have more pressing things to deal with, but I don't know what to do." Davis said.

I gulped down the remains of his beer and shrugged. "I ain't no Dear Prudence, Derek. Your girlfriend's dad had you beat up. For what it's worth, you think a little retribution would make you feel better? Kick the shit out of an old man? That's not happening. And what would happen if she found out that you attacked dear old dad?"

"Come on, you know I wouldn't do that. But I don't think he's so dear to her at the moment. Same reason he had me beat up. He's an old line Christian and didn't cotton to his daughter aborting the baby, no matter how it was conceived and by whom. Probably hates her more than me to be honest with you."

"Still," I said, aware that I was slurring my S's.

"He won't even take her calls. No email. Nothing."

"Your best revenge is to steal his daughter away. Much as he might think she's a baby killing Jezebel now, he'll be hurt much more by the thought that she flipped him off in favor of your Satanic Majesty."

Davis was mildly surprised at my urging restraint. "Boy, that doesn't sound like the Riley King I know. You've always responded in kind when someone came at you."

"Older and wiser, my friend. Older and wiser."

My cell buzzed and usually this late, I let it go to voicemail, but I glanced at the number and picked up. Derek tried not to eavesdrop, but he couldn't help noticing my grave expression as I listened to the voice on the other end, interjecting only occasionally. I rang off with a clipped thanks.

I said, "More background on Serpente. Seems like he lifted quite a few shekels from the Russkies on the way out some years ago. That explains his seed money down here and why he changed his name. He kept out of sight for a long time. Plastic surgery. Even so, he was camera shy. I never thought about it, but as much as he got involved in society stuff down here, I never saw his picture in any of the local rags. Kept a low profile for a guy that rich."

"Don't suppose the commies have a statute of limitations, eh?"

"Nyet. They're a vengeful lot. That was an old FBI buddy on the phone. I sent him a picture and a little bio on Serpente/Zubov and asked him to check his sources and see what he could dig up."

Despite my overindulgence of drink, I was immediately sharpened by what Logan had told me.

"So, what else did they find?" Davis asked.

"Serpente did collections. He was the money guy, always had muscle with him to intimidate, while he played the kindly banker. Like 'please sir, pay me so my animal friend doesn't hurt you.' That kind of thing. Collected from slumlords who ran subsidized housing from people who barely spoke English."

"Yeah, even though he's a creep, I don't think his physical presence scares anybody. But it explains his interests here in scamming the low rent districts."

"He works better with implied violence, rather than the real thing. Always hinted that the guys backing him were capable of ghastly things. And that was true, at least when it came to him."

"So why did he steal from them and then come down here?"

"Feds turned him. One of their insiders found out he was skimming. So they threatened to expose him unless he helped them. That's the dirty truth about what you need to do sometimes to get the goods on these guys. But the Russians somehow found out. Cut off his balls and stuffed them in his mouth."

"My god, I wish you hadn't told me that. How did he survive that?"

"He didn't, at least for the record. His FBI handler was keeping fairly close tabs, found him bleeding out, rushed him to the hospital, saved his life. Obviously, he was going to be of no use to them for futures. So they put out word that he was dead. They were priming him for WITSEC when he split. No one knew where. Until now. Guess he had squirreled away enough to get a little work done on his mug and get started in Charlotte, which was kind of a two horse town back then."

"But still, he must have had contacts down here. Although you said the locals were afraid of him."

"I suppose he was so good at playing Steve Buscemi that no one tested him. Or maybe you're right, he did know someone already. He was a better actor than a goon. Smart guy in his own way."

"What if the mob finds out he is still alive?"

"Like I said, they tend not to forgive or forget. Despite being this far away and the change in appearance, I imagine he'll always be looking over his shoulder. It's a lousy life."

# Fifty Two

## Derek Davis

"Randee, what have you done?"

Davis was in his now spotless condo where Blankenship had taken up temporary residence at King's insistence. It was mid afternoon and the image he saw on her monitor was unmistakable.

"What I said I was going to do all along. Expose this man through the internet."

"But we asked you to wait. And you agreed."

"I did wait. Three days. And nothing from Riley King. Nothing from you even though we're living in sin. Not. The more I thought about it, the more I came to the conclusion that your situation has nothing to do with this. So if Serpente didn't come after you in the first place, why would he now?"

Derek ran his fingers through his hair in frustration. "Randee, I know this isn't about me. It's about protecting you. King probably never told you this, but when he was in New Jersey, two women he was working for got killed. Both clients thought that they were in no danger from the dangerous men they were involved with. So he's extra cautious now about exposing his friends to anything like that."

"He didn't tell me that, no. But this is different. My internet kid says there's no way they can trace this to me."

"So you're trusting your life to some 17 year old kid? King was FBI, and he tells me that these professional hackers can track anything. And Serpente already knows you've got a burr in your saddle over this. It's possible he poisoned your cat. Randee, for a smart lady, I don't know."

"Nobody pushes me around, Derek. Besides, I've got another trick up my sleeve."

"Pray tell, Randee. What?"

"I use whatever resources I have. King mentioned that he knew this radio guy, Patrick Henry. Well, I called the man yesterday and got through --- saying that Riley was a mutual friend. Originally, I thought he could narrate the video but I realized it didn't need narration, it speaks for itself with a few captions. So I had a better idea. Mr. Henry couldn't have been nicer. I told him about the corruption. He said he'd look into it, then an hour later his producer called and said to put up the video and be listening at three today. That Henry was going to talk about it. It's almost three now."

"And did King tell you that Patrick Henry knows Serpente and has the hots for his wife? Randee, this isn't New York and you aren't dealing with people on the school board. You're dealing with criminals."

"I get that. I do. But I won't back down. This man has been ripping off the public and endangering lives. Look at what he tells those poor workers. *Asbestos. Don't worry it can't hurt you.* You think he'll be there when they get mesothelioma in ten years?"

"All we were asking was that you give us time to come up with a concerted effort. Now you've gone off on your own. I need to call King. You stay right here and don't do another thing. Please. If you don't care about yourself, think about the guy's wife. Think about me."

"Grow a set, Derek. It'll do you good."

# Fifty Three

Charlene had disappeared. She left a note saying she was staying at the farm of one of her friends. Serpente had no idea where she was and couldn't find out. I wanted to send someone out to stand watch but she refused to divulge her location. Despite my qualms about my past with women in danger, I had to trust she knew what she was doing and I couldn't spend time trying to track her down, now that Randee had prematurely started things in motion.

If Charlene was telling the truth, it actually could work to my benefit. I could operate without worrying that Serpente would send muscle to my house if he got wind of the fact that she was staying with me. I still assumed I wasn't even on his radar screen, unless he regularly checks his security disks at home.

After Davis had informed me that Randee had acted on her own and disregarded our warnings, I insisted that she and Derek find a cheap motel and check in under assumed names, paying cash. I girded myself for the prospect of Patrick Henry's three p.m. monologue on Serpente. It was too late to contact Henry and beg him to back off, not that he'd listen to me anyway. If it promised big ratings, he'd sell out his own mother.

To say his little speech wasn't what I expected would be an understatement, a term that could never be applied to one of Henry's rants.

"Give me LIBERTY or give me DEATH," the stentorian tones of some mid-Atlantic wannabe echoed in my little Bose speakers. It was followed by a crashing guitar solo, bass and drums thumping on my subwoofer as Henry began his spiel.

"Good afternoon, fellow lovers of freedom and justice, as we count down the hours to the end of the dusky tyrant's reign over our oppressed souls. I am Patrick Henry, a lone voice in the wilderness defending our constitution and the sacred intentions of its divinely inspired progenitors.

"Today it is my holy appointed duty to expose another fraud perpetrated by the left that threatens our very way of life."

Despite the overheated rhetoric, support from Henry's substantial radio audience might just tip the scales in Randee's favor. Strange bedfellows, indeed.

"I'm talking about a man whose Italian forefathers entered our country legally on Ellis Island, back when we welcomed the fine European stock who have done much to enrich our culture. He came to our fair city decades ago with nothing but the shirt on his back and a hardy work ethic, a man willing through the sweat of his brow to make our community a better place."

*Where was he going with this?*

"He wanted to build honest housing for our citizens but the liberal demons in control had other nefarious plans. Rather than construct his buildings and let the free market dictate, they placed before him a gauntlet. First --- he must construct accommodation for the undeserving poor, the forty seven per cent who suck from the public teat. Help them luxuriate in air conditioned comfort watching pornography on their flat screen televisions while eating bon-bons. They do this at our expense, while the rest of us slave in the hot sun to pay the confiscatory taxes necessary to support their idleness. Taxes that allow these welfare cheats and illegals to defraud hard working patriots who make this country great.

"Now I know you have little time to browse the internet given the honest day's labor you undertake to put bread on the table, but I must direct your attention to a website that I fear will turn your stomach."

He then reeled off what I assumed to be the URL of Randee's video.

"On it, you will see Mr. Serpente's workers, attempting to upgrade one of his well appointed apartments under threat of blackmail by a Yankee carpetbagger. A licentious woman who must have descended on our fair city on a broomstick. She contacted me, falsely citing the name an acquaintance, and begged yours truly to help her in her quest to extort this fine citizen. Her goal was to escalate the amenities enjoyed by society's leeches. Well, madame, and I use the term only because my sainted mama taught me to respect even the lowest of God's creatures, Patrick Henry does not support sloth and socialist corruption. He refuses to endorse extracting hard earned cash from the pocket of a man who has labored for three decades so that he and his lovely wife, a former Miss North Carolina, might occasionally enjoy some of life's simple pleasures. And to what end? To further subsidize the underclass threatening to destroy our city like a swarm of New York cockroaches. No, this shall not stand!!"

I had not listened to Henry's program in a dog's age and this was why: he took a simple plea for safe living conditions and turned it into an angry screed against liberalism.

"So my fellow Americans, I charge you with a mission. Visit this unholy website. Flood it with your comments in contempt of what this Yankee harridan is trying to accomplish. Her name is Randee Blankenship, probably a member of a certain tribe. Stand tall with God on your side, and He will reward the Righteous. Hit her servers so hard that they will explode in a fiery holocaust that will expunge this evil from our midst and restore the reputation of this hard working, honest American. I have spoken."

With that a Sousa march led into commercials, mostly for used car dealers and male enhancement products.

*Well, Randee, you got what you wanted. A spot on the most listened to afternoon talk show in Charlotte.*

# Fifty Four

## Derek Davis

Derek had promised an email detailing his building experience to the Mexican fellow at the real estate seminar. He was only sending it to be polite since the idea of moving to Mexico was so out of the box that he didn't take it seriously. Stir crazy from being cooped up in the motel with two women now that Liz had joined them, he cut and pasted verbiage from a promotional brochure his company had handed out when the market was hot along with an attachment about New Hope. Fulfilling his promise, he thought no further of it until a strong reply came within a half hour. The gentleman was impressed by the C.V. and wanted Derek to meet with him before he left town, perhaps later that evening?

Why not? Even though the meeting would likely amount to nothing, he had nothing to lose. He agreed to a seven p.m. get-together in the one of the small conference rooms of the hotel in Cornelius where the man and a colleague were staying. Maybe these fellows had connections stateside that might lead to something in the future.

The man he had met at the conference introduced him to the CEO of the venture. The man's face reminded Davis of a young Nick Nolte, only he was darker, rapier slim and well kempt. Dapper, immaculate in a dark woolen suit, white shirt and silk tie. Bronze skin, sporting a narrow mustache, salt and pepper hair clipped short. His name was Alejandro Salazar, and he was as deferential and mannered as his underling.

"Mr. Davis. I wanted to meet you in person. I hope I haven't inconvenienced you but we have a late morning flight tomorrow." There was a lilt to his tenor voice, true and clear.

"Not at all, Mr. Salazar."

"Yes, you see when I saw the site plan for the village that you had drawn up, I was quite impressed. It shows foresight. I share your idealism about what housing in the next decade could look like."

The man was attempting to be complimentary, but his efforts were making Davis feel worse. He was about to be stripped of most of his assets, not to mention his dream of New Hope. At least someone understood his vision and had endorsed it.

Salazar went on. "I must tell you, our concept in San Miguel is not quite so ambitious. It's a small project, but one I think you'll find aesthetically pleasing."

He gestured to another sheath of papers and plans on the table, and invited Derek to look them over. The drawings were indeed beautifully rendered, with far more detail than the standard sales brochure.

Salazar had the floor. "Mr. Davis, may I call you Derek?"

The man spoke perfect English, to the point that Davis suspected he was born in the states and had emigrated to Mexico, and not all that long ago.

Salazar said, "I did some research on you prior to our meeting. I was very taken by how you have run your business. You've conducted yourself honorably in all your dealings. You have shown vision far beyond the average developer and I firmly believe that had world economies not interceded, New Hope would be rising on the site today. I want to make you a proposition. I don't know if you've heard of San Miguel?"

Davis said he had. "I did some research as well. It seems you have quite a little jewel up there in those mountains."

"It is one of Mexico's most picturesque villages and we own a controlling share of this development, just on the outskirts of town. It is considerably more than halfway built out and despite the hard times, it has sold well. I need a man who shares my beliefs in sustainable construction to supervise the final phases of the project. The commitment would be for two years. You would need to be present on site on a daily basis. You would stay in a completed villa with all the amenities you are used to in the U.S.."

Asking Liz to leave the States for two years with him was something he never thought she'd consider. Since this offer was so unanticipated, he didn't even know what *he* thought of the concept.

"Now I must caution you, I'm not a man who likes to be kept waiting. To me, if one hesitates, it indicates a reluctance that I cannot accept in those who work with me. I need to know that their commitment is as strong as my own. But since I've caught you unawares, I'm willing to give you seventy two hours to reply."

He slid an envelope across the table. "Contained in here is an outline of your responsibilities and our compensation package. I know nothing of your personal situation but I'm sure you will want to discuss this with counsel and those you hold dear. I look forward to hearing from you. Please feel free to contact me with any further questions and I sincerely hope that you'll respond in the affirmative."

Davis smiled at the awkward phrasing but remained non committal, not wanting to offend his hosts by turning the offer down out of hand. The three men stood and made cordial farewells; Derek imagined it would be the last time he'd see either man.

He held that belief until he reached his car. He started the ignition, flipped on the dome light and opened the envelope. When he saw the figure at the bottom of the page, he knew that he and Liz had some serious business to discuss.

# Fifty Five

## Randee Blankenship

Randee was beside herself with good news. "I can't believe it Derek. It's been two days since that horrid man gave his little speech on the radio. But my site has gone viral. It's the talk of the town."

"Yeah, how about that? Meanwhile Liz and I are babysitting you in this crummy motel."

"Don't be such a pill. We've had great dinners with Riley at Mickey and Mooch. And you two are moving to Mexico for a couple of years. I visited San Miguel a while back. It's beautiful and this Salazar man sounds like a great boss. What could be better?"

"It would be nice if we didn't have to keep looking over our shoulder in case one of Serpente's goons finds us."

Liz looked up from her Kindle. She had read three books while in relative captivity and didn't seem to mind. She had been immediately enthusiastic about living in San Miguel as Mrs. Derek Davis. She saw it as a fresh start, away from the hot mess Charlotte had become for both of them. Two years in the mountains of Mexico could be viewed as a long vacation, and who knows, they might even like it enough to stay permanently.

Liz said, "Derek, you need to get out. Go bowling or something. Randee and I will be fine."

Blankenship agreed. "Yeah, Derek. Scram. We girls will just chat about cooking and shoes and stuff. Right! But my Lord, you wouldn't believe some of the obscene comments I'm getting on the site. Patrick Henry's followers are a bunch of cretins. But luckily, his rant has attracted so much attention that normal people have taken notice and the tide has turned. I don't think we'll need to stay underground much longer. I think we're going to see Johnny Serpente frog marched on the evening news in short order."

"Well, revel in your victory all you want but King made me promise to keep an eye on you. Even though the damage is already done, Serpente could come after you out of sheer revenge."

Randee just smiled and said, "Over soon, kids. It'll be over soon."

# Fifty Six

I was driving to Ballantyne with Charlene. She wanted to collect her valuables before alerting Serpente that she planned to leave him. I wasn't on board with the timing but short of physically restraining her, there was nothing I could do. Although given my past with women who insisted they were safe, physical restraint might be the best alternative. At least if I accompanied her, I could minimize the chances that the Snake would take out his frustrations on his bride.

She acknowledged my reticence but rejected all my warnings. "I know you ain't comfortable with this, but there's no way he'll be at home. He'll just try to go about business as usual, go to work and stay under the radar."

Under her lightly applied makeup, I could tell she hadn't been sleeping well. Telltale circles under her eyes would be visible to even the most casual observer. And Charlene rarely attracted casual viewing.

I said, "Are you going to tell me where you spent the last few nights? I'm not the jealous type, so if it's a guy, no sweat."

"I stayed with my friend Marcia's sister near Asheville. I took long walks in the country. I had a lot of thinking to do. Still do."

"When was the last time you spoke to him? What have you told Johnny?"

"Nothing yet. That's why I want to gather up some things. Just some jewelry and clothes for now. Things I'd be upset about if he decides to light a bonfire to my stuff when I drop the bomb that I'm leaving. It's not like he'll be like Chris Stapleton and say *there's nobody to blame but me.*"

I'd heard the country song she'd referenced and although I found it cute, it was just a song. Husbands and wives have been known to destroy the other's treasured possessions out of spite and Charlene had no doubt accumulated a lot of possessions while with Johnny.

I said, "Just reconsider the timing, that's all I'm saying. My source in the CMPD tells me that it's likely there'll be indictments coming against him. You may be walking into the lion's den."

"I think I just need some space for a while. That's what I'll tell him. No mention of divorce. I just need to pick another time and place to break the news."

"In a crowded restaurant is SOP. That way, the person getting dumped is less likely to make a scene. I'd hover close by in case he does. You know the U.S. Attorney of the Southern District called him in for questioning yesterday. The world's closing in on him and he may expect you to stand by your man. He'll think you owe him that much."

She reached across the center console of the Audi and touched my hand, a slow lingering touch. "Whatever happens Riley, you're a good man and I appreciate all you've done for me."

We were having a conversation like two people united on a mission, not potential partners in romance. Her manner was dry, almost clinical. Maybe that's what it comes down to when it's between two people who have been around the block a few times. You don't have fanciful images about walks on the beach, crackling fires and storybook princess weddings. You just need a lover who won't drive you crazy. Was that John Mellencamp? I'd have to ask Stone.

"You're sure you don't want me to come in with you?" I asked.

"No, that would be awkward if he is there. I did try calling him to find out where he is, but everything went straight to voicemail. Even his golfing buddies haven't spoken to him over the last 24 hours. That shitstorm your friend started probably has them running away from him as fast as they can. I'll go in with my cell phone. I'll call you before I open the door and keep the line open. If he's there, I'll say something like 'Gotta go, Johnny's here'."

"You've seen too many episodes of *Covert Affairs*. Just don't get into it with him if he is there. Just tell him you have to go, you just came by to pick up a couple of things. Say there's a car waiting and you'll come back later."

"Riley, I'm telling you, ain't no way he'll be home. But he is, I'll just gather up whatever I can and say that say that Marcia or Doris are waiting in the car. They'll back me up. They have in the past."

How many times and with how many men had Marcia or Doris covered for her? And strangely, in her seeking counsel on how to drop Johnny, she was foreshadowing how she was going to deal with me. In the few days she had lived under my roof, there were no overt come-ons, not even mildly ribald flirtations. It was almost as if I had been struck from her list of prospective lovers and re-classified as hired muscle. In some ways this was a relief, in others, I was disappointed that I hadn't enjoyed her bounty at least once.

But if I was to be her protector, how could I allow her to enter the house she shared with Johnny by herself? How many times had Elizabeth Huntington and Paige White assured me that they would be safe? Two women I worked for who were no longer around because I believed them. Although I had told Charlene I'd wait in the car while she gathered her things, I was going straight to the unlocked front door the second she was out of sight. That way if I heard anything concerning, I could be at her side within seconds.

I said, "All right, you have your mind made up. I hope whatever you think you need to take with you is worth the risk. If he shows up while I'm outside, you sneak out the back and we'll patch out of here. Not that I'm afraid of him, it's just cleaner that way."

"I don't suppose you're afraid of anybody, Riley. I wish I could be like that. As independent as I like to think I am, it scares me to be back out on my own. I've got some money stashed, but a lot of my friends have sued for divorce and even when it's amicable, it's not amicable."

Even though I was now certain Serpente had no part in Davis' assault, my business with him was far from over. With all the internet fury over Blankenship's video, the authorities had indeed called him in for questioning and Johnny would likely be out of business soon. But even if incarcerated, he could still reach out and hurt Randee or Derek, if only out of vengeance.

"All right, Charlene. We're here. Just tread lightly and be careful. If he is there just make your excuses and get out, okay?"

"Will do, Riley. She leaned over and kissed my cheek. Just that innocent act excited me. Good thing nobody has found a way to bottle what she has going on, or the population explosion would overwhelm the planet. She said, "I really appreciate this, darlin'. Shouldn't take more than ten minutes."

"I've heard that before from women who were packing. See you in an hour."

"Piggy pig. I'll be back in ten. Time me."

I watched her shapely bottom as she walked down the drive. I tried not to think of the time I'd seen her practically naked in this same spot. She peered into the main level garage and walked around back, presumably to check the lower level parking area. She emerged a minute later, winked at me from the front door and pulled out her phone.

"Looks like the coast is clear, Riley. The SUV is gone. Start the countdown. Ten minutes."

"Hey, remember what we said. Keep the line open. Just in case."

"I almost forgot. I'd make a terrible sleuth. I'm going in now."

She disappeared behind the massive doors. I waited a few seconds, then followed. Through the tiny phone speaker, I could hear her rustling about. I imagined her stopping somewhere to check the mail that had come in her absence, then mounting the stairs toward the bedroom. There weren't any workers on the premises so I assumed the master bath was complete. My mind wandered to that small remodeling project that set this all in motion. I actually was a little curious to see how the room had turned out. I wished Derek could see it too, and share his expert critique. Well, no matter what, *that* was not going to happen.

I heard the whoosh of a door opening. The master bedroom? Then a slight creak of another door. The master bath?

The quiet was broken by a horrific scream.

"Charlene? Charlene, what's wrong?" I shouted into the phone.

"Oh my God, Oh my God. Riley. Oh my God. Come. Come quick."

A Snake? Blood? Charlene was tough but even the most courageous women (or men for that matter) could be unnerved by a copperhead. I grabbed my gun and sprinted up the stairs, Charlene's sobs still filling my ears.

Someone had indeed killed a snake. But it was not of the reptilian persuasion. Lying face up, naked, eyes wide open, was John Serpente/Dmitry Zubov.

There was no need to feel for a pulse. Amidst Charlene's screams, the caked blood behind the body told me this hadn't just happened.

# Fifty Seven

"We've got to call the police," Charlene was screaming.

"Calm down. Yes, we have to call the police. But first you have to tell me what happened."

"What happened? What happened? You know what happened. I came up here and found my husband dead on the floor of our bathroom. That's what happened."

I had dealt with hysterical people of both sexes in these situations. Most of the time, I could tell if the hysteria was manufactured. Guilty parties often overplay their grief. The normally unflappable Charlene had come unglued for real.

"Riley, what are you doing? Help me. I need you."

I spoke sharply. "Charlene, he's dead. What you have to do now is concentrate on yourself. I hate to hit you in the face with this, but if I were investigating this, you'd be number one on the suspect list."

"What? How can you say that? You think I'm capable of killing anyone, much less my husband?"

"It doesn't matter what I believe. You left him. You stayed with me. You've cheated on him before. Unless you've got a rock solid alibi for where you were at the time of death, you're the main focus. That's the way cops work. They're not Hercule Poirot. They take the path of least resistance."

Her body shuddered. She turned abruptly and raced down the hall. I could hear retching sounds as she emptied the contents of her stomach. I waited a moment before venturing down the hall to the main bath.

"Are you all right? You need help?"

Her muffled voice responded. "Give me a minute."

I gave her two. Her face was damp from splashing water and she bore the sickly smell of vomit and the mouthwash she had used to cover it. Right now, she was the least sexy woman in the world.

"I'm going to call a cop I know. He won't catch the case, but he can direct it toward someone who won't jump to conclusions. There will be probably a dozen people here an hour from now. Detectives, forensic guys, medical examiners, techies. You'll be led to a quiet room. They'll ask you about the body, how you found it. They'll act all sympathetic. Try to comfort you. But the whole time, they'll ask you leading questions. Questions designed to root out inconsistencies if not outright lies."

"My God, you really believe they'll think I did this?"

"Short answer, yes. They'll want to know your whereabouts over the last few days."

"What'll I tell them?" Her eyes were moistening again. She needed a lawyer. I could give her rudimentary legal advice, but my expertise was in trapping criminals, not defending them.

"Nothing and everything. Just don't lie. They'll catch you in every single one of them and use them to undermine your credibility. Tell them how you found the body and where you were over the last day. I'm no ME but the body still had some warmth, so I'd guess he hasn't been there more than twelve hours. But you need to get an attorney here pronto."

"Won't that make it look like I'm guilty if I bring in a lawyer and shut my mouth right away?"

"Look, these cops are going to think you did it anyway. You've got to protect yourself. They'll find out about the nights you stayed with me. They'll ask why. It will be embarrassing but it's better they think that you're an adulteress than a killer. Sorry to be so blunt, but we've got to protect you."

"But we never slept together. Don't that matter?" Her shoulders dropped and she made a move toward me. "Am I going to jail? I don't think I could take that, even for one night."

"They can't have anything to book you on you now. They'll investigate. They'll find out you stayed with me. We can't lie about that. I'll just say you needed a place to hide after you decided to leave him. The Derek stuff will come out. Do you know a good criminal attorney? If not, I can recommend one."

"Yes. There are a couple at our club."

"Friends of his, too?"

"More like acquaintances. I think they were lusting after me more than they were friends of Johnny's"

"Call the one who was Johnny's closest friend. If this ever goes to trial, the fact that he was willing to defend you will look good to a jury. Call the lawyer now. I'll call my cop friend. Just say nothing detailed to the police until your attorney gets here. Then make sure you talk with him in private first. He may have a different strategy. You'll stay at a hotel tonight. We can't spend any time together for a while. Just say the least you can and remember, don't lie. If there's something your lawyer doesn't want them to know, just say you're in shock and your brain isn't working now."

"But I didn't do this. Ain't that the best defense?"

"It helps. The best thing I can do for you now is to find out who really did do it. That's the only way you'll ever get off clean. Unless I do, people will always think you did it and got away with it."

I needed to weigh my options as well. I could just leave and hope that Charlene would keep my presence at the scene a secret.

Bad idea.

Even if I did trust her completely, a good investigator could figure it out and pretending I wasn't there would make me look guilty. Besides, even though Shabielski was a trusted friend, calling him would leave a cell trail that could be traced and I couldn't ask him to lie about it. That would risk his badge in a high profile murder investigation.

My best option was the same one I outlined to Charlene. Tell the truth. She feared that her husband might get violent and I came along in case things got out of hand. I'd provided her safe haven as a friend for a few days. Yes, I knew Blankenship and Davis but I trusted that the video and the authorities would handle Serpente. In fact, I had never even met the man.

As I went over the story in my mind, I realized how fishy it came off. It sounded much more believable that I was the mastermind behind this whole series of events. In retaliation for what I thought was Serpente's assault on my friend, I had killed him and stolen his wife. I'd recruited my friends to blacken his reputation to create other suspects with a grudge against the man.

If I were still a fed, I'd buy that scenario over the one I was peddling.

# Fifty Eight

The staff at 131 Main was cleaning up around us, every so often dropping hints that it was time to clear out. But a couple of stern looks from me sent them scurrying.

Derek was curious. "So what happens next on Serpente? Charlene lawyered up yet?"

I said, "Yep. She has nothing to say on advice of counsel. God, how I hated hearing that shit when I was on the other side. Made me want to come at them even harder. But she's better off not saying anything yet. Considering the shit storm Randee started, suicide wouldn't be out of the question except there was no gun present."

"Yeah, maybe he would have wanted it over on his terms. Must be hard to live with the prospect of months of trials and then prison."

We sat silent for a while. Davis didn't have an easy answer or consoling words. He was probably thinking about his own role in the man's demise. He said, "Was Serpente a monster? Worse than the people I did business with in Charlotte that's for sure, but only by degree. Councilmen --- politicians who for a generous contribution, make life easier for a slap dash builder of cheap housing. Building officials he may have bribed? None of them turned him in, except maybe the new plumbing inspector and he disappeared, so who was worse?"

I said, "Sure, he wasn't the only one culpable, just the main one. I could make the case his use of asbestos after it was found hazardous constitutes negligent homicide. You think the building inspectors here were greedy enough to let that ride?"

"Hell, they still use it in Canada --- actually more countries allow it than ban it. But I think an inspector would draw the line there, unless the bribe was life changing. But did the lack of insulation and fire stops ever directly cost anyone their life? They might overlook that on purpose."

I waved for the check. "We may never have the answer to that. Even the cancer. Who's to say that it couldn't have been caused by smoking or genetics? They'd have to autopsy everyone who ever lived there and see if they detected asbestos fibers in their lungs. Who's paying for that?"

Davis said, "I just have a hard time believing that there are a lot of people in my business who would be so cavalier with public health. That's why I think Serpente mostly had to pull the wool over their eyes. I'd never knowingly endanger the health of anyone who had put their faith in me by using any product or technique that may prove unsafe."

"And that's as it should be. But think about it. Hard times for builders and subs. And these inspectors don't make big money. What if a couple of them had gambling debts or a drug problem? Or Serpente had blackmail material on them? Desperation causes people to do things they might not do normally."

Davis said, "I guess. I was just thinking that I never really had to make that choice. My clients could afford a premium price for my peace of mind and not think twice about it. What about the people that Serpente built for, those who wanted to enjoy the American Dream but couldn't afford it? Would they quibble over substandard material or dangerous working conditions if it meant they could have a home of their own?"

I said, "Derek, you're a compassionate guy, I'll give you that. But Serpente had to know the consequences of ripping off the mob. The man's sins caught up with him. There's no way you should fret that he's gone."

"But did he deserve to die in his bathroom?"

"Elvis did. Hell, if it was up to me, I'd rather see the old snake rot in prison. Serpente's death will probably go into the files as unsolved. And nobody will care much, maybe not even his widow."

I drank deeply and paid the check with cash. For all my outward cool over what had happened, I shared Derek's angst. I'd roughed up an innocent basketball player, a kid who could have been me thirty years ago. And I'd clumsily caused the death of a small time crook, when a more deft handling of the case could have exposed what was undoubtedly a larger conspiracy amongst public officials. Now they could lay all the blame on a dead man who couldn't blow the whistle on his cohorts. And my dalliance with the beautiful Charlene had fizzled, although that might be for the better.

But even though the darkest clouds had passed, there might be an even worse storm behind it.

# Fifty Nine

"So I'm not quarantined after all? Then why the cloak and dagger routine, Shabielski?"

The Charlotte cop was outfitted for a leisurely jog. Running shorts, sweat pants underneath, torn tee shirt bearing a *Lakewood Blue Claws* logo. To the casual observer, he and I looked like a couple of middle aged runners prepping for a ten K. The pace was slow enough so that we could converse without too much exertion as we did wide laps around Renaissance Park.

"Brass wouldn't appreciate me talking to you this soon. They want to give the appearance of investigating, even though they've shut it down. Keep the media in the dark, which given the way the Observer has pretty much been turned into a pamphlet, shouldn't be too hard. Sorry the paper dragged your name into it, but that should quiet down soon."

"Logan told me since his feds in New York told the locals here what they know about Johnny, they dropped any interest. And you can bet the New York bureau isn't going to follow up on some small time Charlotte hood who got what they think was coming to him. That was predictable."

Shabielski picked up the pace. He ran six miles every a day and could run me into the ground if he chose to. But his superior fitness level wasn't foremost in his thoughts today, although his competitive nature subconsciously enjoyed the advantage.

Peter said, "By the way, ran into Patrick Henry the other day. He said you owed him a thank you."

"Why is that?"

"Said that because of his rant on the show that day, the old lady got it done. Nailing that pig Serpente. Website went viral. Much more effective than the little plug she was looking for."

"That crafty son of a bitch. I wonder if he believes half the shit he peddles on his show. I've always had my doubts," I said.

"Intrepid as always, Ivanhoe. You didn't know that all along? Here's another little tidbit for you. You're right in that the feds did call my guys. So if any of this stuff does see the light of day, the cheeses here will use the FBI pulling rank as an excuse for their lack of progress. But they put the kibosh on this one way before your boys intervened."

The increased blood flow to my brain hadn't sharpened my focus enough to piece together what Shabielski was talking about. It took me a while to follow where my friend was leading.

I said, "When?"

"Don't bother yourself with a timeline. I've already put it together."

"Lay it out for me. What do you have?"

Shabielski grunted. "Goes without saying, you didn't get this from yours truly. Dig it?"

"How long have you known me?"

"Too long. Anyway, here goes. A full scale media circus into Serpente's business interests would uncover some connections to some folks who wouldn't want to be connected to him."

I said, "Of course. He must have greased a lot of palms. Some of his cronies are pretty high up on the food chain and wouldn't appreciate the scrutiny. So how are they playing it?"

"They've already started leaking stuff to the press about Serpente's previous life. They let some key reporters know that the feds are taking over, something to do with a Russkie hit man and RICO bullshit. They love a good mob story like that. Only loose end is the lawyer your gal hired. But he's connected politically, so no doubt he'll agree to low key it. They've basically told him that she's in the clear and not to open a can of worms."

"That's interesting. Her attorney called me and lets me know that he's advised her not to speak with me for now. Claims that given my profession and our relationship, it might look like we planned this together. Said I should just let it fade away. I guess they're still playing it safe."

The Charlotte cop stopped running. "That's to throw you off the real scent. All part of the act. I'm going to tell you something that you're not going to like. Let's sit."

Shabielski's face darkened and sweat was pouring off his shaved head as we stopped at a park bench under a massive maple that had shed most of its leaves.

"Riley, you're not the first smart guy who lost it over a pretty face. And a killer bod. So don't take this too hard."

I said, "Hey man, if you're about to insinuate that I killed Serpente to win over Charlene...."

"Hear me out. I know that you'd never do anything like that, no matter how hot the chick was. But listen to me. We confiscated computers at the scene. We had a tech guy check search histories. Charlene did a big time search on you right after you met."

"Okay. That's not unusual in this day and age, is it? I researched her as well."

"Fair enough. But here's what's bothering me. She got into media reports of cases involving the Russian mob in New York. Your name was mentioned in a couple. She then checked into some gory stories about how they deal with traitors."

I had a sinking feeling. I now saw her end game but tried to convince myself otherwise.

Shabielski built his case. "She gave you his real name. Volunteered it to an almost total stranger. But by then she knew about your background. She gives up a secret that she had to know would be fatal if it reached the wrong ears. Coincidence?"

"Cops don't really believe much in coincidence, do they?"

"Also, some of the folks we interviewed told us she was talking about a way out of the marriage for some time now. Before you guys met. Then voila! you give her an exit strategy on a silver platter. She tells you his real identity, encourages you to investigate his past, and by the way, has you along for the ride when she discovers the body. Did she inspire you to call Logan about the mob connections?"

"Yeah, she did actually. I thought it was a long shot but I figured it couldn't hurt and he might be able to help come up with something that he could pin to him. Wait a minute, you're saying you think *she* capped him and made it look like the mob did it?"

"That's one of several possibilities. I'm told she had an alibi, but friends lie for friends all the time. So she may have done it herself or more likely paid someone to do it for her. Plan B was that she had you set up to take the fall, if necessary. You had motive, expertise on how to cover up crimes with your FBI experience. Or if we look a tad more benignly toward the lady, she tricked you into revealing Johnny's whereabouts to the Russian mob and they really did take care of old business. The last possibility is that this was all one big happy coincidence. Take your pick. I can't prove any of it. The case is closed, unofficially of course."

It wasn't as if I hadn't considered most of what Peter had sketched out for me, but he seemed to think that Charlene had been behind this from the day after we first met --- leading me along by the genitalia, without actually giving up the goodies. Brilliant!

I was speechless, as if Randee had hit me with her Taser.

Shabielski filled the void by adding, "You know me, I think the world is better off without this sleazebag around. I'm just giving you a heads-up. It was me, I wouldn't trust this chick. When the dust settles, you could ask her to fess up but I'm betting you're not gonna get a straight answer."

"So you plant this seed, old pal, and you expect me not to try to find out?"

"Advising against it, Sherlock. I imagine she's quite a number in the sack, but if she's capable of fooling you once, she's capable of doing it again. I'd steer clear. You have a sweet girl waiting for you in Jersey. Don't let your dick get in the way. Just saying."

"Thanks, Pete. And of course, you're not going to be rooting around on your own, are you?"

"Hey, like I said, world's a better place without him. I learned my lesson in Jersey. Some battles just aren't worth fighting. But I do promise, if something comes up that might ease your mind a little, I'll pass it along. We might even be able to be seen together in public in a few weeks. Gotta go now. Take care of yourself."

He patted me on the knee and sprinted away. I sat for a moment, dazed by what I'd just heard. I mopped my brow with a ragged sleeve, then took off in the opposite direction, running hard at first then slowing to a walk.

With Serpente gone, my only stake in the matter was Charlene. Charlene had seemed really upset upon discovering the body. Was it an act? Had she actually found it earlier and lured me in as a witness to attest to how shocked she was? She had to know that she'd be an immediate suspect. Did she have a co-conspirator, one of her *perennials*, who could wield enough influence to make any charges go away if it came down to that? Or if the worst case happened, would she have turned on me --- actually accuse me of the murder, claiming my lust for her drove me to it?

She was a tough woman who had seen hard times and landed on her feet. The only scenario that kept her clean was that this was all just a coincidence. Just because cops didn't believe in coincidences, it doesn't mean that they never happen.

In the end though, at heart, I am a cop.

# Sixty

Jaime, that sweet girl from New Jersey, called ostensibly to inform me that Stone was on his way to Charlotte with Bosco, but I already knew that from Rick. She was currently in California, three thousand miles away, dealing with movie moguls.

"So, when were you going to tell me?" she asked.

"Tell you what?"

"It's a small world these days, Riley. I'm on all kinds of social media. I've had several friends ask when we had broken up and why didn't I tell them. Local news isn't local any more. A story in the Charlotte Observer can be read anywhere in the world now. She's a very attractive woman. A bit closer to your age than I am, I guess."

I cursed myself for not telling her about Charlene earlier when I had the chance. I was a coward then, fearing she wouldn't understand. Now I couldn't blame her for attributing darker motives.

I said, "Jaime, you know the papers. You know how wrong they get everything. How wrong they got your mother's story."

"So you're denying that this woman, this Miss Carolina, lived with you?"

"No. I'm telling you, there's much more that isn't out in the media and hopefully never will be."

I told her about how Serpente had come to my attention as a result of Derek's beating, an incident that seemed decades ago. How I'd first encountered Charlene while trying to ascertain if there was a connection.

"The more we looked into this guy Serpente, the dirtier he seemed. She claimed to be surprised that he was anything more than just a slightly shady builder. But when she found out the truth, she left him and was fearful that he'd strike back."

"So my White Knight offered her shelter from her gangster hubby? Is that it?"

I said, "I know you mean that sarcastically and maybe you have a right to feel that way. But you and I talked a lot about how I didn't take better care of your mother. I could have stayed with her the night she was killed and maybe she'd still be around today. You know about Liz Huntington, the woman I could have done more to protect and she's dead too. You really think given what I've been through the last few years that I'd turn my back on another woman who needed my help."

There was silence for a moment then she said, "Riley King. Protector of battered women. I saw the pictures in the paper. I Googled her. Come on, Riley, she's gorgeous, she looks like Faith Hill, for God's sake. Did she sing you to sleep with country lullabies?"

"All right Jaime, of course, I was tempted, I'm human. I'm sure a lot of the guys you'll be dealing with in Hollywood aren't exactly beastly looking either. But I trust you. And if you did meet somebody, I'd have nobody to blame but myself. I moved away."

"Why? I wasn't worth staying for? You couldn't put up with another New Jersey winter to be close to me?"

"Jaime, we've had this discussion. This is where I want to be now. I haven't asked you to choose between me and your business. We thought we could make this work until..."

"Until when, Riley? Until I move to Charlotte and leave the agency. Turn my back on the people who work for me and become a housewife? Is that your ideal ultimate outcome?"

I was starting to feel like Don Draper and his bi-coastal wife Megan on *Mad Men*. Jaime had taken over her mother's business and made it blossom. And yes, I was putting my lifestyle and business ahead of her. But so was she.

"I don't know the ultimate outcome, Jaime. I just know that you're important to me. This Charlene woman, I probably will never see again. It's possible she set this whole thing up with her husband and was using me for cover. I still want you to come down for the holidays if you can. Maybe if we're together for a couple of weeks, I mean really together, we can come to some sort of conclusion as to what we both want. That's the best I can do."

"Why didn't you tell me about her?"

"I was going to. When you called me about Bosco. I'm sorry I didn't. I wanted you to hear it from me. I guess I just got so wrapped up in this case, that.... I don't know, that sounds lame doesn't it?"

"It does." She sighed deeply. "Give me some time, Riley. Don't call me. Let it breathe. I'll be in touch when I've sorted this out. Just leave me alone. Please."

I had nothing more to say. "Take care of yourself. Say hi to Indiana Jones."

---

# Sixty One

"You sure you want to do this, Riley?"

Rick Stone and I were travelling south on I-77 in my Audi A5. It was just past noon, but the December sun had not shown itself all day, choosing to hide behind some lifeless gray clouds. Combined with a gusty wind, it felt about as cold as it gets in Charlotte; that is to say, a few degrees below freezing.

"Unfinished business. Call it what you will, but I can't let this hang."

"I guess you could look at it that way. But there are risks."

Stone pulled the passenger visor down, flipping the mirror flap to shield him from the low sun. He said, "I suppose that's one of the reasons you're bringing your old foxhole buddy. I must say, Bosco really seems to like your house. Sorry he had to mark his scent on your nice wood floor. Making himself right at home. You know, I could get used to it here myself. Golf on great courses, pretty much twelve months a year. Do my show from your place."

"Works for me."

"Hey, what's going on with this Charlene lady? You haven't mentioned her lately. Still hasn't been in touch?"

I reached down into the console for coffee before replying. "Nope. Enough time has passed. I expect she never will."

"So..... I've been afraid to broach the subject because I know you're *tetchy* about it, but do you think she killed him? You told me Shabielski put that bug in your ear. You buying it?"

"She didn't pull the trigger; that much I believe. Logan up in New York says that TSA confirmed that one of the guys the Russkies use for wet work booked a round trip to Greensboro that day. Rented a car that came back with almost three hundred miles on it. Enough to drive to Ballantyne, dispatch Zubov and come back. The feds could send a team down to work over the rental for trace, but it's probably been used and cleaned since. Realistically, they couldn't care less about it. Passed the info down to the locals and Shabielski says it got filed where the sun don't shine."

"So .... did she set the whole thing up?"

"I guess a case could be made. But any argument I could make if I were prosecuting --- the defense could swat down in a minute. I'll probably never know the truth, at least from her."

"She may have just realized that you were merely shelter from the storm, but not somewhere she'd want to live."

"Dylanesque. Between you quoting classic rock and Logan using show tunes, do either one of you ever have an original thought?"

"*If there's an original thought out there, I could use it right now.* Sorry, I can't help it. That's obscure Dylan, from Brownsville Girl."

"Please, I got enough of that from Davis in the hospital after his beating. At least he was drugged up. What's your excuse?"

"Ain't got one. So what about that long cool woman in a black dress? Charlene."

"What am I going to do? Make this a personal mission?"

"The old Riley King would have done that. You never liked loose ends. Isn't that what we're doing today?"

Coffee again.

I said, "There's one other thing that tips the scales in her favor. A friend of Derek's wife's is married to one of the attorneys for Serpente's estate. Told her something interesting."

"An attorney breaking privilege. Fancy that."

I said, "It'll be in the public records someday. Serpente's will. The big news is a piece of his net worth goes to *Habitat for Humanity*. He left a chunk of money to his club, God knows why. I guess someday there might have been a John Serpente taproom or something but not now. Charlene won't be getting much. Walking around money for a couple of years. Even the house was in his name only, so unless she contests it, she'll be needing to get a job someday."

Stone said, "And no doubt the pre-nup would have paid out more. Yeah, divorces and estates can get tied up for years. No wonder she wanted to take out her jewelry and stuff the day you found the body. Hope she eventually got it. Wow. He probably realized at some point that Charlene was only good for eye candy --- no real love there. I actually could feel a little sorry for the man."

"Let's not put him up for sainthood quite yet. He did collections for the mob and then betrayed them. And Davis tells me that there's no telling how sick his workers and tenants will be someday. I don't know that whatever he bequeaths will be enough to buy his way into heaven. It's funny, after all the work I did on this, I never met the man. He was a cipher to me. Never saw him until we found his body."

Stone said, "Well, look at the bright side. You got a few nights of great sex. *Habitat* gets a big donation. New affordable housing will have someone better building it."

"You don't believe me that I never slept with her, do you? And if *you* don't, I must be kidding myself that Jaime ever will. Well, here we are. You sure you want to help me follow through with this cockamamie wedding present plan?"

"At your service, as always my friend. Sports talk is a little boring these days. I could use some excitement. Just remember, *in the end, the love you take, is equal to the love you make*. Don't beat up old man Devereaux too hard. The dude is over seventy."

# Sixty Two

## Jack Devereaux

The tack room was clean and well organized. It would never smell like a jasmine garden due to the proximity of six large animals, but Jack Deveraux was proud of how he kept his workshop. Age had crept up on him slowly and with the passing years, he ceded more of the care and feeding of his horses to others, but he still remained more hands-on than not.

He hadn't changed his routine much over time. His wife had her bridge group Tuesday afternoons from one to five, cocktails served throughout. She would invariably come home half in the bag, although given her progressing dementia, he saw little difference in her demeanor. What it came down to was that he carried the responsibility of preparing dinner on Tuesday night, the maid Rosalita's day off. He dutifully tucked his wife in right after NCIS. The rest of the evening was spent in solitary reading --- often the Bible, accompanied by glasses of brandy and a Bach choral arrangement.

So after lunch, he retreated to the tack room workshop and busied himself with whatever chore needed attention until four, at which point he'd feed the dogs and rustle up some grub, as he liked to put it. His wife arrived home at 5:15, and after freshening up, dinner was served promptly at five forty five. He occasionally ordered take-out, but lately he had taken an interest in cooking meals from scratch. Perhaps, subconsciously he was preparing for the day when she could no longer cook at all.

Veronica Deveraux still insisted on making dinner most nights. Unfortunately, more and more, gas burners were left on, freezer doors remained wide open and utensils were mislaid. The frequent burnt offerings signaled the end of her culinary duties and food preparation mostly fell to him or Rosalita.

Routines can be comforting but they also can be dangerous if an enemy knows them too well.

# Sixty Three

Deveraux gave me a hard look.

"What are you doing here, King? What do you want?" The old man's voice showed no fear, his eyes darting about for a possible weapon.

"Just to talk, Jack. Some things you ought to know."

"It's Mister Deveraux. I have nothing to say to you.. Especially since any communication we have will undoubtedly be related to that son of a bitch friend of yours --- Davis."

"That's fine. Just listen then. Two weeks ago, Derek Davis married your daughter."

If Deveraux was shocked by the news, it didn't register on his face. "I have no daughter."

"I see. Well, there's a woman named Elizabeth Deveraux Davis who claims otherwise."

"No daughter of mine would kill a baby. Even if it was Davis' bastard. And no son- in- law of mine would allow her to do it. Married two weeks ago. A little late, don't you think?"

I gestured toward an old chair that Deveraux kept in a corner but the old man refused to sit. "I'll tell you the whole truth. You can choose to believe it or not, but I promise you it's exactly what happened. Liz and Davis stopped seeing each other for a while. He'd fallen on some tough times financially and didn't feel it was fair to burden her with his problems."

"I know all this. You're wasting my time. He was too pig headed to ask me for help, which back then, I foolishly would have given."

"Call it pig headed if you will, but the man didn't want to be beholden to anyone. He made a business here in Charlotte and had a great run. But more to the point, Liz wasn't pregnant by Davis or anyone else. And you won't have any grandkids by her either. She had tumors on her ovaries. Benign, if you care. And by the way, Davis had no idea even that Liz went to Europe --- much less why she went."

"If that was intended to vindicate him, it was a pretty feeble attempt. Some man she married. He couldn't even face me himself to tell me this. That's mighty cowardly, boy. Frankly, I'm a little surprised by that. If nothing else, I thought he had some balls."

"Derek doesn't even know I'm here. Your daughter is deeply hurt that you cut her off the way you did. They are moving on with their lives. I suppose you won't care that she's in Mexico now. Davis has taken a job there. It'll be two years at minimum."

"That's her choice, one of many mistakes she's made. Won't be the first or the last. You may think that the little tale you've just woven changes things, but it doesn't. My attorney is preparing a new will and she will not be part of it. "

"That's entirely up to you. I just thought you should hear the truth. Again, she and Derek don't know that I'm here and probably wouldn't approve."

"My wife told me she went to Europe to abort her unborn child. Now you come with this story that she wasn't even expecting. Now who do you think I'll believe, a woman I've been married to for fifty years or some sleazy private dick?"

I felt sorry for the man. Obdurate as he was, he hadn't dealt with the reality of his wife's Alzheimer's. He was in for a rough ride and it would only get worse.

"One final thing, Jack, while you're doubting your son-in-law's character. He knows you hired those goons to beat him up. He hasn't told Liz. Probably never will just in case she may want to reconcile with you someday."

Jack Deveraux looked puzzled for the first time in the meeting. "I don't know what you're talking about."

"Let's add lying to your list. Davis was beaten up and spent two days in the hospital. The two men who did it cut your grass and tend to your shrubs. So I'm wrong to assume you hired them, Jack?"

"I don't have to listen to this. I know nothing about this attack and I had nothing to do with it. If I've sinned, it might be in that I now take a certain amount of pleasure in hearing about his misfortune."

"Wow. You really believe that, don't you? You really believe that you did nothing to punish Davis for what you thought he did to your daughter?"

Deveraux stepped forward, his eyes blazing. I knew that tempers might get out of hand; that's why Stone was outside the door listening. We had arranged a code word for trouble, at which point Stone would burst in and break it up. If Deveraux got hurt and pressed assault charges, in a "he said, he said" situation, since I was there uninvited, any judge would likely side with the old man. It could mean my license.

Deveraux stopped short. "Listen, you insignificant piece of trash. Yes, I meant to punish him. But hiring people to beat him up? Never! That crude vengeance is beneath me. That's something an ignorant gangster might attempt. No, I might choose to teach your buddy a lesson in a different way. Hypothetically, now."

The man's eyes went from fiery to cold. "You know that I sit on the board of several banks. Maybe one of them held the note on that property he owned in Denver."

The dramatic pause was unnecessary.

"I think you can piece together the rest." His cruel smile left no doubt that he wasn't speaking hypothetically. "I'm going back into the main house. In five minutes, I'll dial the police if you're not off my land. If you try to stop me, anything short of killing me will result in criminal charges on so many counts that Roman Polanski will be welcomed back into the country before you are."

He started off and then turned back.

"And by the by, for your information, I was aware that he had married Elizabeth in a civil ceremony that no self respecting preacher would endorse. Now I suggest you leave, before you dig a hole so deep that even a rat like you can't crawl out of it ."

He slammed the door on his way out, satisfied that he had won.

"I guess you won't be sending them a wedding present," I said to the man's back. I'd done what I set out to do. Thrown the truth in the man's face. And even though old Deveraux was defiant now, when he had time to think about what had transpired, he might eventually be forced to recognize the fact that nothing his wife tells him can ever be taken at face value. She is now living in another dimension most of the time, divorced from any rational definition of reality. That's hard to accept, even for the most intelligent and compassionate among us. Deveraux might then come to the realization that he'd needlessly alienated his only daughter.

The next question was --- is he too stubborn to admit he was wrong and beg her back into his life? And by then, would she be open to accepting an apology from the man who had caused her so much pain when she needed him most?

I hoped that the old man had someone close to care for him in his dotage.

# Sixty Four

Davis and I were consuming a few adult beverages at the now bustling Brickhouse Tavern. I wasn't exactly sipping mine, downing them at a two to one ratio to Davis'. It was game day; Davidson had just clobbered the College of Charleston. A large contingent of fans had descended on the restaurant to celebrate the late afternoon victory.

"When you see this area of San Miguel, you'll understand why Liz has taken to it so quickly. It's gorgeous. And most of the neighbors are American ex-pats so it doesn't feel strange at all. The pay is great and I can probably sock a lot of it away."

"Well, not to go all gooey on you, but I'll miss you two." I was on the verge of sloppy now and Davis seemed concerned. I guess he thought my drinking was starting to get out of hand and he wouldn't be around to be a moderating influence. I wasn't worried. If you can't get soused at a good friend's send-off to ole May-he-co, when can you?

"I know. Two years can go by quickly, though, to be honest it wouldn't be such a bad place to live permanently."

Any trace of the beating had vanished, and Davis was finally getting used to the new contour of his nose. Those who knew him casually said he looked younger, even more handsome but couldn't quite pin down the cause.

Davis shrugged. "Have to admit, it's pretty scary, moving to another country, even if it's just for two years."

"Not to mention getting married. I'm still a little surprised you left Liz down in Mexico less than a month after you got hitched. I think I'm entitled to an explanation." I shot Davis a Groucho Marxian eyebrow waggle.

"Her call. She wanted to re-do the interior of the villa. Personalize it. It's her wedding gift to me. Besides, she's only there alone for a week. My flight's tomorrow. Still taking me to the airport?"

"Sure. Tell me more about this Salazar guy. Seems like he came charging in to rescue you at the last minute when you'd just about lost hope."

"Kind of mysterious. I tried to do a little background check on him. Even recruited one of Randee's computer geeks to help. Didn't want to trouble you with it. Seems like he didn't exist on the web until recently. Couldn't find anything about how he made his money initially. He tells me he's a private person but he's almost like a ghost. Just appeared in San Miguel and started building this beautiful development on the outskirts of town. Environmentally friendly, architecturally correct. There's a lot about the place online but almost nothing on him. He's not Donald Trump, that's for sure."

"At least there's that. And you say he didn't appear as a native Mexican? Like he was born in the States."

"Yep. Guy's a real poltergeist. Almost eerie the way he comes off. Don't know how to describe him really but his checks clear. 'Scusi, got to hit the men's room."

In my semi-inebriated state, my brain started making connections. On my last big case in New Jersey, the feds had faked the death of a reputed mobster and sent him into witness protection. The man had been an informer for years and would be in grave danger from a number of sources if his whereabouts were known. But I had gotten a cryptic postcard from San Miguel a few weeks after the storm subsided, and I thought I recognized the writing. Could Tony Gazza be masquerading in Mexico as Alejandro Salazar? And would he dare venture back into the country to recruit capital for one of his projects there?

Would plastic surgery and a trail of false documents render him invisible? It sure hadn't worked for Serpente.

Contemplating this as I sipped my upteenth drink, I spotted a familiar face with a small group of women a few tables over. I debated whether I should say anything, but decided a friendly hello couldn't hurt.

"Hey, Julie Monahan, it's me. Riley King."

"I know who you are. Get lost."

"Ohhh-kay. I was just out for drinks with a friend and saw you. Good win tonight."

"Look, get out of my face. You stink of alcohol."

The two female friends at her table were giving us space and with the general clamor of happy hour, you had to be within inches to be heard anyway. "Wait, Julie. I'll admit, I've had a few jolts. I'm with my friend who was beat up. He's why we met in the first place. I wanted you to know how it all turned out."

"I'm not interested."

It had been over a month since last we spoke. "Julie, wait a minute. The situation got resolved and no one from Davidson got any negative pub. We kept it quiet. What's the matter?"

"I think you know."

I searched through the scrambled files of my besotted brain for a response, but none was forthcoming. "No, I honestly don't know what you're talking about. Let's not play games."

"All right, King. No more games. Corey Wade told me what you did. And don't deny it was you. His description was spot on. You work for some gangster. You threatened a kid. A kid! A boy who's trying to rise above his circumstances and make something of himself. All to settle some vendetta for some crook you work for. Please leave."

I could tell her that I lied to Wade for a righteous reason, to find out who had injured my friend, who was anything but a crime boss. But it would be useless. I had lost her trust. I thought

I'd intimidated Wade to the point where he'd never share his story. How and when the kid told her was irrelevant. She knew what she knew and there would be no explanation that would persuade her otherwise. Guilty as charged.

*The wages of sin.* I'd crossed a line. With everything else going on, I've conveniently relegated my tussle with Wade back to the dark recesses. I'd do it again for the right cause. That's who I am. I'd probably been deluding myself all along that someone as wholesome as Julie Monahan could ever accept that. I backed away toward my own table, trying to walk normally. I almost toppled a waitress with a full tray of food as I tripped over a line on the floor.

Davis came back and we called for the bar tab. Stone was on his way to meet us for dinner at 131 Main. It should be a nice night, spent among friends, drinking and reminiscing. Somehow, I wasn't feeling joyous.

# Sixty Five

$F$inal night in the States. Derek insisted that everything was his treat and that I let him drive, since he was still taking it easy on the booze since his accident, as we were now calling it. He was feeling flush as we moved our rolling celebration to the quieter setting of 131 Main. At least here Julie Monahan wouldn't be around to throw a drink in my face on her way out. Stone was late, stuck in traffic.

I was drunk enough to lose any sense of inhibition or timing. I inarticulately spilled out the story of my confrontation with Liz's father. Davis listened politely but didn't say anything until I had laid it all out, in my awkward fashion.

He said, "I wish you had told me you were going to do this. I know you meant well, but I would have liked to have known."

"I wanted to put it to him straight up and see what he'd say. I was thinking maybe coming from a third party, he'd see the light and forgive Liz. Sort of my wedding gift to you both. God damn, I knew the old dude was a cold bastard, Derek, but that topped everything. It was chilly, man."

I glanced around the restaurant, soaking in the rich atmosphere, inhaling the pungent cooking aroma from the kitchen. I felt seriously off kilter and resolved to order something soft on the next round. "Sorry, but I just can't get over a father cutting his daughter loose over something like this. I mean, it's one thing to be pro-life, but he didn't even seem to care that the tumors were benign. That blew me away."

Davis had already accepted it for what it was and had written him off. "He's a stubborn old son of a bitch. Explains how my note got called so suddenly. Bastard probably held it as a trump card all along. And I thought he was doing me a favor steering me toward that bank."

"But it's strange that he would confess to wrecking your plans for New Hope but wouldn't cop to ordering the beating. I have to admit, he sold me on it."

"Yeah, well, which hurt me more in the long run? He was right. Six weeks after the beating, there's no pain and people tell me I look better than ever. The scars he caused by blowing up my dream development won't heal until it gets built, somewhere else maybe. I haven't given up on the idea. That'll be the last laugh."

"What are you going to tell Liz?"

"Nothing." Davis took a long sip of his scotch. "She's sworn she'll never speak to him again."

"I was hoping was that hearing the truth might open up lines of communication. Tough for a woman to be estranged from her dad, no matter what kind of a prick he is."

"Riles, I encouraged her to write him a long letter --- she refused. Now I see that she was right --- it wouldn't have done any good. I guess in the end, she's well rid of him."

"I've got a feeling he'll reach out. Someday, some way."

Good thing Stone wasn't around to sing like Marshall Crenshaw. Drink was mellowing our conversation. Two old friends, spending their last night in the States together. Both of us were too macho to end the evening embracing and mouthing things like, "I love ya, man." But we both knew that change was coming, and things would never again be what they were between us.

My cell vibrated. I looked down at the number and immediately picked up. "Hold on, let me get to a quiet place."

I clicked the hold button or at least thought I did. "Derek, I've got to take this. I'll be outside. Shouldn't be long. Rick will be here any second. Order me a ginger ale, will you?"

"Everything all right?"

"Yeah, just a little unfinished business. Not to worry."

I wobbled into the parking lot. "Okay, sorry, I can talk now."

"It's good to hear your voice, Riley. I'd about given up that I'd ever hear from you."

"Same here, Charlene."

"The lawyers thought it best that we not speak for a while. I'm not so sure they'd approve of us talking now actually, but I didn't want to wait any longer."

We were more alike than I wanted to admit. We live unconventional lives. We have rules, but they aren't so hard and fast and that they couldn't be broken for the right reasons. She had done drugs, slept around. Maybe even set up her husband's execution.

Could I ever trust her? Would I ever know for sure? But if she was just using me to get rid of Serpente, it was mission accomplished. Why would she bother to call now? What else could she possibly want?

Maybe my present state of intoxication made me susceptible to her. If I was thinking clearly, maybe my brain would take over and defeat my lust again. But hearing her voice stirred memories of what almost was.

Things were not good with Jaime. I hadn't heard from her since our last conversation about Charlene and I had honored her wishes not to initiate contact. It seemed we were done, without a formal declaration. That's the way these things usually go. *I don't want to fade away*. Damn Stone. And now that Jaime had kicked me to the curb, I was alone again except for Bosco. Even Julie Monahan had dismissed me tonight.

I came off my reverie and said, "Where are you?"

"The 131 Main parking lot. Wave... I'm in the Beemer. The Z4."

"How'd you know I'd be here?"

"You ain't the only one who can do a little detective work, darlin'. Your friend Randee's Facebook page said you'd be sending Derek off here."

"I'll be right over." I made a note to myself to chastise Blankenship for invading my privacy. Someday it could put me in danger. Matter of fact, maybe it already had. Could Charlene be wearing a wire? Was she there to entrap me into saying something incriminating? What had I done that was illegal? In my current state, was I in any position to judge? Hell, my first thought was to check to see if she was wearing a wire by ripping open her blouse, exposing those luscious breasts. That's how bad off I was.

I walked over to the passenger side of her little sports car. She popped the lock and I motioned her to get out and follow me. We walked over to a dark area of the lot.

I wasn't sure how to react. A chaste kiss? A hug? Handshake? Rip off her clothes?

I settled for a smile.

I said, "Better this way. Who knows who might be tapping either of our phones? They might even have your car bugged. I know I'm being paranoid but I was a fed. They're very good at misdirection." I took a deep breath. "You look great."

"And you look drunk."

"Well, yeah, maybe I've had a few. Probably be cabbing it home tonight."

"I have a better idea. My place. That is, if you don't drink yourself into oblivion."

"I think we need to talk first. Derek's inside waiting, so I'll be blunt. I need you to tell me the truth. Did you set this all up with your husband? And don't play dumb. Did you know that the Russians would send someone down here to take care of business? Is that why you volunteered his real name?"

The accusing words just tumbled out. Under normal circumstances, I would have been a lot less direct but if anyone *was* listening, there could be no mistake about who did what to who.

She stayed cool. "Funny, that's what my lawyer was saying *you* might have done. That you wanted me to yourself and weren't willing to wait for me to leave Johnny, so you set up the hit through your fed friends. I said that there was no way that you'd do that."

As if the likes of Dan Logan would ever agree to that. "You're right, I wouldn't."

"But you think I would?"

"I need to hear it from you. Damn, Charlene, you're so beautiful that I want to believe everything you say. But I need to hear it."

"What do *you* believe? In your heart, Riley? You were right when we first met. I did sell myself short. I didn't think that there could be a man who didn't just want me for more than just a piece of ass But you and me, we had a bond, something special. I don't believe everything you said was just to get into my pants, seeing as how you never did."

She shook her head as if she regretted the non-consummation as much as I did. "But Riley, if you think I'd be capable of doing that to Johnny, you'll never trust me and we should say goodbye now and get it over with. I'll get by, don't worry about that."

I desperately wanted to believe her. But I needed more than just a semi-intoxicated gut to go on. It had been a long day and I'd processed a lot of information. I didn't feel up to making what could be a life changing decision right now.

"I know you will. Okay, Charlene. I got to cut this short. Tonight belongs to Derek Davis. Much as I want to be with you, it's his last night in the states. It's gonna to be a late one. So go home. I'm taking him to the airport tomorrow morning. Then I'll need some sleep. So how about tomorrow night? Come to my place around six. Let's talk some more. We have a lot of catching up to do."

"Chinese, okay?"

"Whatever you bring is okay. Just bring you."

I touched her cheek and ran off quickly, avoiding an awkward goodbye. My life felt like it was in shambles now. The list of regrets I'd been dwelling on resurfaced and pounded through by being. My best friend in Charlotte was leaving for Mexico in the morning. I'd roughed up an innocent kid. I had exacerbated the mistrust between an old man and his only daughter. And to top it all off, I'd gotten a man killed, a bad man for sure, but a human being who did not have to die.

I had no idea what to make of Charlene. She could be my salvation or my destruction. Stone intercepted me on the way into restaurant, having just arrived.

"Was that Charlene I saw you with in the shadows?" he said.

"Brilliant deduction, Watson. It was indeed the lovely Charlene herself. In the flesh, which I haven't sampled yet. Which I've told you many times, but you still don't believe." I was aware I was rambling, suddenly feeling more lightheaded than I had with Charlene.

"I thought you didn't trust her and swore you'd never see her again?" he said.

"She called me. I listened. She made sense. Why, what do you care?"

"You know, you've been on me for my habit of dating girls a lot younger than me and I listen to your advice. I admit, I don't take it, but I listen."

Growing impatient for the lecture that I knew was coming, I said, "So? I thought we agreed that she would have been better off with the pre-nup so it made no sense to kill him or have him killed. The will would take more time and pay out less. She's not stupid. Can we go inside? I think I need a drink."

"And I think you've had enough and that your next drink should be coffee. Since I thought you had moved on and we were done with this, I didn't say anything but I thought of another reason that she probably did do it."

"And silly me, thinking with my pee-pee, couldn't figure it out."

"Lawyers."

"*Guns and Money*. Warren Zevon, who you're fond of quoting."

"I'm not quoting anyone," he said. "I'm serious. You know what top criminal lawyers charge these days. Four figures an hour. Serpente gets indicted. How long would it take to burn through all his dough? From what you've told me, he'd do anything to avoid jail. Win or lose, there'd be nothing left. He dies, his money is intact. And since the locals have no interest in following through on this, no class action suit. His money goes according to the will."

"You've never met the woman. You really think she's that smart? Or devious? She invited me over tonight. I took a rain check for tomorrow. Booty call. Finally, at least let me get something out of this. I'm so fucked up now I can't refute your little lawyer theory, Ricky. I'll pull a Scarlett O'Hara and think about it tomorrow, if you don't mind."

It was my friend's last night in town for two years, and I didn't want to let depression over all of my shit ruin the evening. Rick and I walked a more or less straight line back to the restaurant, where Davis was in a booth. No more Charlene. No more Johnny the Snake. No more Jack Deveraux. Tonight *did* belong to Derek Davis.

"Everything okay, Riles? You look a little unsteady," Davis said.

I said, "Should have eaten a little bit more before drinking scotch neat. Let's order some ribs. Hey, isn't that the builder who almost decked you that night last month? The old guy, back in the corner with that shrew of a redhead who looks out of it."

Davis said, "Yeah, that's Paul Larsen. I wonder how he affords coming here if his house is headed for foreclosure. Probably knows the owner. You know, I did feel bad about my part in devaluing his house. I sent that load of travertine you took out of Serpente's place to him. Never thanked me, but what the hell. I wasn't going to ship it to Mexico and maybe the old coot will redo one of his bathrooms with it. Make his house a little more saleable."

I said, "Damn. Looks like he's coming over here. This is the last thing we need now on your last night here. A fight with someone who's got a bullshit grudge against you."

"Be nice, Riles. He's with his wife. And besides, we have a sober ex-Marine for protection with Stone here."

Stone laughed. Both Larsen and spouse were obviously feeling no pain as they ambled over to the booth where we sat. They had their coats on, ready to leave, which told me that the colonel wasn't gearing up for battle.

Larsen's voice was shaky but his gaze was steady. "Davis. Just wanted to let you know I got that load of stone. No use for it though. Sold it. Just about covered my tab here."

Davis put his palm over his face to hide his *WTF* wince, lest it be misinterpreted. "Well, Paul, I hope it helped in some small way. Again, I'm sorry for what happened to you."

"Yeah well, the missus and I landed on our feet. Found a buyer who appreciated the craftsmanship on our old place and gave us close to what it was worth. Asshole survivalist wanted to be fortified when the black helicopters come but his money is good. Then funny thing, we stumble on a foreclosure for pennies on the dollar and I'm fixing it up the way we like it. Cost me a third of what we got for our place. I'll miss living there but I'm back in business now. Just got hired to build a big place for some hedge fund guy on Lake Norman."

I burst out laughing. Here we were, feeling sorry for the old colonel and he was taking on a lucrative project that Davis might have bid on had he known.

Larsen's wife was not amused. She looked at Derek as if he had just pissed on her husband's shoes. She looked like she was about to say something when Larsen shushed her.

"All's well that ends well, my dear," he said. "You know the ladies. Sometimes they get caught up in emotion more than us. Act impulsively. Darling, I don't believe that you and Mr. King have ever met. And I'm afraid I have no idea who you are sir, but gentlemen, meet the light of my life and the lady who's kept me sane through the hard times. Mrs. Jeanette Larsen."

He beamed with drunken pride.

"But everybody calls her Johnnie."

# Epilogue

The men's locker room at Mecklenburg National was not nearly so lavishly appointed as the taproom. When it was designed sixty years ago, the reigning philosophy was that it would serve as an enclave for strictly male pursuits, the kind their wives would not approve of. In rough order, they were:

1) Graphic talk about females, mostly those they termed MILFs.

2) Drinking to sloppy excess.

3) Gambling (the high stakes variety)

Also on the spousal disapproved list would be walking around buck naked, farting, and attending to matters of personal hygiene best done in private. Stuff that was socially unacceptable in mixed company but endlessly entertaining to grownup frat boys.

Very few women had seen the inside of the men's locker room at the club and lived to tell about it, the boys quipped, only half in jest. For the wives and daughters, tours for prospective members terminated at the thick oak doors. The occasional innocent intrusion by a confused newbie was met by a stern letter of reprimand and the threat of a fine or suspension.

Lurking beneath this double standard lay a more nefarious purpose. It had to do with business. There was still an old boy network that thrived as a subset within the bowels of the locker room, one that excluded newer members whose politics or worldviews did not coincide with their own archaic values.

A tiny gathering of these like minded individuals was meeting there this evening. The locker room was closed for maintenance, according to a posted sign. Attending were a high powered attorney, a long tenured city councilman, and a top ranking member of the Charlotte Mecklenburg police force. These were accomplished, serious men, unlike many of their juvenile fellow members. The locker room attendant, Moses Ginn was present --- ostensibly because he knew where all the best liquor was kept. The men were dressed casually and sat or stood wherever it was comfortable. An unschooled observer would think that they were just loitering about after a late afternoon round.

The attorney spoke first. "Well, friends, I think we have this thing contained. Now look, we've all played golf with the man, but something had to be done to keep this situation from getting out of hand. So no regrets, please. The scenario about the Russian mob seems to have resonated and the press is buying it. Officer, that was well done. I always worry about loose ends, though. Are you sure that every base is covered?"

The lawman said, "I'm satisfied. The FBI said they were more than willing to pass this off to us locally although the media believes the opposite to be true. And what a stroke of luck --- they found that one of the Russian mob's enforcers had actually flown down here that day. Nobody will bother to follow up on that but it reads well."

He took a sip of Johnny Walker Blue and went on. "Yeah, we did let this get away from us early. The kid plumbing inspector who was in contact with that old crone in Davidson was a bad lapse by us. It took a little friendly persuasion involving his family but we also found him a job in the private sector for more money so he'll keep quiet. That builder who was helping the old lady shipped off to Mexico --- that was just good timing. The old teacher? Well, she was appeased by the donation to Habitat in the will, as we thought she would be. I don't trust her a hundred per cent yet. We'll monitor her situation, just in case. So gentlemen, I'm satisfied the trail ended with Johnny."

The lawyer said, "Yes, eliminating Johnny was unfortunate, but it was the right move. Simplest solution is usually the best. The stuff we fed our friends in the media that Johnny was a lone wolf who deceived everybody was pretty credible. Like he'd trick the inspectors by doing one place correctly while fudging all the others. Meanwhile, we can make a show at fixing some of the worst violations with taxpayer money; of course, minus our normal gratuity."

The councilman asked, "And the private detective? You're convinced he'll just let this go?"

The cop answered. "We'll keep an eye on him as well. He came out of this with a bonus, didn't he? I've heard tell the lovely and talented Charlene is sharing his bed these days. I imagine he'll be too busy satisfying her needs to give us any trouble. My sources tell me they think he's developing a drinking problem anyway."

The attorney approved. "You're sure the wife is not going to contest it?"

The policeman was firm. "Positive. We'll never be holding charity dinners for that bitch. She's a survivor. Of course, Plan B would been to pin the murder on her, but a trial might have unearthed some stuff better left undiscovered. It was that or suicide, given the sway we have with the M.E.. But the gangland revenge shooting was the easiest scenario to sell."

The councilman added, "Here, here. We all benefited from Johnny or Dmitry or whatever his name was. But we did get careless in trusting him as far as we did. Even if Johnny wasn't about to be discovered for his misdeeds, we let him get away with some pretty awful things. It's one thing to cut bureaucratic corners, but another to allow exposure to dangerous substances that will result in cancer for many innocents down the road. And the fire hazards? That's not what our group is all about and now we're rid of him. Praise be.

"Our shame is we didn't monitor Johnny more closely. We all believed that he was giving our lesser brethren nicer accommodations at lower cost through the efficiency of the private sector. But not at the expense of endangering them and their children. That is unacceptable. We have learned a valuable lesson as to who we share a bed with in the future."

The others considered the august councilman to be their social conscience. They didn't all fully subscribe to his high minded views, but they deferred to him on matters such as these.

The men stood up, preparing to adjourn the informal gathering. "It's kind of sad the way the little guy felt he had to keep up the gangster routine to impress us. That little ruse of his was transparent from the get-go," said the attorney.

The lawman said, "Come on guys, admit it. You all bought it at first. In fact, some of my fellow officers thought he was still connected to the I-tie mob at the time of his demise. Give the little fellow credit, he wasn't a bad actor. But it's great for us the way everything fell into place. It usually does when you plan intelligently. What was it that old baseball man said? Luck is the residue of design?"

They murmured their agreement. "And Moses, as always, you are appreciated beyond our ability to thank you."

To those who only knew Moses Ginn as someone who kept their shoes clean and made sure their favorite beverage and cigar were waiting for them at the end of a round, the transformation would have been startling. The deferential manner was replaced by a strong air of command. He took a slow sip of the club's finest scotch, Macallan 1959.

Ginn spoke for the first time. "I must disagree about luck, though. It played a big role. Like, if Serpente hadn't come to me with them broken down shoes, I wouldn't have had an excuse for visiting him at his home. I told him I kept looking for a way to fix them soles and that made him so happy. Man invited me upstairs to check out his new master bath. That's when I got my chance to cap him from behind. He had a security system but I surged the circuit and blew out the hard drive --- right out the FSB playbook."

The lawyer said, "You're too modest. You've done yeoman work, Moses. Information is power. You've pulled off the biggest charade since Kaiser Sose in that *Usual Suspects* movie. But I have to say, I'm still a little sorry for Serpy. I think he let that whole episode with that hot little wife and her master bath distract him."

"I'm sad that it came to this, too. We're not killers by nature," said the councilman. "We are respectable businessmen who have a keen knowledge of how the world works. We try to do things honorably when it's possible. But when the chips are down, we do what's necessary. Moses, I'm glad that you haven't had to employ the skill sets you picked up in the special ops more than a handful of times, but they do come in handy when dealing with a situation like we were in with the late Mr. Serpente."

The cop said, "I suppose his biggest flaw was hubris. Who was he to think he could ever be one of us in the inner circle?"

"Here's to you. Mister Moses Ginn. Cheers." said the councilman.

With that, they all raised their glasses and toasted their facilitator. Ginn humbly accepted their encomiums. But the experience with Serpente was cold confirmation of what he'd known for years. Like the little Yankee builder, Moses would never be fully accepted as one of the inner circle, The Troika.

Legend had it, when he returned from serving his country in that useless war all those years ago, the only job Ginn could find was the lowly position he had vacated to join the Special Forces. Despite his training and the particular set of skills he had acquired, no advanced opportunities were open to him.

Shortly after reacquiring his old duties at the club, he overheard whispers of an especially vexing issue facing the Troika, and he quietly proposed a way out. After that initial flawless solution, they trusted he could be relied upon to provide similar services when all other attempts at persuasion failed. When called upon, his actions were swift and untraceable. In return, he lived rent free in a posh building uptown that one of the members owned and generous but unreported bonuses came his way on a regular basis.

Although he had gained their respect, he knew they regarded him as a blunt instrument that one day they might purge from their ranks, denying any knowledge of his deeds. Their consciousness had evolved somewhat: they no longer referred to him as "our nigger" as they once had when he wasn't within earshot. Like tonight, they praised him effusively when he advised and executed a clean solution to their messy problems. But he would never truly be one of them: he would always be *the other*.

So he stockpiled leverage. Years ago, without their knowledge, he had installed recording devices in the locker room and was thus privy to all their secrets, both innocent and dirty. Moses was not a man to be crossed, even if he could never be considered an equal. He accepted their gratitude, their favors and their liberal compensation, living a simple but comfortable existence, serving at their pleasure.

Or so they thought.

# Acknowledgments

Most of the restaurants and locations described in the book do exist. I've taken liberties with the Davidson college campus and their athletic programs. The former mayor of Charlotte was indicted and sentenced in a bribery sting, but that happened well after those chapters were written. The Troika, Mecklenburg National Golf Club and the existence of corruption in the city's program for public housing are fabrications for dramatic purposes.

I'd like to thank all my friends and family for their support. My brother John Neer has provided many insights into the building industry over the years. From a literary standpoint, the great novelist Reed Farrel Coleman has been of invaluable assistance. David Hale Smith helped hone the book to its final state. Michael Harrison of Talkers Magazine has been a lifelong source of wise counsel.

Special thanks go to my wife Vicky, who designed all the graphics and has worked tirelessly on the business end of bringing the book forward for our readers. She is a never ending source of inspiration and her faith in my work keeps me going when my own bogs down.

# About the Author

"The Master Builders" is Richard Neer's second novel, following the success of "Something of the Night". Both books feature detective Riley King and his talk radio ally Rick Stone as they investigate crime along the eastern seaboard.

His work of non-fiction entitled "FM, the Rise and Fall of Rock Radio", (Villard 2001), is the true story of how corporate interests destroyed a medium that millions grew up cherishing.

Neer has worked in important roles at two of the most prestigious and groundbreaking radio stations in history--the progressive rocker WNEW-FM for almost thirty years, and the nation's first full time sports talker, WFAN, over the past twenty-eight. He currently is completing his next novel, "Indian Summer", which follows the same protagonists.

Made in the USA
Middletown, DE
26 June 2016